VENOM

Readers' Praise for *Venom*

'A modern blend of mythology and fiction, presented with a compelling storyline. It stands out for seamlessly blending multiple genres–a twist of thriller with mythology and fiction.'

–Shreya Ghosh

'Venom orchestrates a tale of malice, revenge and enigma in a way worthy of being told and read.'

–Sayantoni Ghosh

'Totally unexpected twists and turns at every page, racy thriller! Finished in one day!'

–Vaish

'What I liked the most about this book, is its perfect blending of mythology and thriller, resulting in a remarkable narration … The language used is eloquent and engrosses the reader from the beginning till the climax.'

–Sushma

An Om Patnaik Thriller

VENOM

SATYARTH
NAYAK

HARPER
FICTION

An Imprint of HarperCollins *Publishers*

First published in 2020

This edition published in India by Harper Fiction 2025
An imprint of HarperCollins *Publishers*
HarperCollins *Publishers* India, Cyber City,
Building 10-A, Gurugram, Haryana – 122002, India
www.harpercollins.co.in

2 4 6 8 10 9 7 5 3 1

P-ISBN: 978-93-6569-951-7
E-ISBN: 978-93-6569-494-9

Printed and bound at
Thomson Press (India) Ltd

MIX
Paper | Supporting responsible forestry
FSC
www.fsc.org
FSC® C010615

This book is produced from independently certified FSC® paper to ensure responsible forest management.

HarperCollins *Publishers*, Macken House, 39/40 Mayor Street Upper, Dublin 1, D01 C9W8, Ireland

For Asmita
For all the thrillers we have shared

Also by Satyarth Nayak

Mahagatha: 100 Tales from the Puranas

An Om Patnaik Thriller

The Emperor's Riddles

Prologue

Jhelum, Pakistan
6 September 2014

'A snake. A massive, mighty snake.'

'What was its name, Nana Abbu?'

'Kalia. The shaitaan lived in the Jumna River along Vrindavan and poisoned its waters. So terrible was its venom that it killed all the fish and frogs in the river. The waters bubbled and frothed and turned blue. No animal would drink Jumna's offering, and no bird would build a nest on the trees by its banks.'

Feroza lifted her head up to look at the Jhelum again. An unrelenting downpour had been lashing it for four days now. The river had become a wound, leaking pus. Chewing up its banks and crumbing the villages it once suckled. Feroza's beloved willow tree was gone. She wanted to ask the bulbul why it sang no more. There were whispers that hundreds of people had already perished in the valley. Many of them across the border in Kashmir. An hour ago, neighbours had fished out her brother's clothes from the stream and then his body. She still wondered why he was clutching his flute. Why he looked way more plump than he really was. Kneeling down, she immersed her hands in the river and stared at the water in her palms.

'Jhelum has become Jumna, Nana Abbu.'

The old man rubbed the tears off his cheeks as if they would add to the stream that was threatening to drink them all up.

'Is Kalia here?' she asked.

Chapter 1

The rishi who was born outside of man
Sat praying for a son to irrigate his clan
His seed to germinate into a warrior brave
Purpose of his life and keeper of his grave
Invoking Mahadev, almighty of the devout
The one who had chained venom in his throat
And thus died epochs to bring forth that hour
When his eyes witnessed a blue pushkar flower
Laughing like that lotus, Shiva raised his hand
A sculptor preparing to breathe life into sand
Your arms shall cradle the desire in your heart
The son you crave resembling me in every part
An offspring with a gleaming forehead like me
Among those fearless Rudras twelve he shall be
Amidst the starry Saptarishis will he find a place
Dusky skin like mine to proclaim his divine race
Thus was born a Rishiputra in the land of the east
His eyes like the night and he howled like a beast.

Chapter 2

WHO KNEW A FACE COULD HIDE SO MANY FACES? THE face on the giant screen was splitting. A circle cracking into two semicircles, like a cell replicating itself through mitosis. Someone cutting the moon neatly with steel scissors. The half-moons became elongated, turning into absolute mirror images of each other. Two faces. Black and white. Eyes like pinholes gouged out. Blank. Unstaring. Unflinching. Negative spaces seeing nothing and everything. Awaiting someone to animate them. Two similar faces with one singular difference. One face was festive as its lips curved into a grin. The other one wretched, its mouth upturned with misery. Thalia and Melpomene.

Twin masks of *Komos* and *Tragoidia*. Comedy and Tragedy.

The audience at the Mumbai auditorium greeted the pair with euphoria. They knew the show had begun. The supreme annual spectacle of them all.

MAQUILLAGE 2018

They were looking at a giant tree covered with apples. Red, like blobs of congealed blood glistening in the halogen light. Clinging to the tree was a rattlesnake. The creature's sinuous length coiled around the trunk like an elastic band as it moved downward in a slow spiral motion. Metallic skin providing a near perfect camouflage but its death rattle betraying its presence. Interlocked sections of keratin vibrating ominously, as if celebrating a sin. The hollow segments amplifying that sound for everyone to hear. For the naked couple that lay intertwined in each other's embrace at the base of the tree. The pulsating tone had awakened them. They stood up facing the audience, their hands shielding their genitals. The rattlesnake hissed as the couple plucked two leaves of fig and masked their guilty flesh.

The *mise-en-scene* changed now to a Roman Saturnalia. The Lord of the house genuflecting before his Slave. The Lord with his white face, pink ears and antlers. The Artemis deer mask. The Slave dressed in polychromatic synthesis and the conical pileus on his head. Saturnalia inverted the hierarchy for one day. And so, the Lord waited upon the Slave who took his place at the table. There was meat and wine. Gambling and dice play. Knucklebones and perfumes. Books and parrots. The feasting Slave raised a finger, signalling the tympanum to play. As the stage trembled with its percussion, the Lord swayed with an arrow in his hand. Footfalls light and gentle. The weapon dance. The arc lights throbbing in tandem with the rhythm as the Lord whirled around the table like a dervish. The audience was clapping. The tympanum pounding. Faster now. As the beats increased, so did the Lord's pace. Faster and faster. The lights dancing and the tambourine screaming. Faster. Faster. The tempo deafening now. The lights berserk. The audience chorusing. The Lord's wild choreography reached the Slave's chair. Right behind him. As the final crescendo exploded, the Lord seized the Slave's head and slit his throat with the arrow. The tympanum choked. The mask was laughing. And the lights flashed deep red, capturing a sea of frozen faces.

The tableaus kept rolling on the stage, conjuring more spectacles. An Aztec priestess enlightening her ruler about statecraft from behind her skull mask. Shakespeare's clown Feste frolicking in a motley mask of red and yellow with tinkling bells. That jester exposing everyone but himself. A Kathakali dancer portraying Bhima gesticulating in rapture as he fetched the fragrant Saugandhika flowers for Draupadi. Krewe members revelling at Mardi Gras, masked as birds, satyrs, mermaids and monks. Tossing beads, coins and moon pies at the audience. Sugawara contorting his Kabuki face as he laid an irrevocable curse upon his people for exiling him from Kyoto.

Then the stage roared.

'I am the beginning and the end. That which will come to pass and that which has. Abstract but concrete. Sacrosanct yet sacrilegious. I open and close portals. Create time and destroy it. I am the Uranic Supreme.'

They watched as he materialised before them. The god with two faces. The bi-cephalic deity. Both visages spoke his name.

'I am Janus.'

The lights bowed as they all gathered around his feet. Adam and Eve and Lord and Snake and Priestess and Feste and Bhima and Draupadi and Krewe and Sugawara.

'I am the Pater. First to receive the sacrifice.'

They bowed their heads. Janus pointed.

'Behold the sacrifice.'

The stage lights folded into darkness as if terrified to see what was about to play out. Only a single spotlight blazed bravely above the proscenium now. Twinkling in that luminescent beam was the star they had all come to see.

The actor who owned the final act. The climax belonged to him as they always did in all his films. The superstar who had been consummating *Maquillage* for the past four years.

Ashwin Tomar.

But the audience was not chanting the man's name. They sat quiet. They knew what was coming. What had made it mandatory that no one shall bring a mobile or camera into *Maquillage*. What Ashwin did every year to crown this phantasmagoria.

The hero was going to make the ultimate sacrifice again.

The light moved to illuminate just his face, obscuring the rest of his body. Behind him a mammoth screen came to life displaying his close-up. That exquisite close-up too perfect to be true. He was smiling. Standing before them in that phosphorescent halo like a messiah about to reveal the truth.

Ashwin raised both his palms to caress his face. His fingers climbed up from his chin towards his head. Slowly. Tenderly. Lovingly. As his fingertips met on his forehead, he closed his eyes. The next moment his fingers curled like talons clawing at his skin. Ashwin opened his mouth and let out a terrible scream as the dermis on his forehead gradually gave way. His fingers moved down, peeling the skin that now hung in shreds over his eyes. The audience shrank in collective horror, but the blood oozing from within him glittered under the spotlight. Ashwin rubbed his palms and covered his nose and lips with his right hand. They watched as the fingers slid down, violently scraping that skin off. Again. Again. And again. Blood from his grated flesh staining his teeth. Filling his mouth and making him spit crimson saliva. The next moment his forceps were pulling his eyelids.

Tugging brutally at both the flaps until they tore, leaving his eyeballs red. The stage reverberated as the star fell on his knees. His mangled close-up was stinking now. Reeking of raw, sore flesh. He brought his fingers to his face one last time. His nails were piercing the area right under his eyes. They were waiting. Watching. Then some looked away as he ripped his cheeks apart. Those who had covered their eyes heard that ghastly scream again as he scratched away the membranes. They saw both his hands holding the tatters still attached to his skull through gelatinous strands of tissue. The scream went on and on as if emanating from below him. From the very bowels of an earth bleeding to death. Penetrating every being in that auditorium. Everyone had become the scream and that scream had become everyone. The sound faded as all the lights came to life one by one. As the final set of luminaries flooded the stage, the actor stood up before his audience.

Under that crust. Behind that shell. Stripped of that hide. Those on stage bowed as Janus crowned the faceless hero.

Ashwin Tomar grinned again as the curtain fell, veiling him.

Chapter 3

THE BUDDHA WAS SMILING.

Officer Parag Suri had just returned from Bodh Gaya. Ever since he crossed paths with Buddhist monks in a previous case at Sarnath, the black holes inside him had started to shrink. Childhood visuals of watching his father and mother gunned down by a terrorist cell had become less petrifying. The bullets less resonant now. The shrieks less deafening. He loved listening to young Samaneras at Gaya. Talking to the Bhikkhu, the head monk. Their words somehow found a way inside his skin and coated his flesh with a strange salve. Those holy walls becoming an amniotic sac that nourished his forty-year-old soul. Since then, every once in a while, Suri would make a pilgrimage to Bodh Gaya and open himself to Mahabodhi. And that Temple of Great Awakening would press a Refresh button. Restore his system and recover whatever he had lost. But one file appeared permanently deleted.

Alia…

He was back now at his police precinct in Mumbai. The officer had been transferred to the megalopolis from Varanasi two years ago. Suri missed his old town's friendly claustrophobia. The reassuring temple bells. Floating clay lamps. Those pyres at dusk that melted your bones to set you free. But the monks had told him that Buddha wanted us to nurture an acceptance of our present condition. He had embraced the Arabian Sea. But he still yearned for the Ganga.

And Alia…

She sat now on his table, framed in glass and gold. Next to her was the picture of his grandmom Alexis. A daring entrepreneur herself, Alexis had inspired a young Suri to hunt for whatever his heart desired. The old woman had gone on to settle in Egypt where she had died two years ago. It needled him now and then that he had never got to bid her farewell. The bust of Buddha on her left was still smiling. The constable standing before him was not. Only minutes ago, Suri had ordered him to smack a young man brought in for drunk driving and the constable had uneasily complied.

'But he's the IG's son.'

'Two words when we meet the IG,' the officer had shrugged. 'Sorry, sir.'

He was looking at a package wrapped in white paper on his desk. It bore his name and a label. The constable shoved it to make place for his tea.

'We found it by the door.'

Suri pulled the parcel and read the words on the label.

EXHIBIT S090218

His penknife tore through the wrapping to reveal its content. A scroll of cloth with three lines printed on it.

For he seemed to me again like a king, Like a king in exile, uncrowned in the underworld, Now due to be crowned again…

Suri read them over and over again. Then he woke his computer up. The mantra on the screen greeted him with a soft ping.

Om Mani Padme Hum...

He fed the words to Google. Precisely 1.17 seconds later the search engine returned more than three thousand results. But the topmost one was highlighting the exact quote. Telling him that the lines on the scroll had been extracted from a poem.

Snake – D.H. Lawrence

Chapter 4

THE MIRROR WAS LOOKING AT THAT FACE AGAIN.

It knew the man was not gazing at it. No one ever did. They all stood before it but never saw it. They only saw themselves. They all drowned in its depths to fish for themselves. Peered inside its soul to see their own bodies. It was itself perennially invisible. A circle of glass. A hollow vessel into which everyone poured themselves but never clung to its sides. They all came, found themselves and left it empty. But did they know that what they saw in it was just a shadow?

Did Ashwin Tomar know?

The mirror knew him well. He visited it more often than others. Groped to see himself more dangerously than others. And loved what he found more pathetically than others. Even now he stood enchanted by what it showed him. That flawless face floodlit by the row of bulbs on either side. Drops of sweat on his skin, like crystal molecules. The mirror had heard that human bodies were as fragile as the glass that made up its body. And yet it saw them anointing themselves. Making love to themselves like Ashwin now. His own face hypnotising him.

The mirror asked itself that question once more. Was it teaching men to be self-seeking? Be oblivious of others?

Was the looking glass the root of all evil?

'You killed them again!'

The director of *Maquillage* barged into the green room. As the door swung, the ovation outside sneaked in. The cheering still on. The director still fawning.

'It's so delightful to see a megastar like you do theatre. And not any other theatre. You take the stage only for *Maquillage*. We are so grateful, Ashwin.'

The actor crashed into the divan. 'Better than last year?'

'Last year?' the director waved his hand. 'Better than ever. You were a miracle. Did you hear the silence right after you ended? Louder than the loudest acclaim I have ever heard.'

'I prefer applause. Cinema is a huge high, but theatre validates you instantly. A thousand hands clapping for you live. Faces reflecting your act. A congregation touched by a single man. Standing alone on the podium as the universe celebrates you. That's why I migrate to this stage every year. Just for the applause.'

'How do you do it, Ashwin? The make-up. The prosthetics. You never let anyone do it for you. You come here and close the door. And minutes before show-time you are ready. All by yourself.'

'Trade secrets.' The actor picked up a knife running the blade over the director's face. 'I will tell you but then I will have to kill you.'

'That will be a death worth dying,' the man laughed. 'What baffles me is how natural that make-up looks. Not a hint of greasepaint or cosmetic veneer. It's almost as if that mask becomes your face. Becomes one with you. Does it? Do you really tear your own flesh? Peel your own skin layer by layer? Is that the stench of blood on your clothes?

Is the actor screaming in agony while his audience claps?'

'Nothing that dramatic.'

'You lie. Tell me, Tomar. What is it like up there when that lights hit you? When you stand alone facing a crowd after that ultimate sacrifice? What do you feel?'

Ashwin lay his head back and closed his eyes. 'Freedom.'

'Freedom?'

'Yes. Liberated. The façade is not my face. My face is my façade. So, I free myself. Remove the wrapper covering me. Remove it on the stage of *Maquillage* where everyone else hides behind a mask.'

'Don't you feel naked?'

'I once asked a stripper that as she removed her clothes one by one. She said she covered herself with her audience. They became her garment.'

'Not sure I follow you, but remember something, Ashwin. The person and the performer constantly feed off each other. Brighter the star, hazier the individual. The stage is an altar of self-denial. Don't sacrifice the real you.'

'My sacrifices are done. No more.'

The director jumped as something rustled below him. It was a woman on all fours. Scooping the actor's costume that bore the stains of his stage-act. Tall with slender limbs and straight hair, she hardly raised her eyes to look at the men. Ashwin gestured.

'My new secretary. Yeva.'

'So sorry. I almost stepped on her.'

'No harm done,' the actor giggled. 'Take all these soiled ones, Yeva, and bring me a fresh pair.'

The director was watching the curious visage on that woman. It was like watching a blank page nod at you. Or a whitewashed wall that offered nothing. Just a pair of ice-blue eyes piercing his body like stalactites. He placed a document before Ashwin.

'Your signature here.'

Picking up his fountain pen, the actor yelled.

'Where's the wine, Yeva?'

She slid across the room to fill a tall glass with merlot. A single sip and the glass lay shattered on the floor.

'Is that my brand?'

'They didn't have it. They said this was as good as...'

Ashwin yanked her and jabbed the fountain pen nib into her hand. The metal tore a vein, squirting blue ink into her blood. The director pulled Yeva away as she sucked on the wound.

'Are you insane? Look at her hand.'

The actor flung the papers at him. 'Get out. Both of you. Out!'

As the door slammed, he picked up the piece of cloth that the director had left behind on the couch. A fragment from the stage curtain that Ashwin always demanded at the end of *Maquillage*. And as always, he ignited it and watched it burn.

Chapter 5

'MORNING, CITY SLICKERS! YOU HAVE JUST TUNED INTO Mumbai Mojo 99.9 FM where we are continuing our special series on Indian festivals. The one we are discussing today is quite intense because it's all about cobras and vipers. You guessed it folks! Nag Panchami it is and to talk more about it, we have Om Patnaik in the studio. The thirty-eight-year-old writer has emerged as quite an authority on the esoteric in recent years. Thank you, Om, for joining us, and we have some pretty cool myths and stories lined up for the next one hour. For example, did you know that Nagpur is actually named after the Naga since the city was once believed to be infested with snakes? How intriguing is that, Om?'

'Hello, Mumbai. And yes, that's actually true. The Nagoba Temple in Nagpur is quite a venerated shrine for snake worship today. Especially during Nag Panchami when ophiolatry is at its peak.'

'Ophio…?'

'Ophiolatry. The worship of snakes.'

'Word of the week, guys. Now let's start from the very beginning. I was reading up that snakes have been worshipped in India since Indus Valley. How did the concept of Nag Panchami originate?'

'The legend behind that lies embedded in the *Mahabharata*. The story goes that Abhimanyu's son Parikshit succeeded the Pandavas and reigned for many years until he was bitten by the Naga king Takshak. The serpent had fulfilled a prophecy by doing this, but the dead king's son Janamejaya swore revenge. He organised a huge sacrifice called Sarpa-satra along with a galaxy of sages from all the three worlds. The single-point agenda was complete extinction of the snake species.'

'That's some sacrifice. Did he succeed?'

'He certainly knew what he was doing. So powerful was the ceremony that thousands of serpents across the universe were drawn towards it and fell to their deaths in that enormous sacrificial fire. But there was still no sign of the serpent that Janamejaya awaited.'

'Takshak.'

'Precisely. Perceiving the power of this ceremony, the Naga had fled to the netherworld and pleaded to Indra for refuge. When Janamejaya found out about it, he instructed the sages to chant louder and louder. Takshak had coiled himself around Indra's bed, but the increased tempo of the mantras began to drag not only the serpent but even Indra towards that fire. This alarmed all the gods who requested snake goddess Manasa Devi to intercede. Manasa realised the gravity of the situation and dispatched her son Astika to try and stop this sacrifice.'

'Why Astika?'

'Astika was wise beyond his years and had mastered the four Vedas. Highly impressed with his scholarly mind, Janamejaya offered him a boon. The young man knew that the king never dishonoured his word. He begged him to end the ceremony and Janamejaya agreed. That was the fifth day of the lunar Shravan month. And that is now celebrated as Nag Panchami every year. The day snakes escaped extinction.'

'Quite a legend.'

'You also have enough folklore that tries to source how this festival began. In one particular tale, a farmer accidentally ploughs over three baby snakes. The infuriated mother serpent gets her revenge by slaying the farmer, his wife and two sons. The daughter of the household pacifies the snake by offering her milk and begs for forgiveness. The reptile relents and restores her family back to life.'

'The archetypal village fable.'

'Interesting you should say that because Nag Panchami also has an agrarian element. Farmers worship the snake deity to bless them with a bumper yield. If you notice the date, the festival falls right at the onset of the harvest season in India. Also, right before monsoon, when snakes are forced to come out of their waterlogged holes posing a threat to humans. So, we appease them to spare us from harm.'

'You said the date was the fifth day of the lunar month of...'

'Shravan. And fifth day or Panchami makes it even more interesting. Not many know that the number five is closely associated with serpents in Hindu mythology.'

'In what way?'

'Friday or the fifth day of the week is dedicated to snakes. Nagas are also associated with five colours. White, black, red, pink and yellow. Five prominent serpents are worshipped on Nag Panchami. And as per the Chakra tradition, the fabled Nagmani is believed to reside in the throat chakra of humans. The fifth chakra.'

'Fascinating. The Nagmani is quite the motif in all snake legends. Does it really exist?'

'You mean that miraculous gemstone guarded by snakes that can bring its owner infinite power and fortune? Sounds too fantastical to be true. But if there's one thing I believe, it's the power of our universe to constantly astonish us. To make that possible which our human minds are too arrogant to believe.'

'Or too naïve.'

'Exactly. That's why I write esoteric. We sometimes need a little more faith than we have.'

'You are a believer, Om.'

'A proud one. You may or may not believe everything you come across. Reject that which sounds improbable but it's crucial that one hears them out. It's so tempting to tick the easier boxes. The practical options. We all look for that peace. You may not have the faith but it's vital that you always have the choice. The choice to decide for yourself. Open your eyes and see.'

'Ah! For those who have read it, *Open Your Eyes and See* is also the title of Om's debut book, which came out a few years ago. One of the most definitive works on the esoteric. I must confess that a few chapters almost made a believer out of me. How come you haven't undertaken anything new since then?'

'I haven't been able to make time.'

'Perhaps you have exhausted all the esoteric our planet offers. You think you might come across something even more extraordinary?'

'One must never challenge life. Who knows what it might throw at your face?'

'Some mention your childhood as the reason why the esoteric attracts you.'

'I have heard of those theories. According to them I never got over the separation of my parents. And I sought answers then and am still seeking answers now. The questions have changed but my search lingers on. Also, that I found no faith in my parents and now seek it in other places.'

'Or perhaps because you are still single. You need a muse, Om.'

'Do I? All this could be true or a pile of crap. But I do enjoy unmasking. Unearthing. There's no greater joy than torturing a question until it screams out its own answer.'

'Your website attracts quite a crowd. I hear it's become a mecca for conspiracy theorists.'

'You could say that. We are a zany lot bickering about everything, from assassination theories to the paranormal. Ancient symbols and modern holocausts. No discussion is too uncanny. We ask newcomers to tread lightly. Some of our forum threads could really tangle you up.'

'But the site has also become a dartboard for critics. They say by positioning fringe theories at the forefront, you and your band amplify the insignificant.'

'Our website is about possibilities. Alternate stories that must be told. Peripheral voices that must be heard. No sane civilization can refuse to tolerate that.'

'I have been browsing through posts by some of your members. Quite unreal stuff. This one grabbed me instantly. A serpent again.'

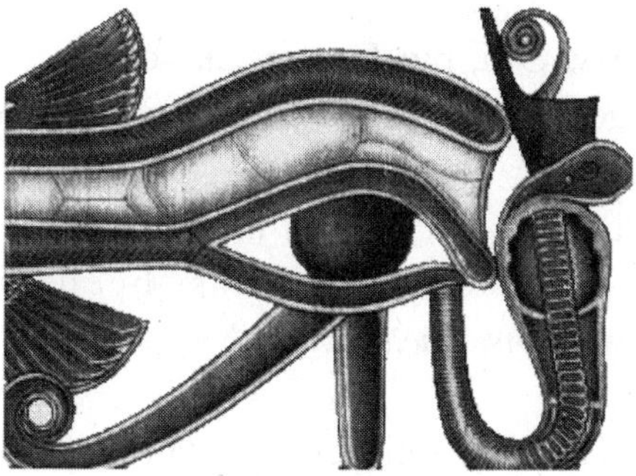

'That's one of our most active members. Goes by the username Zahak. He hasn't posted for a while now. What you see here is his last upload.'

'Interesting name.'

'Yes. Zahak comes from a Persian tale by Firdausi.'

'What's even more intriguing is that this Zahak has been slapping this particular image all over the Internet.'

'Really?'

The RJ googled it. Picasa and YouTube. Facebook and Twitter. Many more content-sharing pages and portals. The image was floating all through cyberspace with Zahak's name pasted across it.

'What is this symbol that Zahak is sharing everywhere? Looks quite eerie.'

'Far from it. This is the legendary…'

Patnaik paused. A familiar beep had caught his ears. The RJ was frowning.

'Is that your mobile, Om?'

'Yes. An SMS.'

The writer was staring at the message on his screen.

'But we are still on air.'

'I know.'

'I am sorry, Om, but I must ask you to...'

Patnaik got up. 'Nope. I will have to ask you to excuse me. I must leave.'

'Leave? But we are right in the middle of...'

'Terribly sorry. This has been fun. *Naga preetabhavantishantimaapnotibiaviboh.*'

'Excuse me?'

'It's the Nag Panchami blessing. Hail the Snake Goddess.'

Chapter 6

THE MAN WAS LOOKING AT THE MESSAGE AGAIN. NO WORDS.

Just an image.

♏

The zodiac symbol of Scorpio. But it was also what the police had named a murderer long back: the Scorpion. A murderer Patnaik had hunted down along with officer Suri. The writer knew Scorpion was dead. Gunned down by prison guards the night he had tried to escape. His phone beeped again. Another SMS from Suri.

Wankhede Stadium

And a third SMS. He gaped at the name.

Akram Qureshi

The cricketing legend. Retired skipper of the Indian team for nine years, he was among the greatest captains to have groomed the home players. His passionate affair and marriage with one of India's most bewitching models had only further intensified his aura. Sixteen glorious years on the green and then suddenly that scandal. A match-fixing controversy during the last game of his career had smeared his swan song black. But it was his silence that Patnaik had never understood. No one had. Why had the man never spoken throughout the BCCI proceedings? Or spoken just once to accept the allegation?

And what had happened to Akram now?

The writer had reached Wankhede. As they escorted him to the Garware Stand, Patnaik knew the official machinery of deduction was rolling all around him. Irregular lines of yellow plastic had sealed entry to the stand proclaiming it a crime scene. He had seen police vehicles lining the entrance next to an all-equipped CATS ambulance. Forensic personnel with cotton swabs and plastic caches jostled with the medical team carrying a surgical kit. And quite a few police officials with inscrutable faces.

'Hello, Om. We meet again.'

Suri was standing at the entrance to the box. The writer waved the symbol on his cell.

'Scorpion?'

'Scorpion is not fucking Moriarty, Om. You know he is dead. That case that brought us together is done and dusted. Scorpion is history.'

'Then why this image?'

'Because I knew this would rattle you. Draw you all the way here, no questions asked. That's what this case needs.'

'You mean Akram? What happened?'

Patnaik set foot inside the box but the officer stopped him.

'Not here. There. The washroom.'

'Washroom?'

He led the way. Two doctors were bent over the former cricketer. A police photographer was flashing his camera intermittently. Others scanning every inch of the space. But

Patnaik was watching Akram. Lying sprawled on the damp toilet floor of the Wankhede. A mass of congealed blood caking his body. Medics were forcing open his drooped eyelid and shining a torch over that pale blue eye.

'There,' Suri pointed. 'His forehead.'

The writer squinted his eyes. Something was stuck on Akram's brow. Something glinting in the hushed lights of the washroom. He bent closer and instantly recoiled.

'Horseshoe? Is that a horseshoe?'

'Right.'

'A horseshoe on his forehead?'

'Yes.'

'But why? Some kind of a statement?'

'Certainly intriguing. Turns the victim's body into an artefact.'

'Still the same cold cop. Not a trace of emotion despite all this gore.'

'I don't see the victim when I see a body, Om. I only see the killer. Handiwork of the bastard who must be stopped.'

The small curled metal was pasted right in the centre of the cricketer's forehead. Patnaik's eyes tiptoed over its contours.

Horseshoe over forehead?

The officer gestured towards the right side of Akram's torso, just below the chest. 'That's what they did to him.'

Patnaik was looking at an enormous white bandage specked deep red. 'Bullet wound?'

'No. Trauma indicates stab wound.'

'A knife then?'

'Far from it.' Suri indicated an object lying wrapped in plastic.

'Stump?'

'Yes.'

'They stabbed him with a cricket stump?'

'Quite handy if you ask me.'

The writer was ogling at the spike of the stump soaked in Akram's blood.

'How deep?'

'His liver's gashed.'

'But you said it's not murder.'

'Not yet. He's alive.'

The writer glanced at the body again. 'You are telling me someone impaled his liver and he bleeds all this blood and still survives.'

'Yes.'

'But that's great news,' Patnaik exclaimed. 'He can tell us who assaulted him. Can he hear us or have these doctors sedated him?'

'It's possible that he might be hearing us. But he can't respond.'

'I don't understand. You said…'

'I know what I said, Om. Akram is not dead. He is in a coma.'

The writer stared.

Coma?

A tap was dripping behind them. Leaking droplets like the words falling on his brain.

Liver

Horseshoe

Coma

Watching Suri place a piece of glass over Akram's nose. Watching the cricketer's breath create a film of mist on that cold surface.

'This is bizarre.'

He heard the officer snicker. 'Bizarre, Om? You haven't seen fucking bizarre.'

They were walking back towards the box. Standing by the glass now, with the stadium stretched out before them. Suri pointed.

'There. The scoreboard.'

It was not displaying the usual numbers. Only a word. A single name in large white font.

VIBHISHAN

Chapter 7

THE SCREEN CRACKLED AS THE STORY CAME HURTLING through. A harried anchor at ISTV Imphal was breaking the news about Akram Qureshi. Unconfirmed reports that the legendary cricketer may have met with an accident at Wankhede. But Atharva was hardly paying attention to his television. The priest was watching what his daughter Indira was doing.

The girl sat tethered to a cane chair. Loops of thick coir swirled all over her body, fastening it to the wood. It was as if she had been made one with that frame to sustain the rope twining around her like a creeper. The coils standing upon each other to imprison her in a vertical helix. Wreathing her torso, the rope had been knotted at the front and the back of the chair. Atharva was looking at her fingers working at the front. They were not coaxing that knot. They were commanding it to let go. Probing and prising to locate that one weak spot that would betray the arrangement. Surrender before her and in the process bring the entire edifice down. Feeling the knot throughout, she paused. She had found it. Her forceps tugged. Gently. Mildly. Then ferociously. Holding the joint by the hair, she wrenched one loop of the braided rope. Detached it further and further. Then another loop. And another. As the coir unfurled like a tendril, she pulled it apart, demolishing the knot. The first bastion had fallen. The rope loosened now but still encircling the girl like an adamant meridian. Her fingers travelled behind her back invading the other one. The second knot was thicker and took a while longer. A valiant resistance notwithstanding, it finally unravelled before the tyranny of her fingers. As Indira stood up, the rope slipped and collapsed at her feet like a weary hula hoop.

Atharva shivered as she laid her eyes on him. Large grey eyes that stood out against her pale face. Scar mark across her right cheek. Despite all these years, he still flinched when Indira looked at him. That gaze penetrating his skin and fingering his core. Scanning his flesh, pulling them apart strand by strand. Entering his mind and exposing his heart. Was this why his wife Jupita sometimes tied up their daughter when she was busy with chores or out of the house? Tied her up to avoid facing those eyes? Wondering how someone so fragile could have a vision so piercing? But Jupita's defence had always been that she wanted to safeguard their child who had been proclaimed autistic by doctors. Besides, Indira loved to stray outdoors, which only made matters worse. The priest had tried to stop Jupita numerous times but she single-mindedly persisted. And these days her arguments only made Atharva smile. Like he was smiling now.

Not autistic…If only Jupita knew what Indira really was…

And so, it had become a strange parlour game. The daughter waiting for her father to return from work and stand as her loyal audience as she would liberate herself. No matter how rigidly Jupita girdled the rope or how elaborate her knots were. Indira had never spoken a word in her life.

Never called Atharva *pa*. But he knew that she loved him to watch as she triumphed over her trap. Loved that look on his face marvelling at her stunt. He was doing it again.

Marvelling at how she did it every time. Marvelling because she was only seven years old.

The child was strumming the sacred white thread around Atharva's body. News about Akram was still on. ISTV Imphal confirming now that he had been rushed to the nearest hospital. The priest watched Indira walking up and standing before the television screen.

Chapter 8

SILLY POINT WAS THE NAME OF AKRAM'S VILLA, NOT FAR from Wankhede. A sprawling structure on the Mumbai seafront, its Corinthian stones flew high like a cricket ball pounded by its owner's willow. Today, however, something else had dwarfed the mansion. Suri sputtered in disbelief as he got out of his vehicle.

'Is that even possible?'

A rainbow arched across the sky over Silly Point. It would have hardly evoked much interest but for the fact that it did not display the usual seven-fold palette.

'It's red, Om. Only fucking red.'

'Yes. That's called a monochromatic rainbow. Extremely rare but is often sighted.'

Entering the villa, Patnaik was instantly struck by how quiet it was. Soundless. Wordless. But the place did not seem mute because of what had happened at Wankhede today. This was a silence that had been living here for a while. Breathing this air. Sleeping here every night. Silly Point was tight-lipped.

Like Akram was during his trial…

They were welcomed in the lounge area and informed that Akram's wife would join them presently. Ornate couches and crystal centrepieces glittered under a delicious little chandelier. Long-stemmed roses peeked out of a vase to stare at the wall before them. A wall planted with framed photographs hoarding assorted moments of Akram's life. This picture here was when he had been named one of the four Wisden players of the year. And that photo there displayed his arms waving the Champions Trophy. This one was a candid click with teammates inside a champagne-soaked locker room. And that one was with the President at the state dinner. One of him as a child holding a plastic bat. One of his son licking a cricket ball. Patnaik was standing before the largest one. Akram hitting a sixer with his trademark feral swing.

'I remember when he had played that shot.'

The officer chased his gaze. 'I know. Quite a match that.'

'I can almost hear the stadium exploding behind him. A thousand voices cheering for one man.'

'But going by what has happened at Wankhede today, someone's clearly not a fan.'

The writer dropped into the couch. 'What was he doing there?'

'Watching a Ranji match.'

'And no witnesses?'

'None.'

'How come, Suri? A man is attacked in Wankhede and a peculiar word is typed on the scoreboard. A match was on the whole time and nobody saw a thing?'

'The assault happened in the washroom. The attacker obviously chose a private space. Minimum risk. The word was typed on the score screen after they found Akram unconscious and raised an alarm. It must have been the perfect distraction.'

'After they found him? So, whoever did this waited for that moment to type out the name?'

'Looks like it.'

'Must be quite vital then. Vibhishan. But what?'

'I was hoping you would tell me. What about the horseshoe?'

Patnaik shrugged. 'Horseshoes have been used as talismans for ages. The belief apparently originated with Saint Dunstan. He was the Archbishop of Canterbury and a blacksmith by trade. They say when Satan asked him to make a horseshoe for his hooves, the Archbishop clapped on a pair which caused him enormous pain. Dunstan removed them only after Satan swore never to enter a house that hung a horseshoe on its door.'

'A good-luck charm.'

'Yes. Being the core component of blood, the metal also symbolises a life force.'

'We had plenty of blood in that washroom.'

'And he didn't die. Someone almost carves his liver, and he only slips into a coma.'

'You don't seem too happy that he's still alive.'

'Don't be absurd, Suri. I am relieved. But also extremely puzzled.'

'And that brings us back to Vibhishan.'

Patnaik glanced again at Akram's photograph on the wall. The officer nodded. 'I know. Vibhishan is the archetypal traitor who betrayed his elder brother Ravana by supporting Rama. And Akram betrayed his team. Is that the link? You think this is a hate attack?'

'Possible. But why now after all these years?'

'Once a traitor, always a traitor.'

'You are convinced Akram sold out?'

'There's hardly any doubt, Om. The evidence. His own stance. Guilt's fucking clear as glass.'

'You might be looking through the glass darkly, officer.'

Suri froze. He had recognised the voice that spoke those words. The lady of Silly Point.

Patnaik stood up scanning her face. One of the most celebrated models of her time, that visage had not fought with her passing years. Not clung to its waning youth as so many faces did. Instead it had allowed age to carve lines and remodel its contours. Not an empty paper but a parchment filled with tales. It had lent itself freely to the elements to play with it. He was not looking at a plastic landfill. This was a face where rivers had flowed to create a valley of flowers.

The officer was apologising. She nodded weakly. 'One has got used to it now. What saddens me is how his legacy lies under a shadow. And there's nothing I can do to pull it out.'

Patnaik shook his head. 'It does not. Not for admirers like me who know he could never have betrayed the game.'

She walked closer and shook his hand. 'Mr Patnaik. Pleasure to meet you. I haven't read your book, but I have heard you are a believer. I see that.' She motioned them to sit.

'How's he doing?'

'Still comatose. They are doing what they can.' Her right hand had picked up a cricket ball and was tossing it repeatedly.

Suri coughed. 'We are terribly sorry to detain you. I know you would rather be in the hospital with him.'

'Doesn't matter, officer. There's hardly anything I can do. Besides I need to know who's behind this.'

'You did not accompany him to the match today?'

'No. I was at a charity auction.'

'And is there anything you can tell us about the assault? The horseshoe or the word on the screen?'

'Nothing. I have heard the details at Wankhede. The whole thing appears terribly theatrical.'

'Suri and I were discussing whether it could be a hate attack,' the writer said.

'For that match-fixing scandal you mean? We know there are still a few out there who would love to see him drop dead. Perhaps that's what this really was. Strange how love can die out but hatred endures.'

She indicated the wall. 'I call it the Wagon Wheel. When I don't find him anywhere, I find him here in these pictures.'

'That's a sweet one.'

'Akram and his elder brother. They used to fight a lot. Still do.'

The ball paused. She went quiet as if she no longer sat in that chair. As if she was entering those frames one by one. All of them once more. Finding her place in every memory. The men understood. They waited for her to come back. When she returned, she asked a question.

'If I tell you what really happened will you keep it to yourself?'

Suri bent forward. 'I thought you said you had no idea who attacked him.'

'I wasn't talking about that. I meant the match-fixing.'

She was staring at Patnaik now. Was she pleading with him to let her speak? Asking them to share her load? He held her hands gently, and she began.

'Akram was tremendously happy that day. They had

won every match in that series and were clear favourites to clinch the final now. I remember he was about to leave for the stadium when that call came.'

'What call?'

'The call that changed everything. It was the team manager. He had discovered that the vice-captain and two other players had issued an enormous pay-off to the rival team to lose the series. Akram's team was not winning because they were better. They were winning because their competition had been underperforming throughout.'

The woman shivered. 'I will never forget the look on his face. Pain. Harrowing pain. And then that rage. When he left, I knew our lives would never be the same again.'

'But we never won that final.'

'Yes. Minutes before the match he had a closed-door meeting with the rival team. And he paid them thrice the amount that his teammates had offered.'

'You mean?'

'Yes. He did not bribe them to lose. He paid them to make sure they play their natural game.'

Om and Suri looked at each other. 'He paid them to win.'

'Cricket was his life. The integrity of the game was above everything else. He had been deceived and he knew he had to correct it. We won the series, but that final was a shameful defeat. It was his way of teaching his younger teammates to value the game. Respect the arena. That there can be no short cuts to holding a trophy aloft.'

'But no one understood that.'

'No one. The press found out about Akram's meeting with the other team. They had no idea what had conspired behind those doors, and Akram remained quiet. They made a monster out of him. He was now the fraud god of cricket. The trial began, but his silence continued.'

'He covered up for his teammates.'

'They were young. At the threshold of their careers. He was due to retire.'

'Were they repentant? Did they thank him?'

'He never asked. They never did.'

She ceased. The writer gently removed his hand. 'So that was it.'

She laughed as the ball jumped again. 'Big questions can have such small answers. Frustrating, isn't it?'

'I feel terrible,' Suri cleared his throat. 'I should have trusted.'

'Faith, officer. It's probably the most difficult magic. Never easy to conjure.'

The house was still silent as they left. They recognised it now. The silence was not unspeaking. It was unspoken. Unvoiced. It implied. Silly Point wanted you to understand. Outside, the rainbow still stretched as if the sky had slit its wrist. Or perhaps it was Akram's blood. The red devouring its own spectrum.

Chapter 9

WHEN TRANSLATED, KALPATARU MEANT ETERNAL TREE. CAST in gold and studded with gemstones, this wish-granting tree had emerged during Samudra Manthan or the Churning of the Ocean of Milk. Installed in paradise by Indra, the tree had shaded sages like Durvasa to meditate upon the universe. It was now the name of the pharmaceutical company owned by Ashwin Tomar. Kalpataru developed, produced and marketed life-saving drugs and was also involved in clinical research. The company's twelve-tier glass edifice was one of the most imposing landmarks of Mumbai's Carter Road. And right below the earth where all its glass ended, coiled a subterranean bunker of cement and stone. The first three levels were car-parking areas while the lowest depth was an abandoned basement. Yeva entered this darkness and switched on a bulb.

Another day was over and she was home.

The heated tungsten flamed as bright as it could but ignited the darkness only partly. The place was moderately furnished with Yeva inhabiting just a quarter of this derelict zone. The rest of the basement was a dumping yard where battered furniture, laboratory apparatus and cardboard crates stood heaped upon each other. Plastic vials fought for space with fractured glass ampoules and flasks. Dust had blinded computer screens, and strips of expired capsules were poking their heads as if clamouring to be heard: they seemed to say that they could still heal. The wasteland largely synthetic except for cobwebs with decomposing cadavers sucked dry. The wall on the right held up a painting. An orange fire turning a green forest black. And before that wall rose a pole.

A wooden staff.

Yeva was slumped on her bed, breathing the usual rancid air. Getting up, she splashed cold water on her face. Water beads clinging to the mirror, reflecting her jubilant face. Changing her clothes, she pulled a drawer and picked up a hypodermic from inside it. Opening her mouth wide, she lowered the needle down her throat. A second later, her fingers climbed the syringe and pulled its piston up. Up. Up. She took it out gingerly and looked at the tube. The hollow was no longer empty. It held blood.

Akram's blood.

Holding the syringe, Yeva walked towards the staff. The wooden figure of a serpent was twined around it. As soon as her fingers opened the reptile's mouth, the basement blazed white. Pure white. It was as if she had cracked an enchanted egg and its yolk had smeared everything with light. The object nestling inside the wooden jaws was flashing like a hundred suns and thousand moons. Trying to blind her once more.

Standing at the centre of this phosphorescence, Yeva took it out.

Placing the object on her left palm, she dangled the hypodermic above it. Her thumb pushed the piston slowly. Gently. Coaxing the syringe to share its fluid. The blood passed through the needle and oozed from the tip forming a red globule. Glinting in that luminous glow. Sliding from that cold metal. The drop shivered and gradually detached itself from the needle. She watched as the blood descended on that luminous object. Covering it. Colouring it. She brought the object closer to her eyes. It was blue now. A very faint blue. Yeva smiled.

Miles to go before I sleep…

She carefully deposited it back inside the serpent's jaws. Tossing the syringe away, she returned to her bed and switched on the nightlamp. The shelf next to her was stacked with books. Yeva pulled out the Amar Chitra Katha sitting next to a Kafka.

Chapter 10

The Rishiputra grew in years dwarfing one and all
Like a shooting Asoka tree, he stood singularly tall
His brain like a magnet sucking every possible skill
Mystery of every weapon and how to defend and kill
Dhanurvidya or archery, the boy did gleefully seize
Brahmavidya of the self, slipped his soul like grease
Bigger and bigger his arms now to wield every arrow
But the heart too stunted to grieve at another's sorrow
Thus rained knowledge soaking the Rishiputra's mind
But his belly remained dry, not a morsel could he find
So frugal was their shelter, that family and all their ilk
That the boy's brow blazed, but he had never seen milk
Beguiled by his mates, one day, like a cat fooled by mice
For what he drank as milk was but water paste with rice
Soon students with virgin arrows lined up big and small
The rishi prized each one of them but his son most of all
Epics fall short to measure the depth of a father's heart
Love for his first-born son that never from him does part
Even as he enlightened them with each knack of the bow
He whispered celestial secrets only for his son to know
But one disciple's aptitude was as unflinching as his aim
Born in the month of snow, Silver Prince was his name
His bow twanged liked thunder when out his arrows flew

Hitting every mark like on flowers dropped morning dew
When that Prince slayed a reptile to save the rishi's life
The man's affection spilled over planting seeds of strife
The Rishiputra saw his father doting on the Silver Prince
Pupil owning art and heart and began resenting him since
His father depriving others to make the Silver Prince shine
Pained his soul and his eyes now poured forth secret brine
But the rishi remained unseeing as only a loving eye can
It never saw his divine child was becoming a lesser man.

Chapter 11

EXHIBIT I260318

Suri was fingering the new package he had found at his doorstep. His name and the label on it again but wrapped in a different paper this time.

Red paper.

He was looking at what appeared to be a small pitcher. It had a stem-shaped cylindrical neck and an oblong body like a beetle. Two expansive handles sprouted from either side on top and curled to merge with the main torso below. The officer grazed the pitcher's surface lightly. The material was ceramic. Painted all over its bulging body was a mythical scene. The central figure depicting a warrior clad in full armour and head gear. His right hand wielded a sword while his left seized a mammoth monster by the neck. The animal's forked tongue lashing out at the warrior as if making a frantic attempt to inject a load of venom. Both figures exuding loads of testosterone as the earthy tones of ochre, black and crimson joined hands to create an illusion alarmingly real.

Minutes later the Internet answered. The caption on his screen solved the mystery.

Amphora with Cadmus slaying the Serpent Dragon

Chapter 12

THE MAN SITTING BEHIND THE DESK WAS SMILING AT YEVA.

'I knew you would come. I had been waiting.'

She advanced towards him almost as if her body was being transported without her own physical effort. 'Waiting for me? Am I fulfilling a prophecy?'

'You fulfil your destiny. And part of mine.'

Yeva picked up a book. '*Investigating Inequality*. Interesting. You still love to teach. Educate them all.'

'I know nothing else.'

'But is it serving any purpose? Altering basic human nature?'

'That's the ultimate goal. We begin with harnessing the animal within man.'

'Animal? You make that sound as if man is the nobler being here.'

'You don't think he is, Yeva?'

She shook her head. 'I have come across quite a few. The caveman inside men is still not extinct. And it continues to kill. Kills for food. Kills for wealth. Still kills to survive. You talk about inequality? The greatest inequality is how natural selection has given way to human selection. Men have usurped that privilege. They lord over the planet now and decide who lives and who dies.'

'And you want that power? The power men have attained by the virtue of their mind?'

'A brilliant mind no doubt but bursting with such arrogance. Sitting atop the food chain now, men are fingering the cosmos. What good do your books do?'

He flicked the table-lamp switch. 'There's darkness in the sky, Yeva. Why does the sun shine then? It's easy to condemn the dark but difficult to become the sun. To burn and illuminate the universe. There is much evil in this world and you can only balance it by doing good. Make that beast within us aware of the choices it has. And hope that it chooses what's right.'

'Have you made the right choices? What about what happened last year? That girl on the university roof?'

'Nothing happened.'

'I heard you didn't do anything. Still the same silent spectator? Powerless to raise your voice against injustice?'

'Not everyone can comprehend power, Yeva. Inaction may not always be a sin. Even you can choose not to do what you are doing.'

'No. I have chosen.'

The man smiled. 'You remind me of Karna.'

'Karna?'

'Yes. His soul had turned pungent like yours. Years of persecution driving him into the arms of Adharma. He had attained greatness and could have been greater still, but he lacked the courage. The courage to choose the right option. An oppressed heart must develop the compassion to deliver others from injustice. Channel its anger to reform society. Simply scratching one's own scabs heals neither the man nor his world.'

Yeva laughed. 'That's exactly what I am doing. Seeking therapy for old wounds.'

'By coming here to wound me?'

'Does it matter? You will live to see another day. All of you will. How does it feel to be you? To be thus?'

'Feels blessed,' he folded his hands.

'Not tired? Saturated?'

'Sometimes. I do find the world closing upon me. But then I think of all that I have done and all that I can still do.'

Her eyes turned moist. 'Not everyone feels as blessed as you. I have seen that agony. The desire to end it all.'

'One can neither end nor begin anything, Yeva. We cannot be alpha or omega. We can only accept being a part of the continuum. Make sure we evolve and so do others around us.'

'A bleeding soul cares nothing about the world. It demands revenge to end its pain.'

'That's a myth. Revenge can never soothe you, Yeva. The pain you talk about is evil. It has contaminated you like Karna. Don't consume yourself. That circle can only imprison. Break that bond. Free yourself while there is still time.'

'Time hasn't come yet. It will soon. And you shall see what it brings forth.' She picked up a red marker and wrote a word on the white board behind the man. 'Wish me luck.'

'But you will fail.'

'Another prophecy?'

'Just natural law.'

He could feel her body throbbing ruthlessly. Yeva was smelling the man's skin now. He watched her eyes change and closed his own. Hearing children faraway reciting tables.

Six times one…six times two…six times three…

Chapter 13

KRIPACHARYA

Teacher to the royal clan of Hastinapur, his birth was oddly enough the outcome of a celestial conspiracy. Maharishi Gautam's grandson Sharadwan had grown up to be an invincible archer. So fierce was the young man's skill that his arrows sent shock waves even among the gods. The one to panic most was Indra, who hastily dispatched nymph Janapadi to seduce the archer. Born out of this scheme were Kripa and his sister Kripi, who were later adopted by King Shantanu of Hastinapur. Revered by many, he had stood by helplessly when Draupadi had been disrobed. Survivor of the Mahabharata war, Kripacharya's name was made forever immortal in the pages of the epic. But why had it been written in red letters on the whiteboard in a classroom at Mumbai University?

Patnaik was asking himself the question again and again.

Why Kripacharya?

Below it lay Lalit Trehan's body slumped on his chair. Academician and sociologist, Trehan was one of the most prized minds of the country. A champion of egalitarianism, his contribution to education in India had won him the Nobel Prize last year when he had just turned forty. For Trehan, literacy was the core competency that turned men into agents of economic boom. And now he lay in a coma in his own classroom.

'Just like Akram.'

Suri nodded. 'Same attacker. Horseshoe on the forehead. And penetration wound on the left scraping the liver.'

'Liver? Again?'

'Surprised?'

'Confounded. I thought Akram's injury was a random wound. That the assailant simply went for the body part closest to him, but this doesn't seem to be the case. Two bodies injured in the exact same place. The same organ damaged. Hardly coincidence, Suri. Is the attacker deliberately targeting the liver?'

'Looks like it. And Trehan is in coma too.'

'But why? Why liver?'

'If I had the fucking answers, Om, you wouldn't be here.' The officer pointed at the letters on the board. 'Vibhishan was written in white. This one's in red marker. Do the two names mean something together?'

'Can't think of anything,' Patnaik scratched his chin. 'Both men existed in different yugas. Vibhishan was part of the Ramayana while Kripa hails from the Mahabharata. They never crossed paths. Not until now that is.'

'Didn't they both fight wars?'

'They did. Vibhishan fought along Rama while Kripa was forced to fight against the Pandavas. He was one of the few who survived that eighteen-day carnage and was later appointed teacher for Arjuna's grandson Parikshit. Hardly any connection between these two names.'

'There has to be a common factor. The modus operandi

is exactly the same in both cases. Definitely the same bastard at work.'

'Any witnesses?'

'None again. Trehan was here checking papers after college got over. It's Holi the day after tomorrow and almost everyone left a tad early. The watchman found him and informed us.'

Suri went on to snarl at two reporters who had somehow filtered through the police cordon. Outside, the press was clamouring for a statement. News trickling in that the chief minister might arrive, further accelerating the chaos. But Patnaik heard nothing. Just the sound of various words clinking inside him like pieces of glass.

Horseshoe…Akram…Vibhishan…Trehan…Kripacharya… Liver…Coma…

The officer's hand on his shoulder pierced his trance. He handed him his cell. 'You better see these too.'

'What are these?'

'Pictures of two objects that have landed on my table in the past few months. Both addressed to me.'

'Related to these attacks?'

'Akram was assaulted after I received the first object. And now Trehan meets the same fate after I get the second one.'

He displayed the two envelopes in which the objects had been parcelled. Patnaik gasped. 'White and red. Colours both the names—Vibhishan and Kripacharya—were written in.'

'Not just that, Om. Look at the numbers on each envelope. The first one is 090218. Akram was attacked on 9 February 2018. This one says 260318. Today's date.'

The writer touched the numbers. 'You think someone's informing you about the assaults? Warning you in advance?'

'Precisely. Someone knows the attacker's plans and is helping me out.'

'If he wants to help, why not send plain text? Why these cryptic messages?'

'Terrified of being found out probably. Wants to inform us in secret. I have a feeling more fucking envelopes are on the way.'

The sudden sound of glass hitting earth startled them. A female member of the forensic team had made a red splatter on the floor. She was collecting samples of Trehan's blood in test-tubes. The man's torso wound somewhat congealed now and yet leaking. She shivered.

'Who would have thought the man would have had so much blood?'

Patnaik caught sight of her badge.

MANU

He nodded. 'Forensics and *Macbeth*? Not bad.'

As she swept the test-tube debris, the officer handed his mobile to Patnaik. 'Check these out. The objects I received.'

'Have you identified them?'

'Yes. The first one is a verse from some poem called *Snake*.'

'*Snake*? The one by D.H. Lawrence?'

'Ditto.'

'I love that. A childhood favourite.'

'Charming. This other one is apparently called an amphora.'

'Right. Ancient flasks used to carry wine or oil. Looks like a miniature replica. The image on the amphora seems to be Cadmus.'

'It is. Cadmus killing a dragon.'

The writer's eyes widened. His finger was flipping them again and again. 'Do you see?'

'See what?'

'You wanted a common denominator. These two objects are giving us that.'

'What denominator?'

'The poem describes Lawrence's encounter with a snake. And Cadmus killed a dragon. Not just any dragon. A dragon that was an Aonian serpent.'

'You mean snake?'

'Precisely. Both are about snakes.'

'But what does that mean? What do fucking snakes have to do with all this now?'

Patnaik walked towards the window. A rainbow domed the horizon again. Another one that had erased its vibgyor and only retained red.

Curving like a snake…

'Excuse me, sir.'

They turned. Manu stood holding a plastic container in her hands.

'We had found drops of these on the floor. The lab results are just in.'

The writer was looking at the substance inside. Pale amber liquid glinting in the classroom tubelight. Suri took the container gingerly from her hands.

'And?'

'Tests confirm the presence of neurotoxins in the sample.'

'Neurotoxins?'

Patnaik whispered before the woman could answer. 'Venom.' He looked directly into the officer's eye. 'Snake venom.'

Chapter 14

THE ROOTS OF KALPATARU WERE ON FIRE AGAIN. THE basement squinting at the wooden serpent's open mouth as if it was sucking on an ember of coal. Yeva extracted that object once more.

Orb of eternal fire. Chunk of everlasting ice.

She pressed the syringe to pour the second drop. The object was drinking Trehan's lifeblood. Its silver beams speckled now with a richer shade of blue. The jaws of wood closed over it again eating all the stardust in the room.

Yeva opened her journal and picked up a pen.

Yeva's Journal—pg 1

Nilgiri Forest
Tamil Nadu

I was watching them from below.

There were three of them. An old woman in a yellow top and animal-print skirt. She was dabbing her cheek with a tissue and looking at her silver watch. A young boy holding a sack was squatting on the ground. Next to him was an old man in a dhoti and a serpent tattoo on his forehead. They were examining something. Opaque snake skin freshly shed. Its scales gleaming like metal. I had never seen the other two but the old man's face petrified me. He was Irula. I had seen him countless times walking through these forests brandishing a long wooden rod. Always hunting down the same thing. He was on the trail again today. Saying this was fresh skin and would cost more.

I followed them as they trudged deeper and deeper into the Nilgiri. My heart sinking inside me like that sun on the horizon. Should I strike? Slay them all? The old man was twirling his rod. I knew what that piece of wood could do. I had seen it shatter bones. Pound bodies into pulp. They had reached. Gathered around an abode.

The man inserted the rod into the hole like a knife plunging into butter. The snake instantly burst out of the hole. A gleaming reptile resting after sloughing off its skin. Trying to stab its fangs into the old man's thigh now, but the captor was laughing. He had seized its tail while the rest of its body lay coiled around the rod. The snake was shrieking incessantly, but none of them heard it. Only I could. And the Nilgiri.

They were stroking the looped body. The enamel skin.

I hardly knew how long I had been following them, but they finally arrived at a clearing. In the middle stood a large stone cabin melding into the dark except for a solitary bulb at the entrance. The trio entered, shutting the door behind. I circled the structure round and round. Elongated on both sides and not a crack or opening anywhere. Then I paused. The ground so far had been dry but the patch here was damp. I knew what it was. A splintered drainpipe.

Minutes later I was inside a dark room that reeked of human urine and faecal matter. The metal door was slightly ajar. I peeked.

The woman was there and the boy and the old man. Several more humans. One group sat with small machetes in their hands. They were pulling pythons from a heap and chopping their heads one by one. Others nearby were peeling the skin off their decapitated bodies. Did they not know that pythons never died instantly? Their metabolism was such that they remained conscious and felt pain for hours even after being beheaded? Another group was working on cobras. Forcing open their jaws and shoving plastic tubes down their throats. Water was then being pumped, bloating them up, which made it easier to tear off their skin. Some were binding ropes around their necks to prevent the water from gushing out. Many such swollen cobras had their heads nailed to wooden posts. Left hanging in a row to die a slow death. Those whose bodies that had become limp were being slit open from both ends to loosen and remove the skin.

The old man was yelling at the woman. Demanding more money. The boy picked up a dead viper and swung it around the old man's neck. The woman smiled as the viper knotted tighter and tighter. That snake was there too. The one they had captured today. A man had finished knifing through its rind. Tossed now into a pile of skinned bodies.

I never knew who that snake was. I never will.

I wished that day to rid earth of man.

And I wished for something else. I was told that what I was asking for was almost impossible. It demanded asceticism and austerity. Demanded kindling a fire within my kernel through relentless meditation. Only one in a million serpents could step into that dimension.

I wished that day to cross that threshold.

The pen slipped from Yeva's grip. She was hungry. Picking up an egg from the plate on her night stand, she swallowed it and regurgitated the shell. The looking glass before her caught her face. She liked how she looked, but it was time to disrobe. As the night turned darker, it no longer found Yeva on the bed. Only a blue krait glistening on that mattress like a rope of sapphire.

Chapter 15

THE TUNES OF THE TOUDRI WERE LAUGHING AND WEEPING. Strains that perhaps belonged to an eternal song that Atharva had heard before or not yet heard. Indira's affection for the bamboo flute had started a year ago and she adored playing it at dawn when her father stood looking at the climbing sun. Her melody warming his household like the infant rays falling from the sky. And the priest grateful for the same things every morning.

New day…new chances…

The toudri was singing again, and Atharva was wondering why it sounded sweeter than other days. Maybe because today was Yaosang. The rest of the country called it Holi, but here in Imphal it was always Yaosang. A five-day carnival that merged colour play with a roll call of revelries. In a few hours, groups of children would come knocking on every door to collect Nakadeng or money and gifts. Drums and cymbals would announce ongoing rehearsals for Thabal Chongba. The moon dance, when young boys and girls would hold each other's hands and sway to music in a vigorous circle. The sacred flame at Kangla Fort would blaze brighter. And Holi Pala and Eshei songs would resound from Sri Govindajee Temple.

The flute stopped. The priest walked into the central

courtyard to see Indira sitting on a stool. She was sipping on a tall glass of grape juice. Before her sat his wife untying newspaper parcels that held abeer and rangoli powder. Black and white cradling red, blue, green and yellow.

'I see you haven't tied up the child today, Jupita.'

'What's the use, Bamon? You will open her knots like you always do.'

'You still think I release her every time?'

'Don't you?'

Atharva stood next to the woman. 'Why do you refuse to celebrate what Indira really is? Why do you yoke her like an animal? When you loop that rope around her, you don't bind her. You only shackle yourself tighter and tighter. Add more layers to the crust that covers you. How do you breathe, Jupita? I see you all wrapped up like these paper parcels. Undo yourself. Break that shell like your daughter liberates herself and you shall see the colours of her aura.'

The priest tinted his palm with abeer and extended it towards Jupita's face, but she backed off.

'What terrifies you so much?'

'You, Bamon. You terrify me. Your constant attempt to paint a halo around this girl terrifies me. She's a child. A seven-year-old child. Stop making a goddess out of her.'

'I cannot make her anything, Jupita. She is what she is.'

'Yes. An autistic girl who can't fend for herself. Who has no teachers or friends. Who's never read a book or used a crayon. My blood turns cold when I try to imagine what life has planned for her. But do you care? No. You are unaffected. You rejoice in her condition and you want me to join in.'

'I rejoice because I recognise her. Stop dumping your

pity on her. She only asks for your love because that's all she has to offer. And she asks you to respect who she is. Our daughter is not autistic. She is unique. An evolved being. But you choose to remain blind.'

'I am a simple Meitei woman, Bamon. I see what I can. That child hasn't uttered a single word in seven years.'

'I hear her perfectly, Jupita. You can too if you make yourself porous. The day you do that, you shall touch her feet. Rise above the physical. Not her body. Try to look beyond that.'

'Is that what your voodoo teaches you?'

'Voodoo?'

The woman strode towards her husband's bookshelf on the opposite wall. A single sweep of her arm brought down stacks of Agama scriptures tumbling on the wooden floor.

'This Tantra that you have found.'

Atharva picked up a text and touched it to his head. 'I did not find Tantra. Tantra found me. And I am grateful for that.'

'Your wordplay does not dazzle me,' Jupita clutched the sacred white thread around his body. 'Should I still address you as Bamon? Do you remember that word? It means priest. I married a priest. Your ancestors migrated here to become Manipuri Brahmins. Men in your family have been the royal priests of Imphal. You hold a masters in World Literature. You do lectures on Theology. You are revered as a scholar by so many and now you start practising sorcery? How can this house play with colours when you wade in black magic?'

'You are so ignorant. Tantra does not conjure the devil. It helps you achieve spiritual symmetry. Repairs the threads of your soul so you may regain that primal pattern. It unites polarities and makes you one with the cosmos. My life never gave me options. I did not choose to inhabit my mother's womb. Follow my father into priesthood or take your hand in marriage. Gods have relented now. Tantra was a choice and I chose.'

'Yes. You made the choice and we paid the price. Me and her.'

'Indira?'

'Both of us. I was cursed to bear a child like her. And that poor child cursed with a spastic life. Cursed to be unnatural because your Tantra violates nature.'

'Tantra venerates nature. Validates forces that are repressed by culture. Censored by the very society you hold so dear. It's all about infinite probabilities, Jupita. Embracing energies that can truly uplift.'

'But our house has been damned. Look at her,' she pointed at Indira. 'A seven-year-old who merely exists. Makes no demands because she supplies nothing in return. No purpose. No will. Who does absolutely nothing...'

Her index finger froze mid-air. Gawking at the vacant stool. The child was on the floor, bent over the colours. She was clenching a piece of newspaper that lay discarded next to the colour piles. But they were looking at what that other hand was doing.

'She's drawing.'

Jupita hardly moved. Atharva walked. Slowly as if the sound of his feet would puncture this vision.

Indira drawing...

Her fingers were dancing all over the abeer. Running amuck to trace lines and circles over blue and red. Cutting through the red powder to generate a curious image. And now her index finger spiralling through blue. Carving another picture. The floor had transformed into a canvas sheet. Latent energy inside her motoring through the abeer to proclaim that her seventh year had discovered something new. Her nails caked with colour now like shoes kicking that painted dust. Red and blue melding into a purple mist to stain her face. The priest saw what she had drawn. Two creatures under a starry sky.

A horse in red.

A snake in blue.

His mobile flashed as he clicked the images. The next moment Indira collapsed. As Atharva pounced on the unconscious body and rubbed her palms, the newsprint she was holding slipped. His eyes caught a man's photograph on that fragment and the headline above.

LALIT TREHAN IN COMA…

It was dark outside when the priest woke up in alarm. Jupita was screaming. Eleven hours had passed since they had hospitalised their daughter. Doctors had advised them medical observation for the night. Atharva had closed the door of their private ward and opened the window. He had seen Indira go to sleep. The nurse had left and he had crashed on the couch next to his wife. And now Jupita was pointing at her and screaming.

'But she's only seven…seven…'

Atharva squinted. Unable to process what he was seeing. His eyes dilating now. Dilating wider and yet refusing to receive what was being shown.

Indira…

She was up. Drawing on the white hospital bedsheet. Figures in bright red. Red as the blood that was heavily soaking her undergarments. Coating her thighs. The child dipping her fingers again and again in this magic ink that her body had suddenly begun discharging. Smearing and watching that red paint dry. Jupita still wailing.

'Only seven...'

And the priest looking at two familiar shapes etched in blood.

Horse...snake...

Chapter 16

'WHAT HAVE YOU BROUGHT, CAIN?'

'My land's produce, Lord. Fruits of my soil.'

'What have you, Abel?'

'My lamb's produce, Lord. Meat of its first-born.'

Ashwin clapped twice. The sound was not flushed with the harmony of applause. It had notes of discord that jarred. The actor was not pleased.

'With pride, Cain. With pride,' he walked towards the two students playing the Biblical brothers. 'You have just placed nature's bounty at the feet of the Lord. The choicest fruits of your labour. Lift your voice up. Round tones. Don't learn the words. Let the words learn you. Respect what you have brought for the Lord, Cain. Respect it so that when he scorns your yield, that injustice shall stab the audience. Continue!'

The senior playing the Lord looked at Abel's offering with favour but not Cain's. The eyes of the elder brother boiled with fury. The Lord addressed him.

'Why such rage, Cain? Why such sorrow? There can be no forgiveness without the shedding of blood. Do what is right and I shall embrace you too. But as long as sin crouches by your door, I cannot enter. If evil has you, I cannot have you. Fig leaves do not cover transgressions. Can you peel off sin? Conquer your heart to conquer mine?'

But Cain had flung his fruits away.

'If you desire blood, I shall give you blood.'

'Bravo!' Ashwin exulted. 'And then Cain calls Abel to the fields and there he kills him. We turn the lights red. Deep red. The entire stage stained with the blood of the younger son of Adam and Eve. The Lord sees Cain standing alone and realises he is no longer his brother's keeper. The Lord's prejudiced mind declares that like his parents, Cain too has sinned. Theirs had been the First Disobedience. This was the First Murder. And the Lord does what all lords do. He curses him. Action!'

'You have put your sibling to death, Cain. Shed your own blood. I demanded that you slaughter a lamb but you slayed your brother. You are cursed. Cursed for life and beyond. You have tainted the earth with your sin. Made it open its mouth and drink your brother's blood. This earth knows you no more. It will no longer yield fruit for you. No longer fill your hunger or water your thirst. Your body shall quake and you will forever remain a fugitive. The restless wanderer.'

'Anyone who finds me can kill me, Lord. Will you watch over me?'

The Lord made a mark on his forehead.

'I will, Cain. You have been branded. Anyone who executes you will suffer seven times over.'

Cheers rang out from students in that University classroom watching the rehearsal. A little over a month ago, Trehan had lain comatose in this room. Faint bloodstains were still streaking the floor, taking their time to fade. Shreds of official tape still adhering to walls, proclaiming it a former crime scene. Once the police had cleared the room a few days back, the Dean knew he was in for some serious damage control. It was time to quell negative publicity and propel everyone towards a familiar routine. Trehan had been directing the Cain and Abel play for the annual festival and the Dean had instantly reached out to Ashwin Tomar. An alumnus of the University, Tomar had quite readily agreed to conduct a week-long workshop. Even suggested that he would like to do it in Trehan's classroom *in memoriam.* The Dean, seated by the whiteboard now, was applauding along with the others. The workshop's first day had just ended fabulously well and he knew that the star's presence was going to exorcise all demons by the end of the week.

'I would like everyone here to join me in thanking our very own Ashwin Tomar. The busiest actor in the film industry today but he heeds when his alma mater seeks him out. And going by what we saw today, we surely have an outstanding Biblical production to look forward to. Trehan's absence shall be acutely felt, but he would be mighty thrilled that his play is in such good hands. What he may not approve of though, is Ashwin's interpretation of God cursing Cain as unjust. That's unheard of. Are you creating a new version of the tale?'

The star was tapping his fingers on Trehan's chair. 'No. I was questioning. Questioning what the story of Cain has been telling us down the ages. That's what our play must do. Interrogate this legend like never before.'

'Interrogate what? Cain and Abel is a simple tale that teaches us to nurture good and close our hearts to evil. It reminds us of God's love for his flock. He punished Cain but also watched over him. Some Jewish traditions even assert that Cain was born of Eve's union with Satan which explains his immorality. And yet God pledged him security and refuge. The mark of Cain is a symbol of divine intervention. God knows only love, but if you sin you shall be punished. Period. What can you problematise?'

Ashwin pulled the chair and sat down. 'The murder stems from Cain's jealousy that his offering was rejected while Abel's was accepted. The first question that arises here is why were both brothers making an offering? The answer lies in God's statement to Cain that there can be no forgiveness without blood. They were both seeking forgiveness. But both were young lads who had hardly sinned in their lives so far. One was a farmer and the other a herdsman. Why did God consider them impure? Because they were the sons of Adam and Eve. The couple who had committed Original Sin. God believed that the brothers inherited the transgression of their parents. Their flesh tainted like an infection. Do you find carbon stains on a diamond? Sting darts in honey? I hardly think so, but you say he is a merciful God.'

'Both were obliged to make an offering and earn pardon. But the Lord rejected Cain's offering because he had shed no blood. There can be no forgiveness without blood, he declared. What kind of God demands to drink blood? What God asks his followers to anoint his altar with the blood of innocent animals? Cain did slaughter. He had his brother's blood on his hands. But now he was cursed. How can human killing be punished but animal sacrifice rewarded? How can the same God who forbade Abraham from slaying his son, ask Cain to slay a lamb? But the Dean says he is a compassionate God.'

'You say Cain was turned away because he reeked of evil. But I ask you, how did evil come to exist in the universe? Who created evil? Did not God who created everything, also create evil? Then why is Cain punished? Why are we penalised? Cain was not born evil. No one is. Why does the Lord smear darkness over our hearts? Make someone good and someone evil? Is it for his own entertainment? A game he has been playing on the cosmic board since eternity? Creating rules and moving us like pegs? Mere characters that must play out the author's script. He made Cain murder Abel and then punished him for it. But you say God forgives us.'

'Or perhaps God did not engineer evil. Perhaps evil is simply the natural condition of the universe like good. Perhaps he only created good, and that by default meant the presence of evil since one cannot exist without the other. So, if evil is inevitable then God is a helpless entity. Not almighty. Hardly omnipotent. Never supreme. Then why follow him? But the Dean says God is divine.'

'God said he shall watch over Cain. Why did he not watch over Abel? Abel was embraced by the Lord and yet he allowed him to be slaughtered. Can anyone explain that? God promised Cain that no one can slay him as he walks through the earth. You call it love, but I call it misery. Infinite suffering. He who put his brother to death was cursed with deathlessness. Cain would remain an outcast. Forever exiled. A man sentenced for a lifetime and beyond. And just as Cain and Abel were made to suffer due to their parents, Cain's children also perished in the Deluge. An innocent generation burdened once more with the actions of an ancestor. Does sin really travel through blood like a gene? But you say God is still loving. As for the mark...'

The soliloquy paused. The star was looking at the student playing Cain. The mark standing out on his skin as if baked with iron.

'Wear that mark with pride, my friend. God could not scar Cain. He could only sanctify him. Deep down he knew that Cain was extraordinary. That first murderer went on to build the first city on earth called Enoch. The Lord can defile us. Ban us and shame us. But a true Cain achieves his destiny. The mark of Cain is not a badge of shame. It's an anointment. A birthmark of the greatness one shall achieve no matter what. Be proud if you are Cain for you can defy God. Do anything you want. The very name spells that out.'

Standing up he wrote on the white board.

CAIN

And then rearranged the letters.

I CAN

The room remained quiet. The Dean spoke once more. 'You forget, Ashwin. God sacrificed his own son for all of us. Crucified Christ.'

'And resurrected him three days later,' the actor smiled. 'But Cain still wanders.'

Chapter 17

A friend like the ocean deep can be both blue and grey
Waves surging to embrace you or receding far away
The rishi had also been close to the son of a regal land
Little fingers peeling berries or shaping houses of sand
And as a summer bird sang whatever entered its heart
The scion had made a promise as the friends did depart
Come to my imperial palace if you ever desire a thing
I shall furnish you abundantly for I shall soon be king
But when the son had grown to take his father's place
His crown had placed on his head the weight of his race
And so when years later the rishi had reached his court
That royal face had not smiled but in rage it did contort
You are a fool to remind me of a pledge that I had made
We were but children then and our words but a charade
You must plead charity now if cows your hut doth crave
Friendship is between equals not the king and the knave
I am the monarch supreme and you but a teacher poor
Cub and cur have grown and can hold hands no more
Behold how your grimy feet are making that ugly stain
Flee far if you wish to live and never come drifting again
That day the rishi had bled as an arrow slashed his soul
Years passed but his anger simmered like a piece of coal
But now he knew his festering wounds would finally heal

For he had found Silver Prince gifted with exquisite zeal
So when the day came that his pupils were ready to leave
The rishi claimed no other fee but therapy for his grief
Burn his city and melt his gold and throw him at my feet
To gods I pray Silver Prince you bring me tidings sweet.
His word came to pass and that fort came crashing down
It was verily the Prince's arrow piercing the scion's crown
The land was split into two with the scion retaining a part
The rishi gifted the other half to the one carved on his heart
Trumpets sang as Rishiputra was made sovereign of the land
He flung his bow as a royal sword weighed on his rustic hand
Alas! A being brimming with malice can only flourish in strife
Like a wretched animal it bites the very hand that saves its life
So although the Silver Prince wreathed a tiara around his head
His father's mounting love for him filled Rishiputra with dread
Thus seated on his gilded throne as he vowed to be forever just
He also made a silent resolve that his hatred shall never rust
And so while the Silver Prince bedecked him in robes most fair
Rishiputra laughed years later when a woman was stripped bare.

Chapter 18

'OBJECT NUMBER THREE, OM.'

Suri's voice was laying bare his emotion over the phone. Patnaik could hear the furious twang but also that thread quivering.

'What have you got?'

'A snake.'

'Snake? A live one?'

'A picture. A fucking cartoon framed in glass. You better come.'

The officer eyed the black envelope again.

EXHIBIT X070418

The image of an animated python. The reptile sitting upright while the rest of its body lay wounded beneath it. Staring at Suri with limpid yellow eyes. Ninety minutes later Patnaik identified the creature.

'It's Kaa.'

'Kaa?'

'A character from Rudyard Kipling's *The Jungle Book*. The stories centre around a feral child, Mowgli. Kaa the python is one of his closest friends.'

'Congratulations. Another snake reference.'

'Yes. It's becoming the motif now.'

'Next attack's scheduled for the 7th.'

The writer placed the picture on that table. 'Suri. You had said you believe someone is informing you in advance about these assaults. Helping you to try and prevent each impending attack.'

'Yes. Hence these dates on the envelopes.'

'What if they are telling you more than just that?'

'More?'

'For example, the identity of the intended victim.'

Suri's forehead wrinkled. 'The victim?'

'Take a minute here. If this was only about the dates, these envelopes would have sufficed. Why make the effort of sending you all these objects?'

'I have no idea.'

'I have been going over these items. They all point in a single direction. While the envelopes give you the day of the attack, these objects specify the person being targeted.'

The officer indicated the amphora. 'You think that thing was hinting at Trehan?'

'Not the amphora. The figure on it. Cadmus. A perfect symbol for our victim. What was Trehan's lifelong calling?'

'Education.'

'Cadmus was a Phoenician prince. And his greatest achievement was gifting his society the art of writing.'

'What writing?'

'He invented the Phoenician alphabet. Also called Proto-Canaanite, it is the oldest verified alphabet of the world. Derived from Egyptian hieroglyphics, those twenty-two letters went on to become the motherboard for various scripts like Greek, Arabic, Aramaic and even the Indian Brahmi.'

'Interesting. And Akram?'

'The most obvious hint there was the title of the D.H.

Lawrence poem. A snake is an ancient symbol for treachery. The serpent in Eden deceiving Adam and Eve.'

'Like Vibhishan.'

'Yes. Classic figure of betrayal again. But I researched some more and there are even closer connections to Akram.'

'Like what?'

'Cricket. Turns out that D.H. Lawrence had no love for sports. And the one he was most averse to was cricket.'

'Sounds like a fucking retard.'

'Not everyone's a cricket fanatic, Suri. Such was Lawrence's hostility that another English writer Richard Aldington, who lived near him, writes that if anyone had presented Lawrence with a cricket bat, the author would have cracked his head with it. And here's the clincher. You have followed Akram's game all your life. Which international county club did he play for?'

'Nottinghamshire.'

'Exactly. D.H. Lawrence was born in Nottinghamshire.'

Suri dropped in his chair. 'Frankly all this sounds too shaky.'

'I admit that, but there are similarities here we cannot ignore,' the writer's voice hardened. 'Or perhaps you are overlooking them deliberately. You don't want to handle the guilt.'

'What guilt?'

'You know that accepting my theory would mean you overlooked the objects. Connecting those dots might have prevented both the attacks.'

The officer sat in silence. Patnaik was shaking his head. 'You could have done nothing, Suri. Just like evil, the amount of good we can do is also predetermined. One can do only so much. This is not your doing. The blame lies with someone else out there.'

'But I was blind. Even Alia would have spotted it. She had the eyes, Om. Just like you. She would have cracked it for me.'

'Then let's do what Alia would have done. Let's decode Kaa. Find out who's the next target and save his life. Maybe then we shall feel much better.'

'Can you unravel this one?'

The writer picked up the picture. 'I can certainly try. Do you see what's weird about this image?'

'What?'

'Look at the snake's pose. What do you see?'

'He's sitting erect while the lower part of his body is coiled into a pile.'

'Precisely. That's the classic yoga posture for meditation when one sits with his spine perpendicular to the ground and the rest of him curled into a spiral position. Now the sender could have mailed us any image of Kaa. Why specifically this one where he is meditating?'

'So, the person they are targeting is connected to yoga?'

'That's what I think. Another thing. Kaa gets into meditation for a particular purpose. He goes into a trance.'

'Trance? A snake in a trance?'

'Yes. Kaa has the uncanny power to not only go into a trance himself but also hypnotise others. When in a trance, he could penetrate both the conscious and subconscious layers of his mind. Scan his memory that spanned over a hundred years. He also induced a similar altered state of consciousness in his prey, making it helpless.'

'What's your point?'

'Trance can be induced within oneself by various techniques. The most common technique used is again yoga. The kinaesthetic. And yogic disciplines that help attain trance are meditation, mudra and pranayama. Do you see where I am going?'

Patnaik had switched on the television. Surfing channels he paused. Suri was looking at a middle-aged man on a podium performing Vajrasana.

'Somnath? Guru Somnath?'

'The revered face of yoga today.'

'But Somnath…'

'It has to be him.'

'Not so fast, Om. We need evidence. Way more than what we have to act. Just because Kaa is into yoga, we cannot swoop down on the Guru.'

'Not just yoga. I told you Kaa can also hypnotise. And I am sure you have heard the same about Somnath. His persona. His voice and especially his eyes. Brown irises but the right one specked with a bit of blue. They say it magnifies the hypnotic quality of his face. Multiplies his aura many times more, almost entrancing his followers into submission.'

They were gazing into his eye. The blue infusing through the screen to touch their skin.

'I have heard about it. What's that exactly?'

'Heterochromia, Suri. A genetic condition where the eyes develop a difference in colouration. And not just that. You say the next attack will take place on the 7th.'

'So?'

'You haven't seen the papers today?' The writer spread out the City Page on the table. The headline was bold and clear.

GURU SOMNATH TO HOLD
GATHERING ON 7 APRIL

'He has announced a huge prayer meeting at his ashram that day. Perfect opportunity for an outsider to gain entrance and attack. And there's more. What has Somnath been protesting the loudest against?'

'Corruption. More specifically, black money stashed in foreign bank accounts.'

'When Kaa befriends Mowgli, he also persuades him to retrieve an underground treasure lying beneath an ancient city for ages. Another thing. Recently Somnath fought against a sting operation done by a news website. What's the website called?'

'White Cobra.'

'Guess whom do Kaa and Mowgli fight to get hold of this buried treasure? A white cobra.'

Suri glanced at the python. The writer was still speaking.

'Too many coincidences here. I might be making an ass of myself, but this is the best I can offer. You can at least inform Somnath.'

'And tell him what? That based on a cartoon we think someone might slice his liver on the 7th?'

'I know how insane that sounds but...'

'Exactly. Insane,' the officer flung the envelope.'This will have to be handled with care. I'll get in touch with his team. Me and my men will be present at his ashram on the 7th.'

'I will come along.'

'Of course, you will, Om,' he nodded as Somnath entered meditation on the screen. 'If anything goes wrong, we need someone to take the fucking fall.'

Chapter 19

THE WORD SHRADHANJALI DENOTED PAYING A TRIBUTE. An unconditional offering of one's devotion. And so, Guru Somnath's ashram called itself Shradhanjali Peeth. Scattered across an area of twenty acres, the ashram was a confluence of ancient wisdom and contemporary chic. While its activity centres serenaded Yoga and Ayurveda, they also performed avantgarde surgeries. Meditation co-existed with ultrasound and ECGs. Herbal gardens lent themselves to science camps while pharmacies stocked time-honoured potions. If the peeth vociferously broadcast pranayama on television, it also silently conducted clinical trials and organic farming. Shradhanjali believed that science and religion were siblings holding hands all the time. Born out of the same cosmic womb, they wondered at the same wonders and sermonised the same truths.

As a multitude descended on these premises today, Suri's men encircled the dais. Eyes and guns scanning everything. Everyone. The apostles flourishing banners. Sadhus coordinating the stage. Singers chanting and devotees seated on the ground. They were waiting for their prophet. A messiah who would have all the answers. Suri was wondering if Somnath could handle the questions slicing his mind.

Who? What? Why?

Patnaik handed the officer a glass of buttermilk. 'Relax. Your security appears watertight. Nothing shall happen to Somnath.'

'I hope something does happen,' he crushed the empty plastic. 'That will prove you right and tell us who's behind this shit.'

Suri turned as the Sadhu Sreshth approached them. Somnath's aide-de-camp. 'I hear you have been looking for me.'

'What time does your programme begin?'

'Programme?' the Sadhu Sreshth smiled. 'It's a movement by our Guru. A fight for justice. For truth. Does truth mean anything to you, officer?'

The word greeted Suri like an old friend. Someone not long ago had asked him the same question.

Alia.

The gathering had begun chanting. Hands up in the air and joined together. Fluttering like tongues of a divine chorus serenading all that was endless.

Om tryambakamyajamahesugandhimpushtivardhanam
Urvarukamivabandhananmrityormukshiyamamratat

'I need to meet Gurusreshth,' Suri said.

'He is preparing for the session. No one can meet him right now.'

'I was not requesting you, Sadhu Sreshth. You asked me about truth. The biggest truth right now is that his life could be under threat. We…'

'I know. We have gone through the information you mailed us. We never allow police personnel on these grounds, but your fears have forced us to modify our procedure. You got what you wanted. Do your duty now.'

'I am doing just that and you have to cooperate. Let me

see him. Your movement needs Guru Somnath. Are you going to risk his life over protocol?'

The Sadhu Sreshth stood undecided and then gestured them to follow. Entering the portals of Shradhanjali, he steered them towards the central chamber. The heart of Shradhanjali. Its *sanctum sanctorum.* The room was stacked with bare essentials. A small pile of sindoor lay next to jasmine flowers and a tray of bananas. Over the fruit rested a large laddoo gleaming like the morning sun. One of the walls had a huge mural of Lord Rama holding a stone. Sitting before a small pool of floating candles was Guru Somnath. He was meditating. The calm saturating this space, far removed from the carnival outside. They waited as he opened his eyes.

'Who's it?'

'I. Suri.'

'If you are I, then why Suri? If Suri, then who's I?'

The officer stared blankly, but Patnaik was smiling. Looking into the Guru's eyes. That touch of blue said to amplify the magnetism of Guru Somnath. Mesmerise his flock to yield absolutely.

Like Kaa.

The Sadhu Sreshth introduced him. 'Om Patnaik.'

'I see you and your friend are here to shelter me.' The Guru smiled.

'Yes,' the officer stepped forward. 'We have reason to believe that you might be under attack today. Could we request you to cancel the gathering? Turn the congregation away? The less people around you the better.'

Somnath had picked up the *aarti* tray. His hands pirouetting before Rama's mural now. 'What do you see the lord doing, Mr Suri?'

'Lifting a stone.'

'Creating the first step. Paving a path over water. He could have turned back, but he kept walking. We all chart our own courses. And once you have done that you must walk. The road sticks to your soles and you cannot abandon it. I have cast my stone too. I must step on it now.'

'Must we test our fate, Gurusreshth?'

'Our fate? When Hanuman was flying over the ocean to Lanka, he was tested by Surasa, the mother of snakes. She did everything to devour him, but he escaped her pit to fulfil his ordained task. If my fate chooses that I remain safe, I will hardly need your assistance. But if fate wants me to stumble and sink, there's precious little you both can do. In fact, you may even end up as instruments of my doom.'

'You must place your trust in us.'

'I only trust the power of resolution, officer. Once you resolve, you can do anything. Engulf the sun. Lift a mountain. Set the universe on fire. My resolve is to conduct my session today. The attacker's resolve is to assault me. Your resolve is to thwart his plan. We are all determined here. Let's see whose resolution makes it to the finishing line.'

The officer walked out through the door. 'Fine. I shall make final inspections and then you may arrive at the dais. But Om will stay here with you. I want no one else in this room.'

The Sadhu Sreshth opened his mouth, but Suri silenced him.

'No one.'

Patnaik watched them leave and turned towards the Guru.

'I am here.'

Somanth was looking at him curiously. He spoke again,

but his voice now held an eerie tenor.

'You are an author, Mr Om. Have you heard the story of Apostle Peter?'

'You love stories?'

'Everyone does. Apostle Peter vowed to offer his life to Christ. But the night Jesus was arrested in Jerusalem, Peter denied knowing him. Denied him not once but thrice.'

'I know.'

The Guru was peering at something behind him. The writer turned and froze. A woman stood in the middle of the room. A woman swathed in black. Her face hiding behind black as well but not her eyes. Blue eyes standing erect.

'Who are you?' Patnaik's tone had become hollow.

She was approaching him. Her eyes burning holes in his face.

'Who are you? How did you get here?'

The woman did not speak. Patnaik turned to see Somnath bowing before the mural. Sitting down on the floor in Siddhasana. Cold breath was chilling the writer's neck now. He spun to find the woman's face right next to him. Her eyes fixed over his as if nailed by a hammer. The more he gazed into those blue pits, the more he found himself powerless to look away. That void dragging him inside. Pulling his entrails into a bottomless hole. Were his senses draining out of him one by one? Did he not know his body anymore? Rooted to the spot while that basilisk hauled him out of his flesh and bones. Sucking him like a succubus. He was no longer Patnaik. Just an extension of this woman who had transferred her mind into him. A puppet held by a lasso of neurons. Awaiting to be brought to life solely by her command.

He heard what she wanted him to do.

Patnaik moved. Now he was pasting the horseshoe over Somnath's head. Now he was making the man bleed. Reaching for his liver. Handing the woman a syringe. Now he was scribbling all over Rama. Sitting alone now inhaling the smell of the Guru's open wound.

'Om?'

Was Somnath calling out to him?

'Om.'

Not Somnath. It was Christ hanging from the cross.

'Om.'

Nails stabbing his hands and feet. Someone picking up another nail and placing it on his torso. Right above the liver.

'Om.'

The hammer striking. The nail spearing through his flesh. Closer and closer to his liver.

'Om.'

Penetrating his liver now. Eating his body and drinking his blood. Christ looking at him.

You denied me, Om.

You denied me.

'Om!'

The writer's body quaked as if something was squeezing out of him. He saw it now. His scarlet fingers. Somnath bleeding on the floor. Suri calling out his name. And another name scrawled in black over the feet of Rama.

HANUMAN

Yeva stood outside by the dais. A furious wind had suddenly descended pulling the stage down. Blowing away everything but the red rainbow spreading through the sky.

Chapter 20

EIGHTEEN...EIGHTEEN OF THEM

Patnaik was counting again. He had counted the bars nine times already. Right to left and again left to right. The figure remained steady.

Eighteen.

He smiled.

'Not many faces smile in my lockup, Om.'

The officer was entering the cell. The charred cigar between his fingers glaring at the solitary prisoner with red eyes. Watching him toying with the iron bars.

'I smile at the irony, Suri. You left me there to keep an eye on Somnath. And I cut him up.'

'Yes. His liver's damaged, and he's comatose. What the fuck have you done?'

'I don't know, Suri. Did I really do all that?'

'We have evidence, Om. Your fingerprints all over the horseshoe. Your handwriting on the mural. Your palms coated with Somnath's blood. Do you deny any of it?'

The writer closed his eyes. His voice sagging under an unseen load. 'None. I deny nothing. But where is that woman?'

'Woman. That invisible woman,' Suri echoed. 'Who is this fucking woman you keep harping about? How did she fade in, and where did she fade out?'

'I have no idea, but I know she was in the room. Looking at me. Not Somnath. Only me.'

'You say she was draped in black?'

'Yes. I only saw her eyes. Blue eyes.'

'What's the last thing you can recall before I entered?'

'Her eyes fastening themselves upon my face. Melting into my skin. Whatever followed is a total blur. She was gone. Just you standing before me and Somnath bleeding on the ground.'

The officer's eyes tapered into slits. 'This blur sounds like hypnosis. Are you telling me the woman hypnotised you?'

'Did she? But I could not have been willing.'

'What do you mean?'

'I have gone under hypnosis a few times before. One must be a willing subject for it to work. You had left me in charge of Somnath, and the woman materialised out of nowhere. If she did try to entrance me, I am sure I must have resisted. Resisted hard. But it appears as if she still got me under her spell. That requires extraordinary power.'

'Is that going to be your defence, Om? Hypnosis?'

'I am sorry. You reached out to me for help, but I have only made it worse.'

'You have. This case has been screwing my department, and they had no one to pin it on. But now they have you. My seniors are pretty sure about your guilt and that you must have carried out the previous two attacks as well. I have been ordered to investigate you.'

Patnaik smiled weakly. 'You wanted me to take the fall.'

Suri leaned against the prison bars. 'Fuck off, Om.'

'You really think I assaulted all those men?'

'Think? I am afraid to think now. I know you, Om.

I know the person you are, but I need something more to hold on to. Law goes by evidence and what we have at Shradhanjali is evidence, I cannot ignore. And this woman you saw makes no sense. Who was she? Why didn't anybody see her? If she attacked Somnath, how did she pull off this fucking stunt?'

'I may have the answers to that, officer.'

They turned towards the source of that voice. Framed at the entrance was a man. Holding the hand of a little girl.

'Who the hell are you?'

A junior cop appeared from behind the duo and saluted Suri. 'He claims to have information regarding the attack on Somnath.'

'And you brought him all the way here?'

'They had been waiting in your cabin for long. He says he also knows about the earlier two assaults on Akram and Trehan.'

The officer scrutinised them both from head to toe and motioned his junior.

'Leave.'

The pair came forward towards the cell. The girl clasped the bars and stuck her scarred cheek into the space between them. She was gazing at Patnaik. The writer winced as he looked at those enormous grey eyes. Then he relaxed. Unlike that woman in black, this child was not attempting to master his senses. Her eyes seemed to be mapping his soul to bond with him. Telling him that they knew all about him and wanted to know some more. He heard the man identifying himself to Suri.

'Atharva Sharma. I am a priest from Manipur. This is my daughter Indira.'

'Why have you brought her here?' The officer frowned. 'This is no place for children.'

'She's not afraid,' the priest said. 'Indira's at home everywhere. She wanted to be here because she alone can guide us.'

'Guide us to what?'

'The attacks. I know about the attacks and who's behind them?'

Patnaik clenched the bars. 'You do?'

'Yes.'

'Me? Is it really me?'

Atharva shook his head. 'It was never you. And you know that.'

The writer slumped. 'Not sure. I wasn't sure anymore. All these hours here I have been going insane. Counting these bars. Tugging at my hair as if that would jolt my memory. Terrified of myself. Wondering if there was a part of me I did not know. A part that could butcher a man. Telling myself I was incapable but then smelling his blood on my hands. Not sure anymore, but you say you know. Was it really her?'

'It was.'

'That woman.'

'She is no woman.'

The two men looked at each other.

'No woman?' Suri asked. 'What do you mean?'

'I mean the truth,' Atharva held out four fingers. 'Four truths that shall set you free. If you drown a fist into the Ganga, you gain nothing. But if you cup your palms, you draw up her water. That water alone can liberate you. What will it be? The palm or the fist?'

The officer remained quiet but Patnaik spoke. 'Tell me, Atharva.'

'The woman you saw was not human.'

'What then?'

'A serpent. She is an Ichhadhari.'

Chapter 21

'ICHHADHARI?'

'Yes. A shape-shifter. A snake that can assume any form at will. Ichhadharis are a cosmic rarity. Only one in a million serpents is able to go through the profound austerities that give it that power. Paranormal power to assume the body of any animal species in the universe. It can invoke the entire spectrum, from a housefly to humans. Your attacker is also an Ichhadhari serpent.'

'Ichhadhari,' Suri chewed up the word. 'You mean like fucking Bollywood?'

'If only it was fantasy, officer. Three violent attacks you cannot explain. An innocent man standing behind bars. This is reality, and so is the evil unleashed by this force.'

The officer was silent. The next moment he joined both his palms above his head like the hood of a snake and started swaying. Indira stared while Patnaik's face flushed cherry red. But Atharva hardly cringed. His gaze remained steady over that awkward cavorting figure.

'Mock me all you want. But do not ignore me. This truth alone can safeguard us.'

'Truth?' Suri sneered. 'I have three men lying in a coma. We are plugging hole after hole to make sure the press gets as few details as possible. My seniors are threatening me like the fucking mafia. And you walk in here offering me a prehistoric joke?'

'This is no joke. Transmigration from one body to another is an established tenet. Shape-shifting is mentioned in the oldest forms of totemism and shamanism. Our physical forms are nothing but an overcoat of energies. The ability to wrap a different body around your soul is not as fanciful as you think. Have you never observed a chameleon change its colours?'

The officer was yelping again, but Patnaik stood in silence. He had not spoken a word. Suri spun.

'You seem fascinated, Om. I know you are this gigantic believer in all things impossible, but don't tell me even you can swallow this and not choke?'

The writer did not reply. Instead he asked Atharva a question.

'What makes you think we are dealing with an Ichhadhari here?'

'Visions. Let me start by saying that certain visions manifested themselves upon me again and again. I practise Tantra, and these were warnings rumbling around me that something was severely wrong. They compelled me to explore them.'

'What visions?'

'Dark divinations from a very compelling source. I began investigating them only to discover that an Ichhadhari now crawls upon the surface of earth.'

The writer was listening. Reading the words his own brain was scrawling.

Poem

Amphora

Kaa

The venom

'Don't they say it takes a hundred years for a snake to become an Ichhadhari?'

'That's exaggerated folklore, Om. No serpent can have that lifespan, and no text specifies such a time frame. It entirely depends upon the snake's resolve. How intense is that desire. Everything else you hear is fiction.'

'That's the fiction here?' The officer laughed. 'Leave. I hate fucking fairy tales.'

'What about things you can see with your own eyes?'

'What things?'

'Red rainbows, for instance.'

The words gripped them both by the neck. The officer's voice rattled. 'What about them?'

'Don't you wonder why you have been seeing so many of those recently?'

'It's not unheard of,' Patnaik said. 'Monochromatic rainbows are pure science and have been sighted down the ages.'

'Of course, but highly rare. Once in a blue moon. But your city has had three of them in the past three months. And each one happening minutes after a person was attacked. Am I wrong, Mr Suri?'

The officer gaped. 'You mean they are connected?'

Atharva continued, emboldened. 'Yes. A red rainbow alone should have told you that something paranormal was at work here. While the visions had informed me that an Ichhadhari was walking this earth, those red rainbows confirmed that. Not many know that a rainbow has always been identified with snakes given their shape. And you have been seeing extraordinary monochromes, because they are denoting an extraordinary serpent.'

'An Ichhadhari.'

'Exactly. The rainbows also pointed at the Ichhadhari's activities. Every snake dares this trial by fire for a reason. Becomes a shape-shifter to achieve a specific goal. When I checked news reports, I found that on all the three days that the rainbows had appeared, a man had also been attacked. A high-profile celebrity. The articles hardly carried too many details about the assault. You won't tell me anything either, but take my word, Suri. This is the Ichhadhari's doing.'

The silence in that room thickened. Atharva held the writer's hands through the bars.

'You are right, Om. Red rainbows are pure science but also an oddity. A disruption of the natural order. The universe is sending out distress signals. Displaying a symptom that its symmetry is being destroyed. And something as abnormal as a red rainbow is looming above all of us.'

The men stood watching each other uneasily. Patnaik could feel his brain straining itself to embrace what the priest was saying. He drank deep every word but a nameless reservation was gagging his mouth. He uttered the line he had often heard Suri say.

'We need proof. Something must back what you claim.'

Atharva took out a voluminous book from his case. The officer peered at the cover. '*Agni Purana*?'

The writer's eyes were devouring the volume. 'One of the eighteen Mahapuranas of Hinduism. Believed to have been recited by Agni himself to Sage Vashishtha. Three hundred and eighty-three chapters hiding such murky secrets that the book's classified as *Tamas Purana*. The Dark Purana.'

'Wrong, Om. It's three hundred and eighty-four chapters.'

'Eighty-four? I am pretty sure it's three hundred and eighty three. I have a copy and have gone through it several times.'

'So have many others. But that's the standard printed edition circulating since the nineteenth century. The English translation followed some thirty years later. This copy I have here is the oldest edition. The complete one. Only two such copies exist in the world today. When the visons hinted at a serpent, I began consulting this Purana. And it has showed me what I am trying to show you both.'

'Showed you what?'

'You say you have read the *Agni Purana*, Om. What is Chapter 294 about?'

'Serpents. Eight cardinal serpents in Hindu mythology and how they are divided among the four castes. Five hundred species of snakes like Gonases and Rajilas that came into being from these primary eight. How seven serpents preside over the seven days of the week. Also the nature of snake bites and how they affect the seven principles of vitality.'

'Right. Now check Chapter 297 in this book. That is the one missing in all editions today. The chapter mysteriously stripped. What is it called?'

Patnaik flipped to the contents page and ran down the numbers. His finger twitched involuntarily.

'Ichhadhari Sarp.'

'Exactly,' the priest jabbed the words. 'An entire chapter solely devoted to this supernatural phenomenon. It describes how snakes acquire this paranormal ability and what powers they possess. But above all it lists the Ichhadharis of the past, present and future.'

'Lists?' the writer's eyes flickered. 'Are you telling me…?'

'Yes. Initially I was not able to grasp the meaning of the shlokas, dates and charts. It took me some time but now I know. This is a lineage graph. Just as Bhrigu Shastra records past and present human lives and predicts future humans who shall be born, this chapter in the *Agni Purana* records Ichhadharis. Those that existed and those that will exist.' He looked at Suri. 'Like your computer database of criminals.'

The officer scoffed, but Patnaik was hooked now. 'How extensive is this database?'

'Hardly that large. You must understand that not every serpent has the prowess to become an Ichhadhari. It needs enormous spiritual courage to cross that threshold of energies. The *Agni Purana* records a total of just six hundred Ichhadharis till the end of Kali Yuga. As per the Purana, three hundred of them have already come and gone. We stand now right in the middle of this chakra. Look at the year computed for the arrival of the present Ichhadhari.'

The writer had already seen the figure. He turned towards Suri.

'It says 2014.'

'Precisely. It has arrived, and it's a female serpent. The first of the next three hundred. Thus, begins the other half of this cycle. An Ichhadhari created in the darkest hour with a purpose to destroy.'

'Isn't that the purpose of every Ichhadhari?'

'Never, Om. Many have taken on the human form to serve mankind. To do a greater good. But not this one. She is pure negative energy. Her aura is stained with anger and hatred. The stars themselves leave no room for doubt.'

Patnaik was studying the astral charts. 'These stars?'

'Yes,' the priest tapped on the lower section of the page.

'Hindu astrology lists twenty-seven stars or nakshatras. These have been grouped into seven categories based on their qualities. We start with the gentle stars categorised as Mridu and move towards the vicious ones classified as Ugra. The five Ugra nakshatras symbolise evil. The most ferocious of them is Magha. Besides being Ugra, this star is located at the conjunction of Ketu and Shukra or Mercury which further compounds its havoc. These twenty-seven stars have also been classified according to the three gunas. Sattva or construction. Rajas or confusion. And Tamas or destruction.'

'And Magha is Tamasik?'

'Precisely.'

'Hang on, Om!' Suri interrupted. 'English, please.'

'Atharva's basically saying that our astrology defines some stars as benign and some as evil. And the worst of the lot is Magha nakshatra.'

'A star harbouring darkness inside its heart. Our Icchadhari has been created in the shadow of this malevolent Magha.' The priest circled a spot on the chart. 'This is the precise asterism when the star was in ascendancy. What do you see printed here?'

The officer squinted at the page. 'A swastika.' The red symbol was glowing on the page like varnish. He shrugged. 'I thought a swastika was auspicious.'

'It is,' Patnaik nodded. 'But the swastika is also a symbol for serpents. It denotes the heliolithic culture of snake worship.'

'Exactly,' Atharva said. 'The swastika under this star here further confirms the arrival of an Ichhadhari. The previous one was created way back in Aryavarta during the Mahabharata times.'

'The Mahabharata? That long ago?'

'Indeed. After all these centuries now, we have another serpent channelling that impossible will to become a shape-shifter. The Purana gives you the exact date and place when she transformed herself into an Ichhadhari – 2 September 2014 at the Nilgiri Forest. Now see this.'

He was displaying a newspaper cut-out.

HEAVY RAINS LASH JAMMU & KASHMIR

'This headline appeared a day after the monsoon burst over Kashmir in 2014. The valley's worst flood since Independence. Check the date mentioned when the rains began.'

The writer read it out. 'Same date – 2 September.'

'Not a coincidence. The floods that decimated these parts of Kashmir and Pakistan started the day this Ichhadhari was created. Whenever extreme negative energy is manifested, nature reacts violently. Transmits an SOS. The floods were an omen the day that evil descended upon us. And these red rainbows are doing the same. We are being constantly warned that a tumour now festers on the face of the earth. It all makes sense.'

'Sense?' Suri waved the word away. 'This is fucking hysterical. You have obviously swayed Om, but that tattered volume is still not convincing me.'

The priest pointed towards the room outside.

'Will those envelopes convince you?'

'What envelopes?'

'The white, red and black envelopes on your desk? I saw them as I waited in your cabin. Labelled as evidence. That means they are connected with this case?'

Patnaik spoke up. 'Yes. We received objects inside them pointing towards the identity of the intended victims.'

'I am surprised you did not see the connection, Om. Didn't the three colours speak to you?'

The writer's eyebrows keeled over, showing his confusion. Seconds later Atharva's words had set his mind on fire.

The three colours...

White...Red...Black

He turned towards the officer. 'Of course.'

'What is it?'

'White, red and black. The first three colours.'

'First three colours?'

'Yes. Hindu mythology lists five divine serpents. They are the primordial Nagas. Each Naga is associated with a singular colour. The first is Vasuki associated with white. Takshaka is red and Karkotaka is black. Not just the objects, Suri. Even the envelopes have been pointing at snakes all this while. Whoever is sending you these parcels knows. Knows that we are dealing with a serpent.'

Suri backed off now as if this information had dented his disbelief. The priest caught the look in his eyes.

'The next two colours are pink and yellow. You might believe us if a pink envelope comes knocking on your door next.'

'It's fitting in,' the writer whispered. 'All the objects mailed to you in those envelopes. Lawrence's poem. Cadmus. Kaa. The snake motif running through all of them. The venom at Trehan's classroom. My hypnosis.'

'Venom? Hypnosis?' The priest pounced on the words.

As the officer recounted the details, Atharva grew more and more uneasy. 'This further confirms that she's a shape-shifter. An Ichhadhari can hypnotise you like no other. It's not just the force in her eyes. The energy radiates from her very core.'

The officer kicked the prison bars. 'Fine, priest. Let's say for a moment I accept everything you say. But you still haven't answered everything. Why is this Ichhadhari attacking these people?'

'That's something I don't know, Suri. What I do know is that she's not alone. She has a partner. A companion.'

'Companion?'

'Yes. This creature is not isolated. Her powers are being put to use to realise an extremely personal goal.'

'And you know who this companion is?'

'I know quite a lot, Suri. The Ichhadhari is a woman called Yeva. And her companion is Tomar. Superstar Ashwin Tomar.'

Chapter 22

THE DROP OF BLOOD WAS HANGING FROM THE TIP. Bloating up into a full circle. Clinging desperately as if hanging from a precipice. Gravity below was dragging it down. Sucking it atom by atom. It was slipping. Pleading Yeva for help only to see a shadow creep behind her. Creeping closer and closer. The shadow raised its hand and yanked Yeva's dark hair viciously. Her face jerked back as her neck arched up taut.

Yeva laughed. Ashwin was stroking her neck. A moment later they were both standing under the wooden staff. Yeva held the object in her hands once more. Her only offspring delivered not long ago.The darkness she had ingested to spit it out as light. They called it the Mani.

'You do it today.'

Ashwin smiled as the jewel bathed in Somnath's blood. Red ink squirting and turning it more blue.

'Thank you, Yeva.'

'Not yet. A few drops more to fertilise this egg.'

The actor peered into the heart of the Mani. Its insides churning. Molecules splitting and fusing as that crystal ball conjured up all those faces again. Faces it had first shown Ashwin four years back.

Chapter 23

THE OFFICER HAD CLASPED INDIRA'S WRIST. HE DREW THE girl gently towards Atharva.

'I don't want your child to see me manhandling her father. I have heard you out. At one point you had almost reeled me in, but this has got fucked up again. Please leave.'

'I am not worried for her. You are my concern. You and those who shall be attacked.'

Suri looked at Patnaik. 'Tell this man to scoot or it shall get unpleasant here.'

'No, Om,' Atharva's voice rose. 'Tell this man to heed my words or Ashwin will keep spilling blood. More bodies and more rainbows.'

The writer stood still. Everything swirling inside him over and over.

An Ichhadhari tamed by Ashwin Tomar?

Suri will never believe this.

He paused.

Do I believe?

He felt the metal bars turning colder. 'Listen, Atharva. I can convince Suri only if you convince me. I accept the power of an Ichhadhari. I have stood pinned before that evil myself at Shradhanjali. I respect the *Agni Purana*. But this allegation against Ashwin Tomar is ridiculous.'

'Raving mad,' the officer added. 'He needs help.'

The priest flashed a print-out before them. 'And who shall help you when she strikes again?'

A large picture showing Ashwin making his way through the crowd at the auditorium right after *Maquillage*.

'Look at the woman walking behind the star. You do recognise her, Om?'

Patnaik was gawking at that face.

'Her eyes, Om. Haven't you seen those before?'

The writer was not listening. He was standing before those eyes again. Blue eyes inanimate inside that image and yet dipping a finger into his nerves. Running a cube of ice all the way down his spine.

'This is her. This is her, Suri.'

'Are you positive?'

'Those eyes. This blue. The same blizzard that froze me at Shradhanjali. She's the one. And she is with him. With Ashwin.'

'Yes,' Atharva nodded. 'Ashwin's secretary. Yeva. She started working for him this year.'

The priest was watching Suri's face. The mask still on but that paint flaking again. A lot more paint.

'How did you locate this woman?' the officer asked. 'Why zero in on Ashwin Tomar?'

The man pointed to his daughter. 'My Indira. She led me to him.'

'What do you mean she led you?'

'Indira's not an ordinary child. She's different from others.'

'I did notice that,' Patnaik said. 'Withdrawn. Hasn't spoken a word. It's as if we three hardly exist on her horizon.'

'And you must have whispered the term autistic to yourself.'

The writer protested, but Atharva had taken no offence. 'Everyone she encounters diagnoses her that way. The doctors have officially declared her autistic because their science doesn't know any better. I know what Indira really is. We both do. Not everyone can comprehend that, and so we keep it to ourselves. That truth is our little secret.'

'Truth being...'

The priest caressed the child's forehead. 'She's an Indigo.'

'A what?' Suri asked.

'Indigo child,' the phrase reverberated on Patnaik's lips. 'Is she really an Indigo, Atharva?'

'She is.'

'No wonder! No wonder her eyes knife through the soul.'

'What's an Indigo now, Om?' the officer rumbled.

'Indigos are unique men and women believed to possess exceptional qualities. Highly evolved with capabilities bordering on the paranormal. They are extremely empathetic and display a strong bond with the energies of nature. Intuitive and affectionate but also in constant defiance of authority. They challenge every institution that hinders progress. Unfortunately, their unusual traits are not always recognised by their families. Most indigos end up misdiagnosed as cases of autism or ADHD.'

'Yes,' the priest laughed. 'My wife Jupita's one of them. She could never see what I saw in those eyes.'

'I know. The eyes of an Indigo pass right through you like an X-ray. Indigo is also the colour of our third eye chakra. The pineal gland which is the node of our sensory faculties. It's highly pronounced in an Indigo which would make Indira extraordinarily perceptive.'

'She is. How else could she have generated those visions that started it all?'

Patnaik stiffened. 'She did? I thought you had the visons.'

'I only interpreted and investigated them. It was Indira who produced every single divination.'

Atharva was narrating her story now. The day she bled. The day she began drawing on Holi. Then drawing anywhere and everywhere. Drawings that still refuse to cease. Showing them iPad images of the first one now.

'She menstruated at seven?' the writer exclaimed. 'Does that even happen?'

'I can hardly explain that,' the priest said. 'I stopped questioning her long back. In Tantra, menstrual blood like semen symbolises renewal. Preparing one for a higher spiritual struggle. Perhaps that's what she was warning us about.'

'These are powerful images. And this was the first vision she had?'

'Yes. She drew two creatures next to each other. I am showing you one of those two first.'

'A snake.'

'Yes. I initially took no notice of the actual drawing. The fact that Indira was suddenly communicating through art was too momentous. She had never drawn anything before. But when she kept spawning the same figures over and over again, I began wondering. Began clicking pictures. Why was the medium relaying the same message in an endless loop? Leaving it everywhere like clues? I started to investigate.'

'And her snake image took you to the *Agni Purana*?'

'Right. The Purana revealed the existence of the Ichhadhari

and the red rainbows further strengthened that idea. And then Indira began drawing a face.'

'Face?'

They saw the priest tapping over his pad. A video of the child filled the screen.

'By now I had started recording whenever she drew,' Atharva said. 'It was enthralling to see her construct each one of them. Almost as if she was possessed and that energy was leaking through her fingertips.'

'Is that a slate she's working on?'

'Yes. It made sense to get her that as the frequency of her drawings multiplied. Something to vent it out on. I would have preferred an art book, but she picked out the slate herself. They are practically inseparable now.'

They were watching her fingers holding the chalk in the video. All five fingers joined as if forming a conduit. Spraying the slate thick with the stream of her consciousness. Whatever was pent up inside Indira had found a release as it flowed through her hand and landed on that black slab. The slate slick now with layers of chalk. They were looking at the face she had drawn. The face they would recognise anywhere.

Ashwin Tomar.

'This is where Ashwin entered the picture,' the priest spoke. 'Indira's image initially led me to speculate that the actor was the Ichhadhari. The female serpent masquerading as a male human. But the *Agni Purana* clearly stated that the Ichhadhari had been created only four years back. That and the assault on Trehan convinced me that it could not be Ashwin Tomar.'

'What do you mean?'

'The day Trehan was attacked, Ashwin was not in Mumbai. He was in Imphal. In my city attending the wedding of the CM's son. I know that because I was present there myself conducting the rituals. Now an Ichhadhari has many powers, but it cannot be in two places at the same time. Ashwin was off the hook, but I also knew Indira could not be wrong. If not the actor, it had to be someone close to him. Ashwin has no family. He lives alone. The only person who constantly shadows him these days is his secretary Yeva. She hadn't accompanied him to the wedding that day. I knew then that she had to be the shape-shifter. Then four days ago Indira drew this.'

They were looking at the new image. Another face. Parag Suri.

'It was clear what she wanted me to do. Reach out to the investigating officer and share my findings.' Atharva turned to look at the writer behind bars. 'But there was obviously more than that. She also brought me here so that Om could corroborate my theory. Confirm that Yeva was indeed the Ichhadhari. Do you see what Indira has done? We needed each other to piece this. She brought us together.'

Patnaik was staring at the girl's drawing. 'A bit crude but an extraordinary likeness, Suri. And she's only seven.'

The officer jabbed at the iPad screen. 'Even if I grant you that Yeva is the Ichhadhari who hypnotised Om, how does that involve Ashwin? That he knows about her and is using her for something? He might have no idea who the fuck he has hired.'

'No, Suri. Ashwin knows exactly who he has hired.' The priest was flipping through a film magazine. He showed them a paragraph circled with felt.

STAR BURNS A BLACK HOLE

'This 2014 clipping reports that a production house had erected a humungous set in Mumbai to shoot a song for their thriller starring Ashwin. But at the last minute, the star refused to picturise on set and insisted that the whole unit move to Ooty. The producers fumed but gave in when Ashwin promised full compensation. The unit reached Ooty on the last day of August. And the *Agni Purana* says Yeva became an Ichhadhari on 2 September. The place mentioned in the Purana is Nilgiri Forest. And Ashwin insisted that…'

'That they shoot in Ooty,' the writer completed. 'The Nilgiris. You have been quite thorough.'

'Why such desperation for Ooty? To reach the Nilgiris before 2 September? He knew. Knew very well who she was and where he would find her.'

'But why?' Suri exploded. 'Why does Ashwin Tomar need a fucking Ichhadhari?'

Atharva sat down on the floor. 'Have you read the *Mahabharata*? Do you know the story of Ashwathama?'

'Ashwathama? What's he got to do with any of this?'

'Humour me, officer. Are you familiar with his tale?'

'Not much. Wasn't he Dronacharya's son?'

'Yes. Ashwathama was born with the blessings of Shiva and had several divine traits. He was a formidable warrior and yet constantly jealous of Arjuna. An emotion that did not change even after Arjuna made him king.'

'King?'

'Drona had once been humiliated by King Drupad of Panchal and he sought vengeance by asking his disciples to conquer him. Arjuna defeated Drupad and annexed his kingdom. Drona split Panchal into two parts installing

Ashwathama as the ruler. Despite this, the friction between Arjuna and Ashwathama never ended. Much like Karna and Duryodhan, Ashwathama forever resented Arjuna's skills and Drona's love for the prince. He went on to commit many more sins.'

'Quite a paradox,' Patnaik said. 'Ashwathama proves that you may be born divine but your negative karma will render it useless.'

'Exactly. Lord Krishna also saw how that Brahman had become a Rakshasa. He laid a terrible curse on him. He made him immortal.'

'Immortal?'

'Yes. Deathless so that he would suffer forever, finding no release. Eternally exiled to roam the earth till the coming of Kalki. Kali Yuga is not yet over. Kalki Avatar has still not arrived. And that essentially means that Ashwathama is still among us.'

'Yes. That's quite a conspiracy theory,' the writer added. 'Browse the Internet and you shall find a million reports of people claiming to have actually seen Ashwathama. Some say he lives near Narmada River. Some mention a fort in Madhya Pradesh while others talk about encountering him at Rishikesh.'

Suri stifled a yawn. 'What has all this got to do with our fucking case, Atharva? Are you telling me that Ashwin knows where this Ashwathama is?'

'No. Ashwin Tomar is Ashwathama.'

Chapter 24

ICHHADHARI

Yeva

Ashwin

Ashwathama

Indira had taken out a box of chalk and was squiggling on her slate. Patnaik had picked up a piece and written the four words on the prison floor.

'Your four truths, Atharva.'

The priest nodded. 'That's all I have to offer. Accept these and we shall be able to act.'

'Ichhadhari. Indigo. Ashwathama,' Suri mouthed the words as he lit another cigar. 'You know what they say, Om. It never rains but it fucking pours. Myth and fantasy have never had any place inside my precinct. All these years I have kept that hogwash out and now a tantrik from Manipur comes and dumps it all over my walls.'

Atharva smiled. 'You lie, officer. I didn't only see the envelopes on your table. I saw the Buddha. The mantra on your computer wallpaper. That's not mere iconography there. You might have a little more faith than you think.'

'And now you tell me that I must believe in Ashwathama to solve this case?'

'If you can accept an Ichhadhari, why not Ashwathama?'

'And also believe that the *Mahabharata* is not a nursery rhyme?'

'It is not, Suri. I fail to understand why people cannot digest that the Mahabharata is not myth but history. And I am not even talking about Dwarka. Vyasa himself classifies the epic as *itihas*. The annals of the Bharat dynasty are documented in the Adiparva. The lineage of kings is exceptionally detailed and even concurs with the Ramayana. The time and place of various events in the Mahabharata have been recorded right down to the position of stars and planets of that age. Not to forget the staggering technical descriptions of formations and weapons used in the war. Even Megasthenes declared Chandragupta Maurya as a ruler in the lineage of Krishna.'

'But how, Atharva?' the writer frowned. 'Even if I accept that Ashwathama still exists today carrying out his punishment, how can that doomed creature be Ashwin Tomar? You do know the nature of Krishna's curse which makes it impossible.'

'What do you mean?' the officer asked.

'When Ashwathama was made immortal, Krishna cursed his body to forever decay. To be racked with every pestilence known to man. Muck would drain from his pores and he would be shunned by all. But Ashwin is a demigod. Worshipped by millions. A face born with the aura to rule. How can that shining star be a piece of festering flesh?'

'I know. I have grappled with that question myself. How can someone with a rotting body be a matinee idol? Someone condemned to isolation stand in the middle of such adulation? I don't know how to answer that. The only truth I know is that Ashwin is Ashwathama. His very name gives that away.'

'Name?'

'Of course. Ashwin Tomar. Observe the phonetic similarity. How it sounds exactly like Ashwathama.'

'I never thought about that,' Patnaik nodded as a grin slowly rippled across his face. 'Intriguing. Very intriguing, but hardly conclusive.'

The priest tipped his iPad screen at them once more. 'This is where we revisit Indira's first image. And I reveal that other creature she had drawn next to the snake.'

'Horse!' the writer gasped at the figure in red abeer.

'Yes. A snake and a horse together under a starry sky. Yeva and Ashwin. Ichhadhari and Ashwathama.'

Patnaik was looking at Suri. He knew the same word had lit up inside the officer's brain.

Horseshoe.

The priest saw their faces change. 'What's the matter?'

'Tell him, Suri,' the writer insisted. 'Tell him.'

'It's the attack victims,' the officer said. 'We found all three of them with a horseshoe pasted on their foreheads.'

Atharva's face bubbled. 'That's perfect. Another reference to the horse. It further cements the fact that we are dealing with Ashwathama. You do know why I say that, Om.'

Patnaik nodded slowly. He drew a line vertically across the name he had written on the floor, splitting it into two. 'Ashwathama. It means he who is horse-voiced. The *Mahabharata* says when he was born, he cried like a horse.'

'Precisely,' the priest said. 'Besides the name and Indira's drawing, the paramount reason why Ashwin must be Ashwathama is his association with an Ichhadhari. His desperate search for that extraordinary being.'

'Why so?' the officer asked.

'When do you pursue someone so doggedly? Only when you have something to gain. Obtain something cherished which only that other person can provide. Think of the most precious object an Ichhadhari can offer and it instantly tells you that Ashwin has to be Ashwathama. That which was taken away from him and that which he now seeks.'

The writer's eyes were sparkling. Atharva knew his words had set the man's cerebral wheels in motion. 'That which gleams like your eyes, Om. The light that blinds others but brightens an Ichhadhari. The fire that alone can purify Ashwathama.'

'What is he raving about?' Suri asked.

Patnaik turned to face him. 'We told you that Ashwathama was a child blessed by Shiva himself. He was born with many divine properties.'

'Yes.'

'The most magnificent of them was a Mani.'

'Mani? Ashwathama was born with a Mani?'

'Yes. A fabulous sapphire embedded on his forehead like a celestial birthmark. A jewel nourishing his body. Making him invincible to every disease and danger. When Krishna cursed his body to forever decay, he wrenched that gem out. With that miraculous shield gone, his body opened up to contamination. It was as if that blue stone had been the reservoir of his immunity. When the jewel was gouged out, it left a gash on his forehead. A gaping hole that would forever discharge blood and pus.'

'What's your point, Om?'

'It's pretty simple actually. Ashwathama suffers because his magical Mani was removed from his body. But if he finds another gem as potent as that sapphire, he could heal his body again. Restore himself to that pristine state. A stone equally incredible like the Mani of an Ichhadhari.'

'Precisely,' the priest took over. 'A simple case of demand and supply. When a serpent becomes a shape-shifter, what's the first object it creates? The Mani. Whenever a story revolves around an Ichhadhari, the pivot is always studded with the Mani. A cosmic cliché, but it has happened in the past and has happened again now.'

'And the snake's Mani is also no fable?' The officer queried.

'Far from it, Suri. The *Garud Purana* is our definitive Hindu text on gemology and clearly mentions the Nagmani or Nagmoti. It's one of the nine sacred stones described as a dazzling white jewel. And the fact that Ashwin has traced the Ichhadhari's Mani further reveals him to be Ashwathama. Mahadev never breaks his promise.'

'Mahadev?'

'As Ashwathama's godfather, he had a distinct bond with him. Not many know that right after he was cursed, Shiva appeared before him and granted him a boon. I came across this story while researching on Ashwathama. You will find it in regional folklore surrounding the Mahabharata. Shiva promised him that the creature dearest to him would manifest itself on earth as a superior being to help end his suffering. Yeva is a serpent. The creature Mahadev loves the most. A serpent who has arrived as an Ichhadhari.'

'But you said she's wicked,' the writer countered. 'Her creation wreaked misery in Kashmir. How can Lord Shiva allow such evil on earth?'

'I don't have all the answers, Om. Ashwin located Yeva in the Nilgiris the day she was created. That, more than anything else, confirms his identity as Ashwathama. Only he would know about her and where to find her. Find the Mani he has been waiting for.'

'Is it really as good as his original sapphire?'

'Almost. Many esoteric texts discuss that sapphire. Names like Shyamantaka and Shiroratna also pop up in these writings. They mention that there are two specific gemstones that can act as a substitute for Ashwathama's Mani. One of them is a complete mystery. No one knows what that jewel is and the texts describing it have not been deciphered well. Roughly translated, it means a peacock egg.'

'Peacock egg?'

'Yes. Pretty ambiguous. Even its existence is hardly clarified. Some believe that this gem was already present when the texts were compiled. Others argue that the jewel came into existence much later and the texts were actually predicting its creation. Either ways it's a riddle.'

'Peacock egg,' Patnaik mouthed. 'What could it be?'

'No idea, Om. The other stone is of course a serpent's Mani. Not as potent as the original sapphire but a worthy successor if Ashwathama can obtain it. And he already has.'

Suri stirred. 'You mean...'

'Yes. She has created the Mani and handed it over to him.'

'How can you know that?'

Atharva indicated Indira's artwork again. 'Look at the serpent. It lies beneath a single star. That's exactly how a Mani gets formed. When an Ichhadhari collects a drop of rain under a particular nakshatra, it creates the Mani. Yeva has done the needful.'

'Then why this mayhem?' the officer burst. 'If what you say is really true, Ashwin's secretary got him the fucking lollipop. So why are these people being attacked?'

'That baffles me too. Why indeed assault all these men? Who are they? Why was the Ichhadhari silent for four years and has suddenly started this bloodbath? Could it be some kind of pact between Yeva and Ashwathama? That she gave Ashwin the Mani and now he's helping her attack these men? Some personal revenge. An agenda that concerns only Yeva?'

'No, Atharva,' the writer shook his head. 'Whatever the motive, it concerns both of them. Probably Ashwin more than Yeva.'

'Why, Om?'

'You are forgetting the horseshoe clamped on the heads of all three victims. Why would Yeva do that? It's a statement. These bodies are not just being bled. They are being desecrated. Stamped with something that symbolises Ashwathama. Stamped on the forehead. That part of Ashwathama that held the sapphire but now carries a rotting wound. Branded like the mark of Cain, he's now branding others. Yeva may be the attacker but Ashwin's clearly the rationale.'

'We need to solve this. Find out the fucking reason behind these assaults. That may perhaps validate all that Atharva wants us to believe. But where do we start?'

'I think Indira is telling us what to do,' the priest took the slate from her hands. It was covered with threes. Front and back. Number three everywhere.

'Three?'

'It's quite clear. The three men lying comatose. She wants you to take her there.'

'Impossible,' Suri cried. 'The location's classified. Out of question.'

'The only question that matters now is why were these men targeted.'

'But those coordinates are beyond public domain.'

'My child is not public domain. She is here to help you out and until you put your faith in her, she stands handicapped. If you want the answer, this is the only way. Can you trust her? Trust both of us like you trust Om?'

Suri was hearing echoes. Similar sounds. Similar words not long ago.

Alia.

Asking the same thing.

Can you trust?

Alia…

Atharva was still speaking. 'Take her there. For those men. For Om's freedom. Take us there once. Then perhaps you shall accept everything I have said.'

The officer stood up. They were watching the child. Watching her play the prison bars as if it was a giant xylophone.

Chapter 25

'UNDRESS.'

She watched as he discarded his clothes one by one. Was this how Adam had stood under the tree? Unburdened. Unencumbered. Willing to unload. Ashwin's perfect frame stood resplendent in the muted light of the room. The body that lenses lusted for. That transformed cameras into voyeurs lingering on and on. Served hot on tabloid and celluloid.

'I said undress.'

'Again, Yeva?'

'Always.'

His fingers rose to detach his skin. Pare off the rind that encased him. He was smiling as the crusts came off. Shreds and lumps falling one after the other on the floor in a heap. Uncovering a frame of diseased flesh stinking up the basement. She smiled.

'The world can make love to Ashwin. I make love to Ashwathama.'

Yeva shoved him gently. He collapsed on her bed staining her sheets. She was standing nude now, her dark hair swaying like a bundle of snakes. He laughed.

'Come, thou mortal wretch.'

She climbed on top. 'You are quoting Cleopatra.'

'Because you are my asp.'

The Ichhadhari placed her mouth tenderly over the sores covering his torso. One by one. All of them. Her lips coated now with the blood that trickled. Puss seeping from his pores clinging to her face. She ran her fingers over his boils. Popped some as if they were bubble wrap secreting slime. His eyes closed as he moaned in pleasure and pain. His body revolting to throw off her weight rubbing against its lesions and yet seizing that intimate warmth incubating it. Her arms looped over his frame. Entwining him as if he was a branch of sandalwood. Her fingers rose to cup the hole in his forehead. The more she wiped, the more that cavity oozed. Red and yellow mingling into a thick foul discharge. It used to make her vomit once. Now she only wept tears into that void.

'Not again, Yeva. Your salt stings.'

His hand was flowing through her hair. His skin and nails cracking and sticking to her strands. She made her way south, pressing the heat of his erection against her face. Engulfing it and running her tongue over the scabs dotting the entire length of the shaft. Her saliva coating the ulcers at the tip. Shuddering violently, he pulled her down and clambered on top. Watching how he had anointed her skin with his fluids. Made her a goddess. Made her a mess. His tongue caressed the contours of her lips and ears. Scooped a drop of sweat from the hollow of her neck. Buried his face in her bosom, biting her nipples. Grasping and sucking them like plates of ambrosia. His wrist bones creaking as he clutched her tighter and tighter. Licking the place where he had stabbed her with the fountain pen.

'I hate hurting you, Yeva.'

'I love it when you do that.'

Going down, Ashwin paused. Poised over her navel. He giggled.

'We are no different, Yeva. We both carry our own craters.'

He squeezed the hollow on his forehead and filled her navel up.

'There now. We are one. Pus and poison.'

His probing muscle was tickling her loins. She opened as he entered. His erection burning her entrails like an electric current penetrating deeper and deeper. Stabbing her now. Stabbing hard. His body threatening to crumble into pieces as it gained kinesis. Pounding more and more. Pounding her the way only a cursed animal could. His hands clutching her posterior and hauling it up so that he could touch her innermost layer. Throbbing as one flesh. One bone. Bodies dissolving into sweat as her fingers climbed his back. Higher and higher and finally grating his skin as he exploded. His curse flooding her gates. Flowing inside her as he shrieked like a horse in the throes of life and death. Smell of hot iron singing their senses.

'You bleed again, Yeva. Bleed again for me.'

'The Ichhadhari becomes the body that pleases you. A virgin body every time.'

He had collapsed upon her like a corpse with a hammering heart. She pulled him closer.

'Have you seen anacondas mating, Ashwin? As many as twelve males wrap around a female. They twist and twine for days in each other's embrace.'

'Sounds redemptive.'

'You love with such passion. It's a pity you never knew a woman.'

'I don't know why. I might have been a different person.' He kicked her. 'You now. Undress.'

She closed her eyes. The next moment his body dropped, because Yeva lay no more beneath him. Just a sound. A hissing sound vibrating through Ashwin's hollow body. Wriggling and writhing. The female krait emerged like a shiny blue ribbon. Coiling and uncoiling around him. Clasping his fingers and toes. Licking the soles of his feet. Entering his pits and cracks. Closing her mouth on his erection again. One phallus tasting another. Slithering up his chest, she reached his face. Probing him all over and finally curling around his throat.

'You are diabolical, Yeva. Granting both desires possible. I think the Bible lies. Eve did not sin with Adam. It was the serpent who burrowed into her.'

Her hissing sound was lulling him to sleep. She rose and spread her hood over him as he slept like a child.

Chapter 26

WATCHING HIM RISE AND FALL.

His body inhaling and exhaling. He was sated. At peace for now. Hours later she was Yeva again. Disentangling herself from him but he clutched her as if they were joined by a vital tissue.

'Don't. Don't sever our knot.'

'Men say serpents are masculine. I am the phallus. What does that make you?'

'The cavity. I have remained hollow since the day he scratched out the sapphire from my body. I am a vacuum, Yeva, and your seed alone can fill me up. Your Mani shall make me whole again.'

'It's mystifying, Ashwin, how I, a mortal, could produce a Mani that's immortal. Sometimes I wish I could be deathless like you. We could be together forever.'

The actor closed his eyes. 'There can be no bigger curse than not knowing the sweet release of death. Dragging your weary immortality on your back because your life imprisonment shall never end. Burning endlessly never to be extinguished. A character on stage forever seeking his exit.'

'But books I have been reading say I too symbolise eternal life. If humans stand at one end of evolution, I stand at the other. I with no gills, wings or limbs am the primordial point of cosmogenesis. The cold-blooded creature inhabiting the cold underground darkness of the very beginning. Plato calls me the first deity of the universe. We snakes are like lines. We don't begin, and we don't end. You only see of us what is visible and yet at either end stretches an invisible infinity.'

'Ouroboros. The snake devouring its own tail.'

'Yes. The universe that feeds upon itself to recreate itself. Like you, we are also an endless cycle of creation and destruction. Self-reflexive like the phoenix, we rise from our own ashes. Our old skin making way for new.'

'You can peel off your skin but not your mortality. Rejoice in that.'

Yeva laughed. 'Serpents alone don't shed skin, Ashwin. I know someone else who does that. A divine magician who strips as the world applauds. Completely unaware of the true nature of the illusion. I pity them.'

He got up and stood before the mirror. Glass reflecting that flawless frame. No longer Ashwathama. He was Ashwin Tomar again.

'Not them, Yeva. I pity him. Krishna. The Dark One who cursed me. He wanted my decomposing body to drive men away. My boils and blisters to make me a pariah. He said the world will turn its eyes, too repulsed to look at me. Today the world pours in to watch me on screen. Watch me uncover my flesh on stage. Their hands groping and begging to touch this untouchable. The outsider now stands centrestage. I have made my body a spectacle, Yeva. The grandest spectacle of them all. Do you know what "maquillage" means?'

'Make-up.'

'Yes,' he grinned. 'They think it's all fake. A cosmetic

façade. They wonder why I don't allow anyone to help me prepare for the show. How do I tell them there's nothing to prepare? I do not rub greasepaint on. I do not put on a mask. I am the mask.'

'And that's why you are the greatest actor they have.'

'Indeed. My mask has melted into my face. The gore and pus inside me are not maquillage. Maquillage is what wraps me outside. Just like that human body you have draped around yourself.'

'You are quite a case study, Ashwin. One blue god destroyed your body and another gave you a new one. An impeccable layer that hides your decay.'

Ashwin picked up Yeva's lipstick and drew lines on the mirror. Three short parallel lines and an eye over them.

'Mahadev. My creator. My saviour. He placed me in this world, and he still provides me sanctuary. Men say Vishnu preserves and Shiva destroys. If only they could see how the Preserver destroyed me but the Destroyer preserves me.'

'Tell me again what our god told you.'

'Mahadev came to me the day I was cursed. He saw how the Dark One had scratched out my third eye. Meted out a curse most unjust. He could not reverse my condition but blessed me with this outer frame. A perfect cover-up that hides my contagion. This blanket cloaks me but does not cure me. Just a bandage around a bleeding wound. He revealed that a serpent shall soon become an Ichhadhari whose Mani could restore me again. And so, I waited. Rotting at the core but glowing outside.'

Yeva touched his face. 'Quite a marvel.'

'Yes. The only other creature that comes this close is Microcaecilia. The female amphibians grow an extra layer of skin to feed their young. An outer lining whose destruction causes no pain.'

'Just like you rip your face and feel nothing.'

'Absolutely. It's a crust all over me that I can remove at will. A veil of skin that coats me again within minutes of my peeling it off. An armour of muscle that lends me that perfect physique. The layer decorates me but also imprisons. And so, when I shred it on that stage, I feel free. My blood and pus flowing as they have been for ages now. Standing as myself without the mask. My audience applauding. Shaming that Dark One every time.'

'I wonder sometimes,' Yeva said. 'Wonder what Krishna thinks when he sees you now.'

'Scratches out his own eyes,' Ashwin snickered. 'I have defeated him like no one ever could. My face outsells him everywhere today. Splashed across more hoardings and banners than his. More covers and many more screens. I outrank him on Google search, and my audiences outnumber his devotees. My theatres more crowded than his temples. I am the bigger idol that everyone worships. Men objectified him, but I have objectified myself. I am cinema. The greatest deception of all.'

Yeva pointed at the *Mahabharata* on her shelf. 'That calls you the same.'

Ashwin took the book out and flipped its pages.

'Vyasa's scrapbook? I know what he wrote about me.'

'All false?'

He smiled. 'All true. I did all that and more. I was a worthy antagonist. I did more damage than the hundred Kuru brothers together. Do you know what's the biggest joke of this epic?'

'What?'

'The word Pandava. Pandu was impotent. These five were not even his sons, and yet they arrived in Hastinapur claiming his throne. It's not hatred I feel for them. It's contempt. They disgust me.'

'Especially the golden boy, Arjuna?'

'Golden? Even his name comes from silver. Argentum. My father had desired me to be the greatest archer of Aryavarta. But he turned blind with Arjuna's skill. His love split and Arjuna got the bigger half. It was for him that my father sacrificed Ekalavya's career, smudging his name forever. A sly dog like all his brothers.'

'You mean the tactics they used to win?'

'That and so much more. They killed everyone using deceit. Lied about my death to butcher my father. Yudhishtir's superego leading to that elaborate ruse. A psychological defence mechanism against the fact that he had lied. They cut off a Brahmin's head. A teacher's head. The worst sacrilege in Vedic society. Killed an elephant when the rules were clear that no one would strike an animal that posed no direct threat. Shared a common wife and watched Shishupal beheaded in their own court. Even made sure that Karna's son Vrishketu would not inherit. And the Dark One acted like a true Chandravanshi, glossing over every profanity and branding it Dharma.'

'Chandravanshi?'

'Yes. Chandravanshis question every law. Bend every rule. Forever ambiguous like the moon that keeps waxing and waning. And so, the Chandravanshi Krishna justified whatever the Pandavas did by constantly contextualising. Duryodhan was no pious soul, but it's the imbalance of justice that stabs me. Krishna even brainwashed Arjuna into wholesale massacre, calling it Dharmayudh. Advocating violence and addicted to sex. No wonder the Dark One degenerated. Freshwater Yamuna turned into saline Dwarka and the flute declined into a chakra.'

'They say Krishna gave half his wealth to Sudama.'

'If Krishna was a true friend, he would have gone to Sudama's house. Not waited for him to come and beg.'

'The hand that blessed Sudama with a new life, turned you into a living dead. Krishna's a paradox.'

'I know. Flies on an eagle but sleeps on a snake. Plucked out my third eye. The epicentre of all that I ever was.'

'Apparently humans also have a third eye. Known as the pineal gland.'

'That Dark One did the same to Shishupal. His own cousin. Removed his third eye and additional limbs. Made sure that Karna was stripped of his divine armour. He burns with envy. Goes green when he comes across a being more celestial. Making me a pariah must have been so orgasmic for him.'

'Is that why Cain resonates with you? You leapt at the opportunity of mentoring that play at the University? Even suggested conducting the workshop in Trehan's classroom.'

'Yes. That was some high,' he smirked. 'Being cordially welcomed into that very space. Walking all over his room. Sitting in his chair. Visualising how you must have opened him up. How he must have winced. They were all so grateful that I was helping them out. And so confused that I was grilling their Bible. If only I could scream that they were playing out my tragedy. Cain too wanders the earth like me with a marked forehead. They say man must die to attain eternal life. But we both who are deathless have been burdened with immortality.'

Yeva held up the *Bhagavad Gita*. 'I think this answers quite a few of your questions. Will you take it this time?'

Ashwin did not reply. Yanking the book from her hands, he snarled, 'I know I have told you to read anything you wish, Yeva. Develop your animal brain, but do not tell me what to do. This book is nothing but lies. He says the body is a transient thing that shall perish. But he locks me in my body. Forever suffering this biological trap.'

'I understand but if you just...'

'Are you rebelling, Yeva? Have you forgotten your vow? The day I saved your life?'

She returned his look. 'No, Ashwin. My vow lives in my fangs. If I remove it, I shall perish.'

'Good girl. What else have you been reading?'

'Finding out about similar Ichhadharis. Aboriginal myths mention Rainbow Serpents that can actually change their sex at will. That's the reason why rainbow flags today represent alternate sexuality. Even Greek mythology mentions a snake woman Lamia. And Sheshnag shape-shifted twice to be born as Lakshman and Balaram.'

'Yes. I have seen Balaram.'

'Is that why you were not too captivated when you saw me first? I hear there have been three hundred shape-shifters before me. I am not the only one.'

'You are my only one.'

She pulled out another book from the rack. 'Take this.'

Ashwin looked at the title. *The Scarlet Letter* by Nathaniel Hawthorne.

'This one you will like.'

The actor was gone. Only his words were sitting next to her.

The day I saved your life...

She picked up her journal. Thinking about that day when she had first met Ashwin. It was the day he had saved her from certain death. It was also the day she had finally set foot into that higher dimension.

The day she had become Ichhadhari...

Chapter 27

THE THREE MEN WERE STANDING BEFORE THE THREE MEN.

This private ward at one of the biggest hospitals in Mumbai was an enormous space. And almost stubbornly white. The walls and the ceiling. Marble flooring. Drapes covering the windows and sheets wrapping Akram, Trehan and Somnath. Monitor screens stood next to each of them like digital sentinels. Charting their vitals and ready to raise an alarm in case something went awry. The only sound was the sound of their breath. Air entering and leaving the three bodies. The ward was out of bounds for most, and men in uniform sat outside making that perfectly clear. Only a few like Suri were privileged. Atharva and Indira had trickled in with him. And Suri had made sure Patnaik accompanied them.

'Why do you have all three of them in a single room?' the priest asked.

'We did that after Somnath's body was brought in. Makes it convenient to monitor, given their similar injuries. Also, easier to secure them in a single room.'

'Security looks pretty tight.'

'It is. Their families and the hospital have been cooperating and the media's being kept away. The news reports out are merely carrying clinical stuff. None of the gory details.'

'I think you acted subconsciously, Suri,' the writer spoke. 'Given the expanse of this room, it appears as if you are making space for more bodies.'

The officer opened his mouth but paused, gesturing at the child.

'Maybe not if Indira can do what Atharva claims. But it's been a while, and I have seen nothing.'

He was right. Upon entering the ward, the child had walked up to the three comatose men. Then she had lain down on the floor. Sedentary like them but eyes wide open. Atharva bent down and placed her slate before Indira. The black slab suddenly puncturing the tabula rasa of that room. They watched her reach for a piece of chalk. Then she pulled her slate near and drew. Drew something that took two seconds.

The priest pounced on it.

'What is it? What has she drawn?' Patnaik's decibels threatening to rise above acceptable hospital levels.

'An eight.'

'Eight?' Suri snatched the slate. The image was reclining on that stone.

8

'What is eight?'

The officer saw both men shaking their heads. Clearly the number meant nothing to either of them. The slate was placed once again before Indira but to no avail. She was scratching the scar on her cheek. Looking at them as if she had communicated everything in that single doodle. The priest was eying the three figures again. A nurse had entered to check on them. He watched her thumb push back Akram's eyelid and shine a tiny pencil torch.

'Love the colour of his eyes,' she cooed. 'Such a beautiful shade of china blue.'

Atharva nodded. She was checking Somnath now. The priest edged nearer.

'His eye's blue too.'

'Hardly. Just a speck. It's heterochromia. Looks scary if you ask me.'

As Atharva moved, his eyes caught the slate lying on the floor. That figure still etched on it but appearing different now. It was as if the number had reinvented itself while they were not looking. He stood processing what he was seeing.

Not eight.

Not eight.

He turned to gaze at the three men in coma. And one world suddenly smearing his insides from brain to ankle.

Blue.

The word hitting him like a speeding train and his body splashing the tracks with blood. But not red.

Blue.

Both blue. But the other?

He quivered as the nurse slammed the door behind her. The two men were staring. He knew they had seen the colour draining from his face.

'You have stumbled upon something,' the writer inched closer eagerly.

'A thought. It's impossible. Impossible. But could it be possible?'

'What is it, Atharva?'

'I must ask something before I speak. You told me about the horseshoe, Suri. One of the baffling things you found on all three bodies. Was there anything else? Any other peculiar details about the attacks?'

'Yes. Two other things. First one's the liver.'

'Liver?'

'That's been the assault pattern. All three bodies sustained liver damage. That part of the body was stabbed injuring the organ and causing massive blood loss. And yet…'

'And yet none of them died. They only entered into a coma,' the priest's mouth appeared to curve into a faint smile. 'What else?'

'Those fucking names.'

'What names?'

'Three of them. At every site, the attacker left behind a mythological name. The first was Vibhishan. Next we had…'

Atharva cut him through again. 'Kripacharya?'

Suri's stunned silence told him it was.

'And the third one was Hanuman?'

'How do you know all this?'

The priest did not hear him. They watched his fingers rise involuntarily and splay across his mouth. His eyes dilating in a terrible ecstasy. His breath screaming through his windpipe and finally whispering slowly.

'I am right.'

He lowered himself to the floor as if his body could no longer sustain the weight of that knowledge. Grateful that gravity had sucked him down. Indira watched her father writing on the back of her slate.

Vibhishan

Kripacharya

Hanuman

'What are you doodling, Atharva?' he heard the officer ask.

'The answer. I think I know why these men were attacked.'

'Do you really?'

'Yes. I had offered you four truths. Asked you both to trust every word I said. But this one frightens me. It razors through me. I want to ask you to believe me one more time, but I am terrified. You will laugh at my face again. Laugh harder than you have so far. How do I demand more of your faith when I am questioning my own now?'

Patnaik sat down before him. 'You know something, Atharva? When I first met Suri, truth for him was only that which could fit in his files. His factual world view. You have placed Ichhadharis and Ashwathamas before him and yet he has got you here today. I am a man charged with assault, and yet he has brought me along, assuming full responsibility. We are both here standing by you. Give us a little more credit for that.'

'Speak, priest,' the officer said. 'We shall try to keep up.'

Atharva took a deep breath. 'These men are the Chiranjivis.'

'Chiranjivis?'

'The Immortals. Hindu mythology lists seven beings who shall remain alive on earth till the very end of time. Seven eternal lives. These are not ordinary men lying in coma before us. They are the first three Immortals. The names you found at each attack site are not random. They are who they are. Vibhishan, Kripacharya and Hanuman.'

The writer felt the earth tilting below him. His fingers curled, gripping the floor.

'Chiranjivis? I remember reading about them long ago. Are you certain?'

'I have no doubt, Om.'

Suri's face did not change. He pointed at Somnath.

'That's Hanuman lying there?'

The priest nodded. 'These Immortals are believed to live on earth through a continuum of lifetimes both present and past. Do you believe in past life, officer?'

'No. I am just trying to make it through this one.'

Patnaik nodded. 'Not sure what to say, but this does explain why none of them died despite the nature of their wounds. They cannot die.'

'Exactly,' Atharva said. 'Liver damage and haemorrhage and yet they survive. They are deathless.'

'Like Ashwathama?' the officer asked.

'Yes. He is one of the seven Chiranjivis as well. But actually the odd man out, which is why he's the last name on that list.'

'What do you mean?'

'It's pretty simple. The first six Chiranjivis either chose eternal life voluntarily or were rewarded by gods to become immortal. But Ashwthama was made deathless to be punished. He never wanted an endless existence but was saddled with it. Immortality is a blessing for the first six but a curse for Ashwathama. And as a cursed creature, he lacks the supreme properties that the first six have.'

'What properties?'

'According to the Puranas, the first six Immortals are all Nilotpal.'

'Nilotpal?'

'It means Blue Lotus,' the writer replied.

'Metaphorically. In more literal terms, it means that each of these six Chiranjivis will have a trait which would be blue. It could be physical or even...'

'Eyes,' Suri clipped him in the middle. 'Akram has blue

eyes. And Somnath has heterochromia. Brown eyes but with a speck of blue.'

'Bingo!' Atharva exclaimed. 'That's what seized my attention.'

'What about Trehan?'

The priest's face fell. 'Him I am not sure. There must be something.'

'There is,' Patnaik nodded. The men turned towards him curiously. 'Something not many know. Trehan and I have a mutual friend who had confided in me.'

'Confided what?'

'Trehan was a blue baby when he was born.'

'Blue baby?'

'It's a heart condition where deoxygenated blood mixes with oxygenated blood throughout the body. The skin and fingertips of the baby acquire a bluish tinge. Trehan had to undergo surgery to correct the defect.'

'That seals it. These are Chiranjivis. We humans are clay, but they are indestructible like diamond. Carbon of this earth.' Atharva was writing on the slate again. Adding the remaining names. 'This is the complete list.'

Vibhishan

Kripacharya

Hanuman

Vyasa

Parashurama

Bali

Ashwathama

'Chinese mythology also mentions Immortals,' Patnaik said. 'But they have eight. Isn't there a Sanskrit mantra, Atharva, that has the names of all the Chiranjivis?'

'Yes. It goes—

AshwathaamaBalirVyasahaHanumanthaVibeeshanaha
KripaParashuramaschaSaptaiteyChiranjivinaha

'Loosely translated it means regular reciting of these seven names ensures longevity. Even today, in traditional Hindu households, when a Brahmin ties a thread around someone's wrist on his birthday, he puts seven knots denoting the Immortals.'

'And Ashwathama is not Nilotpal?'

'No, Suri,' the priest said. 'He also lacks the gunas. The first six Chiranjivis have a guna or attribute each which qualified them to attain eternal life on earth.'

'What attributes?'

'Vibhishan's attribute is Treason. A negative virtue but Vibhishan went against his own brother for the sake of Dharma. His betrayal was instrumental in the killing of Ravan and rescue of Sita. Hence Vibhishan's treason won him Rama's gratitude and the boon of immortality.'

'And Kripacharya?'

'Kripa's attribute is Education. Hardly surprising since he taught the Pandavas and Kauravas. And Hanuman's attribute is Devotion. The eternal devotee of Rama, Hanuman had himself wished to remain on earth as long as Rama's name was venerated. Sita granted him the boon and also added that his image would be installed at every sanctum that housed Rama so that he could forever hear people celebrating the lord.'

'And the remaining three?'

'Parashurama's attribute is Strength. Vyas symbolises Knowledge and Bali stands for Power. The gunas that make them immortal. And that's exactly what Indira communicated.'

The officer flipped the slate. 'You mean this eight?'

'It's not an eight. We have been looking at it incorrectly all this while.'

He took the slate and rotated it. 'Do you see it now?'

They watched the figure transform before their eyes as if it had shape-shifted. And suddenly everything clear as daylight.

∞

'The infinity sign, Suri. Infinity.'

'Yes, Om. Not eight.'

They knew now. Knew that Indira had conveyed everything in that one symbol. The priest had taken out his iPad and opened her first image again. The blue serpent and the red horse.

'Here again she had told me about the Immortals.'

'Here?' the officer looked. 'That's just the two animals.'

'No, Suri,' Patnaik's eyes twinkled. 'He's right. Look at the sky above them.'

'Stars.'

'How many?'

They were all counting. Whispering it to themselves.

Seven.

Seven stars like the Saptarishi.

Seven Chiranjivis.

Suri looked at the comatose cricketer. 'So Akram is Vibhishan? But how's it possible? Everyone knows Akram was born in 1960. If he's a Chiranjivi, how could he be born? And are you telling me he will never die? Trehan and Somnath will never perish?'

'I can't answer all your questions. How the Chiranjivis function on earth is not something the Puranas talk about. One of those cosmic phenomena that we might be able to understand one day. But see how it all fits. Vibhishan as Akram is still accused of treachery.'

'Kripacharya as Trehan continues to educate,' the writer said. 'And Hanuman is Somnath. The perennial devotee. Their gunas remain the nucleus of their lives here, confirming their identity.'

'Yes,' Atharva added their worldly names to the list. 'It also confirms beyond any doubt now that Ashwin is Ashwathama. Only a Chiranjivi would be aware of the identity of the other six Chiranjivis. Just as Ashwin knew who Yeva was, he also knows who these men are. And he's sending Yeva to attack them one by one.'

They saw Patnaik walk towards Somnath. He touched his feet and whispered.

'Now where do we get the Sanjivani to heal you? Why did you not fight back? I saw you go down on the floor and close your eyes before Rama. Why did you not kill me? Kill Yeva?'

'You are right,' the officer remarked. 'Why would Hanuman take it lying down? And why are they being attacked in the first place? You say Ashwin's got the Mani. So why assault these other Chiranjivis now?'

'Rage perhaps,' Atharva said. 'Remember those six chose immortality. It was something they felt blessed to receive. Delighted to be on this earth forever. But for Ashwathama it's a wretched, drawn-out existence never to end. He's lashing out at those who celebrate everlasting lives while he writhes in pain. That would also explain the horseshoes. Branding their foreheads like his own to defile them as Om said.'

The writer shook his head. 'I don't think it's that simple anymore.'

'What do you mean?'

'If he only wants to desecrate them, why stab their livers? Besides, Ashwathama and the Chiranjivis have been on earth for ages. Why suddenly attack them now?'

'I have no idea.'

'Think, Atharva. The seven of them have been around all this while. Nothing had happened until now. Why now? What has changed now leading to these sudden assaults?' He lowered his voice. 'One change. Ashwathama has stumbled upon an Ichhadhari. Or, more specifically, he's found a Mani.'

They felt a wire tightening inside them. 'The Mani? Why would that be a reason?'

'Something you told us yesterday. You said an Ichhadhari's Mani while remarkably powerful is not as potent a gem as the original sapphire Ashwathama was born with.'

'That's true. That sapphire was a celestial stone. Flushed with the dew of Mahadev's essence. A jewel with such prowess that it could even counteract the words of Krishna. He had to first separate it from Ashwathama's body to make his curse effective.'

'In other words, a snake's Mani is not as miraculous. So, acquiring it is only half the battle won. Ashwin needs to make it as powerful as his original sapphire was to counteract the curse and heal himself. And that's why these attacks have become inevitable.'

'What's your point, Om?'

'Blood, Suri. Why is Ashwin getting Yeva to injure these

men? Blood is the vital essence of a being. Concentration of all his energies. The very distillation of his core. And blood of the Chiranjivis would be Amrit. Nectar most virile. Anointing gemstones with blood to increase their potency is an ancient practice. I think that's what Ashwin craves. An elixir to turn the Mani divine. Making the six Immortals bleed to cleanse his own blood.'

'But why target the liver?'

'That I cannot explain. But this is about blood. And more bodies could bleed.' He crossed the first three names out. 'We are halfway through. Three more to go.'

The officer stood up.

'Looks like we have all the answers.'

'Hardly, Suri,' the writer said. 'We don't know who the other three Chiranjivis are. How has Ashwathama become Ashwin? How will his scheme play out? Why is an Ichhadhari so willingly following his every command? How can we stop him? And how do we destroy her?'

'Yeva?'

'Yes,' Atharva said. 'One of the privileges of becoming an Ichhadhari is that you can only be killed in a specific way. I have browsed through various texts but none of them carries that secret. I even invoked Indira to show me the way, but it did not work. We will need to find that out. What about Ashwin? Can you bring him in for questioning?'

'And how do I fucking interrogate him?' the officer smouldered. 'Are you Ashwathama? May I see your pet reptile? I cannot touch him. I cannot even release Om unless we have a similar assault while he's still in prison.'

'So, we do nothing while they attack the next one?'

'I didn't say that. We wait for the next envelope. Figure

out the victim and catch Yeva in the act. That's the only way we can pin down the star.'

'And until then?

Suri's finger circled the image in blue abeer on the priest's iPad.

'How about paying the Ichhadhari a visit?'

Chapter 28

YEVA'S JOURNAL—PG 54

I was lying on grass, twirling my fingers and toes.

I had seen others of my species writhing in pain when their tails got severed or hoods were maimed. Chewed by alligators or clawed by a leopard or trampled upon by man. I had heard stories that when humans lost a limb, they sometimes suffered from a paranormal delusion that the limb was still attached and functioning like a phantom. But I knew nothing about gaining hands and legs.

How did it feel when your body sprouted new limbs?

I still did not know. Lying there on Nilgiri's lap, I was gazing at these hands and legs that had just branched out of me. Fused with my body and yet so indifferent. I turned and lay on my back. I was taking my time. I knew one central command coursing through my spine would soon bring these limbs scampering towards me. Bonded labour following every word.

I smiled. Sprawled on the forest floor that day I had not grasped what I had done. But today I know. The Biblical God had cursed the serpent in Eden to lose all its limbs and crawl on earth forever. But I had defied that decree. I had turned divine. That day at the Nilgiris I had not just reclaimed my hands and feet. A reptile had slithered up the biological pyramid to conquer the highest form possible. The body of man. Man whom God had created in his own image. Man who now thought of himself as god.

I was god-like.

Ichhadhari.

Soul of a serpent but outer covering of a human. And it had not taken one hundred years as some believed.

Heaving my body up, I tried to stand but instantly collapsed. I laughed aloud as I felt the familiar ground below. The soil was my companion. My confidant. For years this earth had held my body close to itself as I had glided atop. We had heard each other's heartbeats. Known each other's secrets. Sensed the slightest changes in each other. It did not want to let go of me. It was pulling me down. Wanting to nestle me again, but I told her it was time to soar. Balancing on my legs, I propped myself up once more. My toes curled but stabilised under my weight. My equilibrium sustained itself as my new body discovered its centre of gravity. I was standing tall, trampling the ground below. Looking at my slender limbs again. Fingers and toes. I walked towards the pond before me. The water had always drowned my body, but this time it could only wash my feet. Was this why man was so removed from nature?

My face…

I was staring at my face. Everything was unfamiliar but not my eyes. They were the same. My own like my soul. My fingers were sensing my hair. My skin. That smooth lustrous coating as beautiful as my enamel snake skin.

Men loved to wear our skin. Now I was wearing theirs.

Wearing and wondering…

If they had such a radiant casing of their own, what drove them to strip my species naked? Not their need. It was their greed. My hands were caressing the contours of my breasts. The fingers slid down plunging into the depths of my navel. Probing a delicate triangle of hair inside my loins. Probing deeper and deeper. Faster and faster.

I closed my eyes. What was this? This sensation? This stimulation? Currents of an unknown pleasure were sparking through my flesh. I was sighing. Wanting to fall back on earth and tell her about it. What pure ecstasy was this, given to man? This inferno? This boiling volcano of self-gratification? My arms were aching now but my finger did not stop. Deeper and deeper. Excavating my new core. Faster and faster. A tidal wave gathering inside me now. Threatening to split my body apart and ooze through every pore. Faster and faster. Faster and faster. Suddenly I screamed as my legs gave way before a nameless force. I looked down to find a python looped around me.

I froze.

The black python must have been watching me from below the dense water reeds. It had lunged with an open mouth and was swiftly entwining me. I was motionless like a slab of granite. Feeling the python's icy body sliding over me. Terrifying. Fascinating. Was this how the human body reacted when we snakes defiled it? I wanted to revert to my real self and stun the python. But I stood unmoving in my new avatar as the creature chained me within its spiral prison. Mesmerised with what another reptile was doing to me. The helix was shrinking now, constricting my spine. The horror rendering me more lifeless even as my eyes widened in awe. My animal instinct had turned blank. The trap was closing in, and I somehow knew that all those human bones inside me were about to impale me to death.

Bang!

The heat of a bullet scorched the air next to my face as it blew the python's head away. I stood still as the coils loosened and slipped off my body. Turning around I saw a man holding a pistol. He came closer and smiled.

'I have been looking for you.'

I asked. 'Who are you?'

'Ashwathama.'

'You saved my life.'

'No. You shall save mine.'

'You saved me. But you are a man.'

'I am not.'

'But you look like one.'

'As much as you do.'

'I am not human.'

'Neither am I.'

'I am here to demolish man.'

'So am I.'

I lowered my face as he fondled me.

'My little mermaid. It's time you fished for your magic coral.'

'What coral?'

'The one that can burn water.'

Chapter 29

THE ELEVATOR AT KALPATARU WAS SLIDING LOWER AND lower down the spine of the earth.

'So, because she's a snake, she has stashed herself in this hole?' The officer remarked. 'Then why become an Ichhadhari?'

Atharva stepped into the basement holding Indira's hand. 'Her human form is just a sheath. It hardly affects her true nature. Serpents have always been chthonic. Living away from the eyes of all. Creatures of the uterine underworld, slithering between cosmic planes above and below.'

'Fucking underworld.'

'You said you wanted to ambush Yeva when she attacked next. Take her by surprise. Why have we come here then, Suri?'

'I want to check this shape-shifter out.'

'You want proof. The cop inside you is still not convinced. Go ahead, but I fear that we shall end up alerting her. She'll see that we have figured out everything and may modify her plans.'

'I don't think so. From what you told us, she's a bloody determined creature if she could become an Ichhadhari. Once she knows that we have caught on, it will be a level playing field. My men have been tracking her since yesterday.

That's her room. Stays out the whole day and returns only by night.'

The door was padlocked. Suri took out his revolver and put a hole through it.

Atharva stared at the fuming barrel. 'Now she knows we have trespassed.'

'That's the idea. She can twist her body into knots knowing she's under our radar now.'

The suspended bulb revealed her lodging. Atharva walked up to the shelves lined with books. *Orpheus Descending. The Strange Case of Dr Jekyll and Mr Hyde. Pygmalion. Beauty and the Beast.*

'She reads.' He picked up a thick volume of poetry dog-eared at *Leda and the Swan.* 'An intriguing selection. Books that reflect what she herself is. Ashwathama's warrior is not just a magical body. She has developed a discerning mind. I was wrong. Maybe her human form is enriching the animal within.'

'What is that?'

The priest craned his neck to observe the wooden object Suri was pointing at. The book slid from his hands and hit the floor. He moved in awe as if he had spotted a minor god taking refuge in that basement.

'Om would have loved to see this, Suri.'

'He's still an accused, Atharva. I cannot bring him everywhere. What is this thing?'

'A Nehushtan.'

'A what?'

'A Biblical motif of a snake on a pole. Refers to the bronze serpent on a staff that God had instructed Moses to install. It prevented the Israelites from dying of snake bites.'

'Why place it here?'

'I wonder,' the priest's eyes were devouring it. 'Nehushtan symbolises healing. One that purifies and elevates. Transmutes the lower into higher. And, if you think about it, that's exactly what Yeva's doing for Ashwin. Making her Mani a sanitiser for his septic body. Maybe Ashwin placed it here to constantly remind her of her task. Her sacred covenant. Or perhaps Yeva installed it. A wooden snake hanging mid-air like an Ichhadhari in limbo. Both human and reptile.'

'I have seen this symbol at hospitals.'

'That's the Rod of Asclepius, also denoting medicine and health. You also have Caduceus, but that has two serpents and a bird.'

Suri scowled. 'That's too many fucking snakes on poles.'

'And we are standing below a building called Kalpataru.'

'So?'

'Symbols depicting snakes on poles have all been derived from legends featuring a serpent coiled around a tree. Greeks describe Ladon twined around the tree of golden apples in the Garden of Hesperides. In the *Epic of Gilgamesh*, the serpent is associated with a miraculous plant. Both the Norse tree of Yggdrasil and the Tree of Knowledge in Eden have serpents around them. And what does Kalpataru mean? A tree in Hindu mythology that grants desires.'

'And we have a snake living under it now.'

'Precisely. That serpent around the tree at Eden caused someone to fall from grace. This serpent below a building named Kalpataru is helping someone attain grace. And it calls itself Yeva. That's Armenian for Eve. The name itself means giver of life. Eve led to the fall of Adam but Yeva is helping a fallen one rise.'

'Fucking twisted.'

'And a cause for concern, Suri. A tree denotes the Axis Mundi or the staff of the earth. A snake encircling it indicates a threat to world order. Evil tainting the elements and coursing through its channels. Yeva might heal Ashwathama, but she'll endanger everything else.'

Suddenly Indira fell on the floor. The chalk in her hand was doodling a snake. A blue snake. Atharva's voice died in his throat.

'She's here. Yeva.'

The officer pulled his revolver aiming around the room. 'Are you sure?'

'Indira's never wrong. She has a bond with animals. The Ichhadhari's here. Hiding and watching us.'

Suri fired at the foot of the Nehushtan. 'Come out. Yeva.'

They waited.

'Show us how you do it.'

'She will not expose herself. And she may not let us leave. We...'

He paused. Indira was sitting in *padmasana*. Legs crossed and eyes closed.

'What's she doing?'

The priest hushed him and whispered. 'Snakes are highly perceptive. If you become intensely meditative, the first creature that shall be drawn towards you is a snake. She's pulling Yeva out.'

'What rot!'

'It's true. Look at images of meditating saints. You will always find serpents around. Why does a snake inhabit the body of Shiva? The biggest mystic of all.'

Indira sat still as if she had turned into one of her own

chalk drawings. Minutes later they heard a footfall.

Yeva.

Time refused to budge. It stood to watch how the two men were watching her. Detecting rage in both of them. A simmering wrath towards this Ichhadhari who had pledged her allegiance to a cursed creature. Disgust at how she could shed so much blood. But there was something else. Something different. Suri's anger also had a drop of doubt. Disbelief. Wondering if she was really a mythical marvel. And Atharva's fury was hiding rapture. A spiritual euphoria that he was witnessing a miracle. The impossible that had slithered out of folklore to stand before him in flesh and blood. A powerful conversion of energy and matter. Sweat was oozing from Suri's forehead. She smiled.

'Not very different, are you?'

He aimed the barrel at her chest. 'Identify yourself.'

'I should be saying that since you both stand under my roof.'

'You are Yeva?'

'I am.'

'Ashwin Tomar's secretary?'

'Ask me what you really want to know, Suri,' she hissed. 'Ask me if I am the shape-shifting reptile.'

The officer lowered his weapon. 'You know me?'

'I do. You. Your future and your past.'

'My past?'

'Those who came before you. And where they went. We have a bond, Suri.'

'Bond?'

'A very old bond.'

Atharva stepped forward. 'What about your bond with

this earth? Are you aware of the price humanity paid when you turned into an Ichhadhari? Your creation triggered the Kashmir floods in 2014.'

'Really? My creation or the ecological devastation you men have been carrying out?'

The priest gaped.

'You uprooted trees in that valley. Encroached upon lakes and wetlands. Shrunk the drainage capacity of rivers. But will you accept the blame? No. Humans never do. Blame the Ichhadhari for the floods like the Chinese blame the Jiaolong serpent.'

'I see you are intelligent, Yeva. But do you deny you are evil?'

'Do you deny you are too? Your entire race?'

'What about Ashwathama?' Suri rolled the name out. 'Do you deny that you are his bloody slave? That Ashwin Tomar is Ashwathama. That he sought you for the Mani and now you go about assaulting the Chiranjivis?'

She paused for an infinitesimal second. Then she clapped. 'Not bad. You have connected the dots.'

'We have, Yeva. We know all about it. My friend here is even wondering if you will change your plans now. Or perhaps abort your mission altogether.'

'Tell him he's a fool,' she flicked her tongue. 'We snakes move in a curve, Suri, but our resolve is pretty straightforward. It hardly matters if you know. Nothing changes. And there's nothing you can do. Your knowledge shall only make your failure all the more bitter. Besides, there's so much you are still not aware of.'

'Not for long. There's enough good in this world to fuck evil. Like my friend, Om. Like this priest here all the way from Manipur. And someone else helping us too. Showing us your every hand. Every move.'

She laughed. Laughed like a cube of ice clinking inside a tall glass.

'You mean those envelopes? All those objects?' The shape-shifter gripped the Nehushtan. She was whirling round and round in neat little circles. 'How naïve you are, Suri.'

The men stood transfixed. The truth skewering both their brains one by one.

It was her…

Yeva…

The envelopes…

Those objects…

Yeva…

'But…but this is bizarre,' the priest stuttered. 'Why would you do that?'

'Just for sport. Men have been sporting with us forever. I picked up the dice too. Besides, I told you I have a bond with Suri. Quite an old bond.'

The officer was hardly reacting. Just hearing her speak.

'Such fun sending him my itinerary. Watching him from his precinct window. Watching him ogling at the envelopes like a moron. Trying to make some sense. He looks pathetic.'

Suri moved and slapped her across the face. 'You were fucking screwing with me.'

She giggled harder. 'The man's angry. Why are you angry, officer? Is it because I am playing or because you are losing? Lost all the three times. I told you it hardly matters if you know. You cannot prevent anything. And we are just half done. I will be sending you more. Three more envelopes to mock you. Three more assaults. And you will keep losing.'

'No, Yeva. The only one to lose shall be you. You and your actor. Take my word and forget whatever fucking scheme you have.'

'That's exactly what many had said when they heard my desire to be an Ichhadhari. Told me snakes have no ability to aspire since they crawl on the ground. But here I am.'

'Spilling innocent blood,' Atharva said. 'The evil that chains the earth.'

She strummed the sacred thread around the priest's body. 'You men are already chained.'

'I can take you in right now,' the officer grabbed her wrists.

'On what charges? What will you tell your superiors? That you have netted an Ichhadhari?'

'Atharva is a tantrik. He can force you to take your true form.'

'How will he do that? By playing a *been* like they do in your cinema? I am an anomaly, Suri. A glitch of nature like Ashwin. How will you explain us to your world?'

'You fascinate me, Yeva,' the priest spoke in awe. 'I knew you must be dark. But you are cerebral too. I saw the literature on your shelf. Quite eclectic.'

'Yes. Ashwin takes good care of me. He wants me to exploit my human form. Appreciate this world as fully as possible.'

'I can see that. The Vedas stipulate that a soul must transmigrate through eighty-four lakh species to achieve the human frame. But you have jumped the line. You have the privilege now to switch on and switch off this human form around you.'

'Human body. The highest form available. God's own

image on earth, they say. But no different really. Same dust as my snake skin.'

'Aren't you enjoying it?'

'Not so much these props you call legs. I feel giddy looking down at the earth I have always clung to. Our locomotion has so much more grace. But these hands are fabulous. Quite useful. I don't fancy my hair and breasts either, but Ashwin seems to relish them. And my voice. I love the sound of my voice. You should hear me hum.'

'And the human brain? Loftier than a serpent's psyche?'

'It's certainly more evolved. You compose operas and solve equations. Cultivate a sense of humour. Contemplate about the purpose of existence. I see the monuments you have erected and the books you have written. You even have the faculty to rationalise. And all this makes it so ironical. So much perception and yet you all are so pathetic. Do you know why?'

'Why, Yeva?'

'Because you lack compassion. That fundamental quality that sustains all creation. You are human but not humane. How can a brain that has created so much, destroy so easily? You who can appreciate beauty more than any other life form, turn this world so hideous? We are programmed by instinct, but you have morality. Aware of the fragility of life, and yet you nibble at the umbilical cord that links you to your habitat. Your brain made you lord of the planet and now you rob the rights of every living being. Choke the universe with a plastic sheet.'

Suri smirked. 'What are you? A fucking greenie?'

'No,' Atharva's eyes had become moist. 'She's a serpent. The species whose whole body embraces the earth. Sensitive to the slightest changes in biosphere. Dwelling in the deepest levels, they feel every action that harms natural balance.'

'Exactly. We have an alliance with the primal forces which Christianity could not handle. They made us agents of the devil. You call us toxic, but your factories have more poison than our entire race. Your climate summits are a joke. We hear how the earth howls, begging for mercy. And then it erupts like it did in Kashmir. But you will soon forget Kashmir like you have forgotten Khandavprastha.'

She was pointing at the painting on the wall. The orange turning the green black.

'What your Krishna did. Ashwin told me how he demolished an entire forest to construct a new city. Your god clothed Draupadi but ripped the cover off earth. You are still doing it. A Khandavprastha burns somewhere in the world every day. And not just forests. You strip us for our skin. Our fur and our ivory. I know natural law dictates that something must die to nourish another. But you men don't seek nourishment. You indulge. It's time we reclaimed this planet now. I have become human to end humans.'

'That's your agenda?'

'Yes. Even your God did that once when he caused the Deluge. That great flood mentioned in the Bible to wipe all you sinners. Nature always avenges itself. And it has chosen me this time to weed you out. Even Ashwin wants the same.'

'Ashwin?' the priest glared. 'I thought all he wanted was to regain his former self. Isn't that why you are attacking these Chiranjivis? To get their blood to fortify your Mani?'

'That's just the beginning.' She looked up. 'What Ashwin has in mind for all of you is beyond your comprehension. Didn't that give you a hint?'

They followed her eyes. A horseshoe hanging from the ceiling.

'We know that signifies your master,' the officer said. 'The beast you serve.'

She was shaking her head. 'Not just that. The horseshoe also resembles an alphabet.' They saw what her fingers were sculpting in the air.

Ω

'Omega,' Atharva recognised it. The next moment the officer saw terror in his eyes.

'What is it?'

'Omega is the last letter of the Greek alphabet. It symbolises finality. The end of everything.' He looked at Yeva. 'What is Ashwathama planning?'

She remained quiet, but Suri erupted. 'What can a fucking loser like him do? Butcher us all while we sleep like he had done on the last night of the Mahabharata war?'

'No. He will not,' she said.

'What then?'

'Nothing.'

'Nothing?'

'Yes. Nothing. Ashwathama will do nothing. You shall destroy each other. All of you. Like that clan by the sea.'

'Don't be too sure. I can see to it that your master rots in a cell for the rest of his eternal life.'

Yeva came closer. Her blue eyes carving Suri's face.

'You do know that we snakes guard our treasure with our life. Try robbing that and you shall be foaming your life out of your mouth.'

'Why, Yeva?' the priest questioned. 'How can someone as evolved as you not see Ashwin's evil? Not see how he uses your rage against humans for his own gain. How can you become his apostle?'

'We serpents worship Mahadeva, and Ashwathama is his child. Anyone blessed by Shiva cannot be evil. Ashwin is not wrong. He has been wronged. I had become an Ichhadhari to eliminate man, and I would have done it with or without Ashwin. It's plain fortune that I met someone who shares the same programme. Who can accomplish it better and faster. He also told me that I have a higher purpose. Fulfilling the promise that Mahadev had given him. I am the chosen one. He has bled for ages and now you all must bleed too.'

'Like the Chiranjivis you stabbed?'

'Yes. Their livers one by one.'

'Liver. Why liver?'

'It has to be the liver. You should know that.'

'Know what?'

'Liver holds the purest blood. It is the holy grail of the body. A receptacle that cleanses that vital element. My Mani is the most flawless part of myself and demands only that powerful nectar. Nothing else can transform it.'

'It's ghastly, Yeva. A Mani could be such a beautiful thing, but you have turned it into a vampire that drinks blood.'

'Perhaps. It's more like receiving the Eucharist. Don't you know the liver's also immortal like the Chiranjivis. An organ that regenerates. That also makes its blood special. Like the eagle feeding on the liver of Prometheus, I swoop down and claim my drop. Three more to go and you can do nothing to stop me.'

Suri placed his revolver on her head. 'I can pump these bullets into you. See if you are truly magical.'

She held the barrel and lowered it slowly to the centre of her forehead. 'Wound me right here just like him. Then I shall be dearer to him.'

He fired, but his hand shook and the bullet ruptured Yeva's eye. As Suri wiped the bloodstains on his face, he saw her fingers probing her fuming socket and pluck out the bullet lodged inside. A moment passed and her eye was whole again.

'Satisfied?' Atharva asked. 'I told you she cannot be killed like that. Their wounds heal right away.'

But the officer shoved the weapon into her once more. 'Where's the Mani, Yeva?'

She laughed. Ice cube tinkling in the glass again but much colder now.

'You are pathetic, Suri. I will destroy you like you destroyed so many of us. Your career. Your life. I shall bleed that wicked blood that flows in you. You hang us upside down from walls. Now I shall invert. Invert the pyramid. Tip the ladder and bring you down.'

She stood no more before them. She lay coiled on the ground, her enormous blue hood fanned out in fury. Atharva grasped the officer's hand.

'It's a krait. A blue krait.'

Suri was seeing it. Seeing the Ichhadhari. Seeing the last flecks of doubt that still clung to his brain freezing to death. Hearing Akram's wife speak again.

Faith, officer…Never easy to conjure.

Indira had walked up to the serpent. She was stroking her

head. The krait lashed out. As the girl backed off, Atharva picked her up.

'Come, Suri. Yeva wants us to leave.'

Getting into the elevator, they saw her watching them coiled under the Nehushtan.

Chapter 30

That we inhabit a universe so relative and temporal
Can a bid to survive be judged proper or immoral?
That idea was not inflaming the Rishiputra's brain
It was a different question making his neck crane
Standing before a mirror, his soul smelling of dread
As he kept on gazing at the very centre of his head
Back in the court he had witnessed a game of dice
Stakes like never before but worth less than a pice
An emperor had lost virtues he had piled all his life
His country and his brothers and their common wife
Dragged by her hair that empress had been shamed
Some voices rearing heads but only to be maimed
Hands had tried to uncover the garment off her skin
But cosmos had turned into a giant sewing machine
An infinite river of cloth had soaked her body frail
Fire of revenge blazing from that cracked holy grail
A truth most horrifying that day did all hearts chafe
Surrounded by family but a woman may still be unsafe
The rishi had folded hands to try and avert her fate
But not the Rishiputra, his own body robed in hate
And when that reptile lies coiled around your mind
You may see right from wrong and yet remain blind
She belonged to his foe, consort of the Silver Prince

Wife to the other four whose lustre made him wince
Loathing for your foe was but natural and prescribed
A sentiment born within and certainly not contrived
Much solace did he derive from that solitary thought
Not guilty for he upheld what cosmic order wrought
And yet the mirror displayed a face slick with sorrow
That singular question still sucking all his marrow
If what I did in that court was unquestionably right
Why does the star on my forehead not twinkle tonight?

Chapter 31

EXHIBIT E150518

'Today!' Suri crushed the label. 'That's fucking today.'

The envelope was pink in colour, as predicted by Atharva. And it had deposited a piece of stone on the table. A rectangular stone with two human figures carved on it. The pair was seated under what appeared to be a skeletal tree barely clothed with leaves. Their hands were outstretched as if reaching out for the fruit hanging from it. The figure on the right was sprouting horns and behind both of them coiled a serpent.

The officer glared at the reptiles on the stone. 'Yeva said she wanted to destroy me. The krait wants to play again. What's this thing?'

'The Temptation Seal,' Patnaik declared.

'So those are Adam and Eve?' The priest asked.

'Yes. It's a replica of the stone cylinder of Post-Akkadian origin dating back to around 2200 BC. Given these elements on the seal, the most obvious interpretation has been the Biblical episode of Original Sin. That prelapsarian moment when Adam and Eve taste the forbidden apple from the Tree of Knowledge. The devil as the plotting serpent watching their disobedience and rejoicing in their fall.'

'What's a cylinder?' the officer queried.

'Small stone seals originating from Mesopotamia to be

worn as jewellery or amulets. The designs were engraved in clay which left a clear imprint in relief. In fact, these seals led to the development of the cuneiform script by ancient Sumerians.'

'What does it say about the next target? We hardly have time.' Tension was dripping copiously from Suri's face. Suddenly he jerked his head. 'Indira! Why don't we get her to tell us who's Vyasa? Draw his face for us.'

Atharva shook his head. 'I did try that. No response.'

'Nothing?'

'None at all. She usually reacts, but today it was like conversing with a wall. Never found her so impervious. We are on our own here.'

The writer was twirling the seal on his forceps. 'What do we know about Adam and Eve that can help us here?'

'I think what we know about Vyasa will help us more,' the priest said. 'Now that we know they are targeting Chiranjivis, that should make it easier to identify the victim.'

'Author of the *Mahabharata* and grandfather to the Kauravas and Pandavas. Believed to be an avatar of Lord Vishnu, Vyasa was born in the Dwaparyuga. Also named Dwaipayana since he was born on an island. Besides Hinduism, he also finds a mention in Buddhist Jataka tales and is considered an incarnation of Brahma in Sikhism.'

'The focal point here has to be the guna. We have seen the previous three Chiranjivis functioning as dictated by their attributes. Vyasa's guna is Knowledge. We already have the Tree of Knowledge on this seal. Where does that lead us?'

The officer shrugged. 'Knowledge would indicate a teacher. Perhaps even a student. A student seeking knowledge.'

'Not any of that,' Patnaik said. 'We already had a teacher

with Trehan whose attribute was Education. I think knowledge here would mean something entirely different.'

'A historian then? Author perhaps? Philosopher? Thinker?'

'Ved Vyasa was a man of many talents,' Atharva said. 'He also—'

'Hold on,' the writer's voice silenced him. 'What did you say?'

'Man of several talents like—'

'What did you call him?'

'Ved Vyasa.'

'Yes. Ved Vyasa. And why is he called that?'

'He divided the Vedas.'

'Precisely. The Vedas were originally a single primordial entity that was split up by Vyasa. Catalogued into four distinct canons. This made the Vedas more easily accessible. In fact, the very word Vyasa means he who classifies or differentiates. He is also believed to have narrated the Upanishads and Puranas to Lord Ganesh.'

'What's your point, Om?'

'My point is that Vyasa is considered a scribe in Hindu scriptures. The first journalist of the universe.'

Suri arched an eyebrow. 'Journalist? You think they are targeting a journalist?'

'Quite possible,' the priest agreed. 'Vyasa was a chronicler. He compiled and documented everything from history and geography to philosophy and art. We could be looking at someone from journalism. It also complements his guna. Knowledge is the primary objective of media. Dissemination of information to make the masses aware and empowered. But does the seal agree with us?'

Patnaik was scrutinising the image on the stone. 'I am

confused. Vyasa is a venerated soul, but this seal depicts only evil. Adam and Eve. The First Disobedience. Original Sin. Fragile flesh that failed to resist temptation. And, of course, the eventual Fall of Man. Why send us something so negative as a pointer for Ved Vyasa? How does this indicate him? Unless...'

A pause most pregnant.

'Unless the Chiranjivi we are looking for is also a fallen soul,' the officer spoke.

'Precisely. Someone preyed upon by temptation.'

'That's impossible,' Atharva said. 'This is about a Chiranjivi. About Vyasa. An exalted being who was rewarded with immortality. How can he fall from grace?'

'Maybe he has in some way or the other.'

The writer was pacing the room now. His body negotiating with this new possibility.

'Look at Ashwathama. Also born divine but gradually corrupted. Let's not forget that these Chiranjivis have been living on earth for an infinite amount of time now. Operating among us in our society. Immortals living and functioning as mortals.'

Picking up a fountain pen, he squeezed a drop of ink on a blank page. The stain slowly diffusing through that white.

'Water is pristine where it originates but becomes scum once it touches the plains. If you are a vacuum, you will suck in everything around you. Maybe we have polluted Vyasa. Our environment reacting upon his soul. Our flaws eroding his flesh.'

'But who?' Suri gritted his teeth. 'You say it might be a journo. How do we narrow it down?'

'That's where the elements on this seal should help,'

Atharva picked it up. 'Garden of Eden. Tree of Knowledge. Anything rings a bell?'

The men stared back blankly.

'Satan. The serpent. The apple.'

Nothing.

'Adam, the Son of God, created in his image. Eve created out of Adam's rib.'

The officer stirred. 'Adam's rib?'

'Yes. A wonderful biblical tribute to gender equality emphasising that both man and woman originated from the same substance.'

Suri bolted across the room and opened a creaky steel cabinet. Delving through a honeycomb of files and folders, he pulled out a thin transparent one and slid it across the table.

'Then that should interest you both.'

They crowded at the edge of the table. An online news report faintly yellow at the edges.

THE CURIOUS CASE OF ADAM'S RIB

'Adam's rib,' the priest gawked. 'What is this?'

'Hardly surprising that none of you know. It was pulled out within minutes of getting posted on the Net. The scandal would have fucking devoured Mahira Khan's career.'

'Mahira Khan. Editor of IBTV news channel?'

'The same.'

'And what scandal?'

'The best there can be. A sex scandal.'

The shock on their faces could hardly mask the curiosity in their eyes. Suri continued.

'This was last year. Mahira was attending a dinner event hosted by Red Apple Productions at Taj. I was among the guests as well. She had a sexual episode with a younger man in one of the corridors.'

'Temptation!' Patnaik whispered.

'No one would have known of the couple's hook-up, but a CCTV camera happened to be lodged at the wrong place. It recorded the entire session. The guard in the hotel's monitor room informed the Red Apple team who confided in me and Mahira. She was distraught but kept her head high and left the matter in our hands. Given that the sex was consensual and no one else knew about it, it made no sense to take the matter any forward. The tape was destroyed, and we all thought the matter had ended. Until this came out the next day.'

He was pointing at the news report.

'This journalist from an online tabloid was also at the dinner and somehow sniffed it out.'

The writer lifted the page. 'I never saw this online.'

'Hardly anyone did. I told you the damage was contained in time. Erased before it could enter public domain. I don't know why I took a print-out, but I might be owning the only copy of this news.'

Atharva was eyeing the title again. 'Why Adam's Rib?'

'It's a condom brand,' the officer said. 'They specialise in ribbed ones. That's what the couple had used that night.'

'But this doesn't work,' Patnaik let the paper slide from his hands onto the table. 'The seal indicates a person who must be a sinner, Suri.'

'And Mahira sinned.'

'Sinned? What you narrated sounds like a sexual encounter between two consenting adults. An encounter even a cop like you overlooked because there was nothing criminal about it. What makes it a sin? In whose eyes?'

'In the eyes of our society, Om. The sin was that we all had to cover it up to prevent society from judging Mahira. For some it would have been about a woman asserting her sexuality. For others it would have been a woman giving in to lust. She would have been ripped apart. Patriarchy would have given her a thousand fucking labels. She agreed to hush it up and that made it a sin.'

The priest's face had deflated as if these revelations were slapping him hard. 'This is ominous. Is everything crumbling down in this Yuga? If Vyasa can be overpowered by his flesh, what hope then for us mortals?'

Patnaik looked at him. 'We could be wrong. Mahira is a woman. She may not be Vyasa.'

'The Chiranjivis are not gender-specific, Om. The only thing that matters is the guna. The central attribute that dictates their actions. Do all the elements on the seal point towards her?'

'They do. Eve as Adam's rib. Red Apple as the event host. You say this happened at a dinner party, Suri?'

'Yes.'

'Some historians also describe the seal as a banquet feast. And this portal here sort of clinches matters.'

He had opened a website. Mahira's author page. The officer glimpsed.

'She writes?'

'Indeed. And only on the *Mahabharata*. Considered an authority on the epic. Talk about irony!'

'It is Vyasa,' Atharva's lips trembled. 'The only thing that will cement it now is the Nilotpal. Does Mahira have the blue lotus?' He began browsing on his iPad. Reading her Wikipedia page.

'What does it say?'

'Born in Bangalore...chemical leak in the hospital where she was born...studied at Loyola...journalism from Northwestern...'

'Wait,' the writer stopped him. 'Chemical leak?'

'Yes. Her mother was exposed a day before Mahira's birth.'

Patnaik was googling Mahira's images on the computer. Selecting one, he opened it.

'That leak. Was the chemical silver?'

'It was.'

He pointed at the picture. The journalist doing a piece-to-camera.

'Do you see it?'

'See what?'

'Her hands holding the mic. Or more specifically her nails.'

Unmistakable.

'Yes,' the priest further zoomed in. 'Blue. Faint but definitely blue.'

'Could be nail colour,' Suri interjected.

'No. This blue also streaks the skin of her fingers. This is not nail colouring. This is argyria. The condition caused by chemical exposure to silver. Looks like her mother was moderately compromised but enough for Mahira to be born with bluish nails. She is the one, Suri. I just hope you aren't too late.'

'Not yet.' Atharva got off his phone. 'I spoke to a friend at the channel. Nothing so far.'

The officer glanced at Patnaik. 'You shall be a free man today.'

'I know. But don't let Yeva bleed her for my sake.'

'You think I'll do that?'

'No. You are a great friend but a much better officer.'

As Suri left his cabin to gather his men, the writer moved towards Atharva.

'Are you fine?'

'Yes. You were right. Looks like we have diluted a Chiranjivi.'

'Go ask him. He might answer your questions.'

'I have another question,' he pointed at the picture on Suri's desk. 'Who's she?'

'That's Alia Irani. She was a journalist. Typical firebrand. She had teamed up with Suri over a previous case involving a killer named Scorpion. We were all on that case. Their bond grew strong but not for long. She was killed by Scorpion. He never got over that.'

'He really misses her.'

'Terribly. Something died in him when she died.'

The officer entered gazing at both of them. 'What now?'

'Nothing,' Atharva hastened to reply. 'I was telling Om that Vyasa finds a mention in Chanakya's *Arthashastra*. The chapter describes how Krishna's Yadava clan butchered each other in a fit of rage and that Vyasa was also attacked in that frenzy. Using this massacre as an example, Chanakya says and I quote:

'Whoever has not his organs of sense under his control will soon perish.'

He got up. 'Ironical isn't it? I wonder if Vyasa has read the *Arthashastra*.'

Chapter 32

'NO, I DON'T HAVE MUCH TIME,' SHE SAID.

They were sitting before the Chiranjivi now, but the face was that of Mahira Khan. The face that blew life into their television screens. She materialised before them every day through invisible airwaves like an oracle making a prophecy. They shared so much history. Together they had celebrated India's world cup triumph in 2011. Mourned the 2004 tsunami. Ducked in terror before the 26/11 attacks and protested against Section 377. But now they knew that history stretched way back. Its roots penetrating Hastinapur the day he had planted three seeds for the Kuru clan. Procreator of the Mahabharata. Journalist revered and reviled. She was dictating a news story, and a junior correspondent was noting it down.

Vyasa.

'I go on air in twenty minutes. Keep it short.'

Perched amidst her laptop, printouts, awards and coffee mugs, Mahira was splitting a large orange into parts. The cabin itself impeccable, with everything neatly sorted and compartmentalised. A blue pool of water outside the glass windows lent her room the illusion of a floating island. And a statue of Ganesha on her table holding a quill.

The officer drained the cranberry juice as the junior left the room. 'Parag Suri. I wonder if you recall.'

'I recall everything. It's been a while since that dinner gathering.'

She popped a piece of fruit in her mouth. Chewed the orange silently as her eyes travelled from the officer to Atharva.

'Did your friend enjoy the story?'

Her face seemed to suddenly crsytallize like liquid turning into gel. Had that memory jolted her into rage? Scratched an old scab? Or had she just become even more indifferent than she already was?

'We are not here to discuss that night,' Suri said. 'We are here because you may be under attack today.'

'Attack?' She placed the orange on her table and smiled. 'That'll be quite a headline. Who'll attack me? And even if someone did, I hardly fear for my life.'

'Of course,' Atharva nodded. 'One less thing for a Chiranjivi to worry about.'

The air clotted in the cabin. His words had pressed a stopwatch waiting for her next move. She was tapping her nails. Silver blue nails. Then her mouth moved.

'Who are you?'

'What matters is we know who you are.'

She got up and walked towards the cabin entrance. The metal buckle on the massive leather belt around her trouser was winking in the LED lights. The officer was telling her all about Ashwin and Yeva and the three men in coma.

'You must listen to us, Mahira.'

She closed the door and laughed.

'I have never been a good listener. That was always Lord Ganesha. I am the talker.' She touched the god's statue on her table. 'We still chat. But he doesn't write anything down these days.'

The men stood up involuntarily. Suri went rigid, but Atharva folded his hands as he welled up.

'This is…this is extraordinary. Ved Vyasa.'

She lowered his hands gently. 'The charm dies once you have seen it, right? As it is, more and more people are now clamouring over my book, claiming it is history and not mythology. And I am glad to see many believing that. Once all that superfluous magic is stripped off, we can finally become as normal as Ashoka or Akbar. Then hopefully you shall see us for what we really are. And familiarity might even breed contempt.'

'Never,' the priest mumbled. 'You are a Chiranjivi. You all are. I have so many questions, and there's such little time.'

'What questions? How did we become Immortals? How do we operate in this world? How do we take birth and die when we are everlasting? My answers will only disappoint you. Hardly as miraculous as you imagine. Egyptians say the Sphinx died when her riddle was cracked. Let me live. You stand enthralled at a card trick but once I explain, you shall only scorn.'

'This is no card trick. This immortality. You being born as Mahira Khan…'

'Yes?'

'It's…it's like…'

'A superhero costume?' she giggled. 'It probably is. Us. Ashwin's body. The shape-shifter's form. It's all a big costume drama.'

'Ashwin's body,' Suri asked. 'It's not real?'

'No. An outer shell of skin and muscle that Shiva blessed him with to hide his corrupted frame.'

'How simple,' Atharva exclaimed. 'How utterly simple.

That explains everything. The Greek God who decomposes inside.'

'What about me?' she sat down. 'Hasn't Suri told you?'

'He has. I am still fighting it.'

'Don't. I could not.'

'Is it us? Our values? Our world polluting you Chiranjivis?'

'I would love to believe that,' she laughed. 'Perhaps it's more to do with the times we are in. This is the finale. The universe hurtling towards the end of Kali Yuga. The peak of its fall when the old becomes the oldest and the weak the weakest. When a tree nears its death, every part of it shrinks and stinks. We evolved with the cosmos. Perhaps we all now decompose with it.'

'You think you sinned that night at the dinner party?' the priest asked.

'Can I broadcast what I did? No. This cop here offered a cover-up, and I readily agreed. I cannot take ownership of what I did, and perhaps that does make it a sin. Perhaps I am the weakest of all Chiranjivis. Of course, none of that finds a mention there.'

She was pointing at the *Mahabharata* lying on her centre table. Atharva picked up the other books next to it. *What The Mahabharata Really Says: An Epic Redefined. The Mahabharata Evolves.* All of them by Mahira Khan.

'You are still fascinated by your own tale?'

'Others more than me. I see so many writers today making a cottage industry out of my epic. All those retellings and reinterpretations. Everyone wanting to be Vyasa. I had to jump in. Everyone must know what my story actually wants to tell. I had started another book but must abandon it midway. After all, how much can a comatose person write?'

Suri looked at her befuddled. 'Are you waiting to be assaulted? You do know the threat that looms over you today?'

'I know. All six of us know what the seventh one is up to.'

'A drop of blood each for his Mani.'

'You know quite a lot yourself, officer.'

'But that's not all. What else is Ashwathama planning?'

'Is he? I don't know anything about that.'

'Something much more sinister.'

'I have absolutely no idea.'

'You are coming with us. And you will tell us who the remaining two Chiranjivis are.'

'I cannot do that.'

'What?'

'Yes, Suri. The *Mahabharata* is all about *purushartha*. Human pursuit. This is your *purushartha*. You must find them yourself. I cannot help you.'

'But they are in danger.'

'So was I, and you found me. If the cosmos wills, you shall reach them too. Or they shall bleed.'

'How can you say that? Isn't Knowledge your guna?'

'Knowledge. Not Action. We know a lot of things. What we choose to do with it is a different matter. Knowledge facilitates us with multiple choices and I have chosen.'

The priest clasped her hand. 'Why invite suffering?'

'To suffer is to be reborn. It rinses the soul like Ganga. Venom is both toxic and prophylactic, Atharva.'

'You will only end up comatose as the others.'

'I know. Those three before me also offered themselves silently. Maybe all of us Chiranjivis are tainted now. Have done things that we are not proud of. This Yuga corrupts us or perhaps our own core is weakening. If the universe wishes to tear us apart, we do not resist any more. Perhaps our blood alone can absolve us now to…'

Mahira paused. The evening *azan* was ringing out from the loudspeaker of a nearby mosque.

Allahuakbar

Ash hadu an la ilahaillaallah

Ash hadu anna Muhammadan Rasulullah

'It's time.' she raised her palms. 'Hayya alas salah.'

Suri opened the door. 'I cannot allow that. My men are posted below, and we will escort you home immediately. You have no choice.'

'I have to do a report in ten minutes.'

'Not today.'

'This is vital. My feature on the latest nuclear treaty.'

'Your pet area. I have seen how strongly your news channel advocates disarmament.'

'Hardly surprising,' Atharva gushed. 'It was Vyasa who had commanded both Arjuna and Ashwathama to recall their nuclear missiles.'

She smiled. 'I saved the world once. Trying to do that again.'

'But the danger…'

'Don't you feel confident enough to guard me here in my studio, Suri? Must I scurry despite the presence of you and your men?' And how do you know Yeva won't attack me at home?'

'How long is this feature?'

'Fifteen minutes. A single break.'

'My men and I shall remain posted inside the studio.'

As they walked out, she messaged someone on her

mobile. The priest pointed at Mahira's belt buckle. 'Interesting design. Yggdrasil?'

'Yes. The sacred Norse tree around which lies the world serpent nibbling at its roots.'

The studio was cold and black except for its pivotal area that held the bulletin set-up. Massive fluorescent lights illumined the middle like a volcano. Lifeless all around but breathing fire in the centre. Outside, Suri's team was securing the whole building. Every entrance guarded and exit sealed. Men stationed on all floors. Eyes on staircases and elevators. Newsroom and edit bays. PCR and rooftop. A firewall of surveillance encircling the building now. As Mahira took her place behind the desk, Suri squeezed her shoulder.

'We are here.'

She smiled. 'You took care of me that night. You can't do this forever.'

'We have covered the place. You are safe.'

'I am not yours to save, Suri.'

As cameras rolled, the On-Air light flashed a deep red. Suri's men were positioned behind the cameras along with Atharva. The officer pacing the studio slowly like a tiger on prowl. Time ticked.

Slowly. Slowly.

The lights came on announcing the commercial break. As the make-up team rushed towards Mahira, a camera-man next to Suri took off his headphones.

'That's strange.'

'What?'

'She hardly ever breaks into a sweat. But look at her.'

The officer gazed at her face soggy with perspiration. Mahira also seemed to be breathing heavily and clenching her fingers once or twice. She looked at him and smiled. As he took a step forward, the lights faded out and the live resumed.

'Almost done,' the cameraman whispered. The priest walked up to Suri.

'She looks ill.'

'Yes. But she was fine when we met her.'

'Something's wrong. Very wrong. Did she just tremble?'

Suri spun like a top. He had not seen the seizure that had rocked her body. He was seeing something else. Tears streaming down her eyes. Face shuddering in pain. Digging her palms into the desk, she pulled herself up with effort as if that simple action was dragging the life out of her. They shrank. They were seeing why. Her white jacket was drenched in blood below. Ripping the earpiece off, she fumbled inside her pockets. The officer saw what she had taken out.

Horseshoe.

Lifting it up, Mahira slapped it against her forehead. Before they could scream in horror, she had crashed on the floor. As her team bolted to surround her, Atharva pointed at the body.

'Her belt?'

Suri's eyes darted wildly.

'Where's her belt?'

They found it lying behind the desk.

'It's unhooked. She opened it and flung it here. But why would...'

His throat bobbed as if someone had stuck a pin. 'It's hollow, Suri. Hollow. See this space running through the entire length of the belt.'

They were holding it in their hands. Touching the blood

in that cavity. Comprehending what it could only mean.

Yeva was in here...

Inside the belt...

The two men looking at each other.

Inside the belt...

'The whole time, Suri. When we were talking to her in the cabin. When we entered the studio. When she was doing her feature. Yeva lodged inside her belt the whole time. Striking her when she went live.'

The priest scrambled on his feet as if an aftershock had stunned him again.

'But that means Mahira...Mahira herself...'

Words trailing off. The line completing itself inside in his head.

Mahira was carrying the snake inside her...

Suri nodded. 'Yes. Mahira. She allowed Yeva to hide inside her belt. She had embraced her fate. It was all scripted. That krait already coiled around her when we met. She was not going to spare herself today.'

'Yggdrasil,' Atharva indicated her buckle. 'Like Yggdrasil.'

'Mahira told me she wasn't mine to save. She made sure. Made sure of that on fucking national television.'

'And all through. She sat all through the live with that snake tunnelling into her flesh.' The priest broke down. 'Vyasa said he was the weakest of the Chiranjivis. He was wrong. So wrong.'

Thirty minutes later, forensics was crawling all over the studio floor. Manu holding a tube of Mahira's blood. Her fingers careful this time not to drop it on the floor. And the two men standing before a pink word on the teleprompter.

VYASA

Chapter 33

YEVA'S JOURNAL—PG 63

I was laughing at the star.

The Arcturus. Derived from the Greek term Arktouros, meaning Guardian of the Bear. The Arabs had named it Al Simak Al Ramih or the Uplifted One of the Lancer. China had christened it Da Jiao. The Great Horn. Polynesians described it as one of the ten pillars that propped the sky up. It was also Hoku-lea. The Star of Gladness. An Orange Giant. They said it was the fourth brightest star in the night sky. The most radiant one in the northern celestial hemisphere.

I was laughing. I knew my star was going to be many times more incandescent.

Here they called Arcturus the Swati Nakshatra. One of the twenty-seven nakshatras of Hindu astrology. The gemstone of Lord Vayu. The eye of Scorpio or the Vrishchhik Raashi. It denoted creativity and the power of imagination. But above all, it symbolised purity. The first drop of rain that fell under this star created that jewel that I craved.

I was waiting.

The sky above was slick with grey sweat. Heaving and aching as it sighed in frenzy. Currents of pleasure tingling its body in blinding flashes. I knew it was coming. They call me chakshushravas. That which can hear with its sight. My eyes were hearing that untouched drop crawling through the veins of the sky. Becoming bigger and bigger until the air could hold it no more.

I opened.

The firmament was quivering. Its moans getting louder. The fireworks more and more radiant. So full of love that it was furious now. The climax thundered. The halo ripped apart the skin of the clouds to release the drop.

The first raindrop landed inside me.

Part of my saliva now. My blood. My venom.

Me.

I closed my mouth to let the alchemy begin. They said a cave in Amarnath hatched a lingam every year. I wasn't far behind.

That night Arcturus was staring at the earth. Staring at my Mani that was burning its eyes.

Chapter 34

FIND OUT WHY YEVA WISHES TO DESTROY YOU...

Patnaik's words were digging into Suri's head like a circle of thorns. He had released the writer. Told him how he had watched Mahira bleed. How the whole world had watched it and was still watching on YouTube. Crucifying him and his men. He had asked Patnaik what to do now and the writer had replied.

Find out why Yeva wishes to destroy you...

Suri sat mulling hard but his thoughts appeared frayed. That circle tightening around his head now. The thorns jabbing and his skin turning red like the rainbow that had appeared again yesterday.

We have a bond, Suri...

Why had Yeva said that? What bond did he have with a serpent? An Ichhadhari? Those objects were lying on a table next to him. The ones she had mailed one by one. Poker-faced when he looked at them but perhaps snickering behind his back. Holding their sides and cackling. Rolling on the table with their feet up. She was laughing too. Laughing at how he had failed every single time.

The officer smiled.

Do snakes laugh? How does that sound?

He pulled the envelopes. Could he milk anything more?

She could have if she were here.

Alia.

He closed his eyes.

I am here, Suri.

Her photograph silent. Her voice reclining on the table.

Look at them.

The envelopes.

What do you see?

He was watching the colours. Letters. Numbers.

Now do you see it?

He leaned. The envelopes fanned out in his clutch like four cards.

Right there.

He held them up closer to his face.

That's it.

He had seen them and yet not seen. Gone over them but never paid heed. Was it because it was so routine? Made the whole thing so damned ordinary? A camouflage for what it was hiding in plain sight. He had looked away four times but not today. Alia was pointing at them. He pulled a pad and wrote them down. All of them.

Now what?

She was speaking. Speaking again.

Hear her words...What had Yeva told you?

He was listening. Hearing voices shaping themselves as letters. Letters becoming words and words giving birth to prose.

What had she told you?

Suri's brain twanged as the voice hit him like a gong. It was no longer Alia speaking to him. It was Yeva. What had she said?

Bleed that wicked blood that flows in you…

I shall invert…Invert the pyramid…

Tip the ladder and bring you down…

He was looking at what he had written. Now he was amidst those letters. Walking gingerly. They were nipping at his ankles, but he was not running away. Still listening to Yeva. And a solitary thought germinating inside him.

A thought making perfect sense.

He saw the letters standing up. Shifting places. Swapping chairs. Falling in slots like a combination and asking him to pull the lever.

Do it, Suri.

The nib struck paper again. He saw what he had written now.

EXIS

Exis?

His face grew rigid. He had only four envelopes so far. Two more were yet to arrive. Two more envelopes. Two more letters of the alphabet. His hand scribbled on the page as if it had grown a mind of its own. Or was she holding it to add those two alphabets? He looked.

ALEXIS

The pen squealed as his fingers strangulated it. He lifted his eyes to look at the photograph next to Alia.

Grandmom Alexis.

Yeva was laughing again.

A bond…A very old bond…

Chapter 35

'YOUR GRANDMOTHER?'

Patnaik's blood was curdling at the sight of the corpse in the photograph. An old woman hanging from the metal bar of a wall. Her naked body skinned from head to toe.

'And you say Yeva did this?'

Suri's moist eyes had smudged out Patnaik and Atharva. The officer blinked his tears out fiercely.

'Yes. Grandmom was an entrepreneur. I never knew what her business was, but she was forever travelling. The last I saw of her was around twelve years ago when she left for Egypt and settled there. I had just joined the academy. News arrived two years back that she had contracted a fatal illness in Cairo that killed her. Her friends informed us that given the nature of her disease, her body could not be kept waiting for long. Since she was Catholic, they interred her there.'

He wrenched the photograph from the writer's hand.

'Bloody lies. They were horrified. Confused. Too disoriented to know what to tell us. The Cairo police joined hands with the hotel to hush it all up. I would never have known a thing. But Yeva. Yeva.'

'Why would she murder your grandmother like this?'

'I asked myself that again and again. Kept making calls to Cairo. Hounding the police and anyone who knew her. It all tumbled out. They told me what she was into.'

'What?'

'Snake skins.'

'Snake skins?'

Suri stammered as if the words had bruised his tongue. 'She used to poach all kinds of snake skins. Illegal trafficking of cobra, krait and python hide from the Nilgiri Forest.'

He saw the horror spreading on their faces, but he was laughing now.

'She peeled snakes. And a snake peeled her.'

Laughing hysterically. Not listening to them anymore.

Patnaik turned towards the priest. 'I don't get this? How did Yeva know Alexis?'

'When we confronted Yeva, she had lashed out violently at humans for trading in snake skin,' Atharva said. 'If Alexis was poaching hide from Nilgiri, that's where Yeva must have seen her. Watched her activities. Perhaps actually seen her killing snakes and borne a terrible grudge.'

'The bond she told Suri about.'

'Quite a profound one. In fact, Alexis might have been the catalyst for Yeva's desire to become an Ichhadhari. Destroy men who were destroying her species. And Ashwin must have helped her track the old woman. That explains her hatred for Suri too. A bond spanning generations.'

The officer spun on his feet. 'Yes. A bond. She killed grandmom and now screws me by scattering bleeding bodies throughout my city. Tells me how bloody worthless I am by sending those parcels.'

The writer looked at the envelopes. 'How did you work it all out?'

'The items. Each envelope is marked 'EXHIBIT' followed by an alphabet and numbers. Standard procedure often used in courts. They had appeared random until I had figured out that the numbers were revealing each attack date. But there was more.'

He indicated the pad on the table.

EXHIBIT S

EXHIBIT I

EXHIBIT X

EXHIBIT E

'This is the order in which they arrived. I wrote the letters down and it made no fucking sense. But then I remembered. Something Yeva had told me, came hurtling back. Do you recall, Atharva?'

'What, Suri?'

'Invert. She had said she will invert everything. Invert the hierarchy. She had been hinting. Hinting all along. Asking me to invert the entire construct here. That's what I did. Inverted this sequence of letters and that gave me EXIS. Two more parcels to go, and it can only be Alexis. Grandmom Alexis. Bloody poaching Alexis.'

'Yeva used camouflage here,' the priest spoke. 'She's a serpent. Her instincts are still rudimentary. She can hardly structure an elaborate riddle. She framed what came naturally to her. What she had been using in the wild for survival all these years. And something so fundamentally simple is always most deceiving.'

Suri flung a sheaf of printouts on the floor. 'From the Cairo police. It's all there. Her trade. Her clients. Her death.

Yeva is right. We humans are dogs. Bloody murderers. It's time someone kicked us off this earth.'

'You are in shock,' Patnaik held him. 'You cannot validate Yeva.'

'Why not?' he pushed the writer away. 'My grandmom was a criminal. A bloody butchering criminal. We all are. Yeva's rage is not misplaced. We are screwing this planet.'

'And so, we alone can set things right. Your life hasn't been easy, Suri, and so you have constantly rejected the idea of something good. That's why you doubted Akram's actions. Doubted the possibility of benevolent Chiranjivis. And now you sit here defending an evil serpent.'

Indira climbed on the officer's lap and put her arms around him. Suri clasped the child in a tight embrace.

'We humans take lives so easily, Om. What right do I have to stop Yeva?'

'Because nothing justifies what she has done. Whatever Ashwin intends to do. Alexis was wrong but that does not make Yeva right. We humans may have botched up the earth. Betrayed our biosphere and the life forms therein, but this is no way to set things right. Who knows what dark scheme lurks beneath Ashwin's glowing sheath? He might bring upon a calamity far worse, and Yeva will be blindly helping him.'

'My grandmom, Om. She has shamed me.'

'And will you shame yourself? We have to foil Ashwin. You have to foil Ashwin.'

'How can I? Don't you see how her envelopes taunt me? I have failed four times. I am no good.'

'On the contrary, Suri. You saw through those envelopes. Cracked her code. That tells me you are still the man this case needs.'

The officer sat cradling Indira in silence. 'Grandmom was the only wholesome memory I ever had, Om. My parents killed. Alia murdered. Recalling grandmom would always fill me with comfort. Now that's gone too. I am all by myself. All by myself.'

Chapter 36

YEVA'S JOURNAL—PG 81

Cairo, Egypt.

I was at Giza Zoo during the day. They said if I paid extra, I could get pictures of myself holding a snake.

She was staying at the Four Seasons on Nile Plaza. That middle-aged woman from the Nilgiris who loved to watch snakes being peeled and diced.

I knocked on her door. Room 555. The three fives hanging from the door like baby serpents. Like the cobras her men had hung from nails.

She opened the door with her left hand. Her right hand held a steaming mug. She had been drinking black coffee. She looked at me and the mug crashed on the floor, scalding the marble. I was not me. Yeva. I had shape-shifted into that man. That old Irula man who had snared the snakes. The man whose neck had been broken with a dead python.

'You?' she squealed. 'You. But you are dead. I watched you die. You can't be. You can't be.' I smiled. She looked into my eyes. 'You are not him. Not that old man. Who are you?'

I spoke. My voice pierced through the form I had taken. 'I am that which you slay. I am that which shall now slay.' I turned into myself. She was staring at my hood. My fangs. And my blue skin.

I was the serpent but she hissed. 'Shape-shifter. An Ichhadhari.'

I became Yeva now. She was getting more and more mesmerised. The power within me bewitching her soul. I spoke to her again. 'You love to strip us. Now I strip you.'

She lifted her hand and stroked my human body.

'You desire my skin?' I asked. 'Or perhaps something better now. My Mani.' The word flogged her like a whip. 'Do you want my Mani?'

She was laughing. Laughing hysterically. 'Yes. Your Mani. Give me your Mani. I will hide it in my mouth like you do. Hold it in my throat like Shiva.'

She opened her lips wide. I lifted the coffee jug and emptied that boiling fluid down her mouth. She throbbed violently as the coffee blistered her tongue and throat. Her fingers clawed at her vocal chords as she tried to scream, but all her sounds had charred and died. The only thing emerging was a thick stream of saliva, blood and coffee mixed together.

'This is how you stuffed our bodies with water.'

Picking up the jug again I smashed a light on the wall behind her. All that was left was a metallic holder protruding from the bricks. I lifted up that woman. Stretching her jaws wide, I rammed her mouth into the holder. She lay suspended from the wall like a piece of meat dangling from a hook.

'This is how you hung us from nails.'

I ripped the tassels from the curtains and bound her hands behind her. 'This is how you tied up our bodies to hold the water in.' I removed her clothes and ran my fingers against her back. I took out the cheese grater I had obtained from the hotel kitchen downstairs.

'And this is how you skinned us.'

The Egyptian queen in the painting watched the strips rolling and falling. The queen clasping the poisonous asp. I laughed.

'You humans can never erase us. We have sinned together in Eden. Look at your palms. We slither all over them. Loop around your fingers. Your very DNA coils like us. How will you ever pluck us out?'

Chapter 37

A man may be remembered by his extraordinary deed
His name also lives on if he fathers illustrious breed
Undying flame handed through each generation down
His splendour igniting every new jewel of his crown
Hence down several ages it had long been decreed
Wipe your enemy out by crumbling his every seed
This task Rishiputra and his friends had now begun
Today they stood encircling the Silver Prince's son
A warrior formidable though his years still a teen
The war longing for fresh meat on this day thirteen
The rishi had generated a spherical military maze
That lad was now entangled in its central phase
They tore him like wolves but he fought like a lion
Blood stains glittering across his armour like Orion
The Rishiputra gored his flesh in front and the back
Twisted his jagged sword to hear his rib cage crack
He knew how Silver Prince adored this strapping boy
He would mourn forever now clasping this broken toy
The rishi weeping tears but his son in frenzy did yell
Smearing everyone with the martyr's blood as he fell
Ganging against one, they had broken a primary rule
It returned to prey on them like a bloodsucking ghoul
Waves bring back to you what you cast into the sea

Elements plot your fall when you deceive with glee
The creator of that labyrinth so proud of his mind
Two days later a simple hoax turned the rishi blind
They lied to their guru that his divine son was dead
The rishi cracked his bow slitting each mortal thread
Hearing his father wailing like an animal far away
The Rishiputra grasped that he had been led astray Like sea flying into clouds from where it was wrung
He too rushed to him from whose loins he had sprung
But by the time he reached, the rishi's body had bled
Rolling under his feet was his beloved father's head
Hallowed rules of conduct the war had already lost
The two armies engaging now to triumph at any cost
Rishiputra spoke not but renounced the war that day
Hoping his arrows would no more crush human clay
Noble thoughts are mud walls that tumble in a flood
He rose again on the final night to sink deep in blood.

Chapter 38

INDIRA WAS HOLDING THE FIFTH ITEM BETWEEN THE forceps.

EXHIBIT L230618

A 35mm film frame. Almost the whole of it was covered with the face of a woman. The woman's eyes were closed but the men had been gazing at her head. This was no hair. This appeared to be a tangled nest of grey snakes. The reptiles growing out of her head as if every neuron in her brain had become a serpent and drilled its way out through her skull. Writhing and dripping venom on screen but arrested in motion inside this scrap of celluloid.

'Medusa.' The writer pronounced. 'Greek monster with snakes on her head.'

'I need some air,' Suri got up.

Minutes later they were sitting in the park adjoining the precinct. Atharva was eyeing the title of the film stamped right below the frame.

THE GORGON

'Looks quite old, Om.'

'Yes. Hammer 1964.'

'Hammer?'

'A British Production House that mostly dabbled in horror, sci-fi and film noir. This was one of the few times that Hammer turned to Greek mythology and borrowed one of its most terrifying demons. The Gorgon who could turn men into stone.'

Suri's eyebrows shot up. 'Men into stone?'

'Medusa was a female monster. Originally a ravishing beauty, she was raped by the sea god Poseidon inside the Temple of Athena. This enraged Athena who transformed Medusa into an ogre. Another version says that Athena herself lusted after Poseidon and transformed Medusa out of sheer jealousy. A hybrid so grotesque that anyone who laid eyes on her face instantly turned into stone. She was finally beheaded by Perseus who used Athena's mirrored shield to watch her reflection.' The writer paused abruptly.

'What's wrong, Om?'

'This image. Something's not right here. Can't put my finger on it.'

'Are those really snakes instead of hair?'

'Yes. She had serpents swarming all over her head. In fact, in Central Europe, a belief exists that hairs pulled out from the head of a woman under the influence of the moon can turn into snakes. Artists like Da Vinci, Rubens and Caravaggio have dedicated their canvases to Medusa while artists like Bernini and Dali have also carved her in metal and stone. Bernini's marble bust is quite a visual pun. She who petrified everyone stands cast in stone herself.'

'And we are looking at Chiranjivi Parashurama.' The officer's fingers tapped the yellow envelope. 'Who's he exactly?'

'The sixth avatar of Vishnu,' the priest said. 'Warrior and mentor, he is the foremost among rishis in Kali Yuga. A disciple of Shiva, he not only acquired the knowledge of scriptures and warfare from the lord but many celestial weapons as well. It is Parashurama who presented King Janak with the bow of Shiva that Rama destroyed to win Sita's swayamvar. In the *Mahabharata*, he mentors Bhishma, Drona and Karna. He rid the earth of evil forces twenty-one times and it's foretold that he shall reappear to mentor Kalki at the end of Kali Yuga.'

'And his guna?'

'Strength. It makes him the *mool purusha*. The alpha male. His weapon is the axe.'

'So, we are looking at a man with massive physical strength.'

'Or a woman,' Patnaik said. 'Remember the Chiranjivis are gender neutral. The frame here also depicts a female demon.'

Suri frowned. 'But we are talking about physical prowess. Enormous strength of an axe-wielding warrior who battled twenty-one times. This sounds like a fucking man. What woman could be that strong?'

'A female athlete,' the writer pointed at the young women on the jogging track around them.

'Athlete?'

'Sure. Female boxers, racers or gymnasts. They all fit the bill. In fact, I would go a step further and propose a name.'

'A name?' the officer's face cracked. 'Already?'

'Given the kind of person we are looking at, this one seems quite likely.'

'What name, Om?'

'Lin.'

'Lin? Lin Zimik?'

'Yes,' the writer looked at Atharva. 'The pride of your state. India's female boxer extraordinaire. A woman with not just physical but immense mental strength.'

He waited as the others mulled over the possibility.

'That's a worthy enough option,' the priest said. 'We should certainly consider Lin, given her multiple achievements.'

'Precisely. A medal winner in all six world championships. The only female Indian boxer to have qualified at the Summer Olympics. In fact, I think she's our only option. This image of Medusa tells me that Lin alone can be Parashurama.'

'What do you mean, Om?'

'Stone.' Patnaik picked up a piece from the flower-bed below.

'Stone?'

'I told you how Medusa could turn men into stone. To use a single word, she petrified them.'

'Yes.'

'Lin's autobiography came out this year. Huge bestseller. You are surely aware of what its called.'

'*Petrous*,' Atharva uttered. The title splashed into his mind like a pebble creating ripples. '*Petrous*. Stone-like which can't be broken. You are right, Om. We must look at Lin seriously.'

'Not enough,' Suri waved the film in their faces. 'We need to substantiate. Besides, Om was saying there's something wrong with this frame.'

'True,' the priest turned towards the writer again. 'What exactly is bothering you?'

'Something's out of place.'

'The only thing swallowing up that frame is Medusa. Something wrong there?'

Patnaik was staring at the celluloid strip looming before his eyes. What had Atharva said?

Wrong with Medusa?

He wrenched the frame from his fingers. The park

existed no more. Neither the two men. Not even he himself. Everything around him seemed to have contracted into this 35mm reel.

Medusa…wrong.

Wrong…but so right.

'I see the wheels turning,' Suri snapped his fingers. 'He's figured it out.'

'I have. Something is wrong here. And quite deliberately so.'

'Tell us, Om.'

'This image. Medusa. It's not from this film.'

'I don't follow you.'

'The image of Medusa you see here in this frame is not from *The Gorgon*. It's been a while since I last saw the film, but this is not how Medusa appears in it. This image has been taken from somewhere else and cleverly superimposed on the reel.'

'Somewhere else?'

'Yes. In fact, from an artefact. Quite a famous piece called *Perseus with the Head of Medusa*.'

'The man who slayed her?'

'Exactly. Installed in Florence, the sculpture depicts a victorious Perseus trampling the lifeless body of Medusa while his left hand flourishes her decapitated head. The same head you see here in this frame. No wonder it was rankling me. This tells you again how visuals can trick the brain. The surrounding scenery overwhelms you to accept the larger picture without questioning the finer detail.'

The officer's forehead furrowed. 'But why? If the film was already about Medusa, why insert her head from another sculpture?'

'Because of the man who sculpted this artefact. Because his name also screams that I am right. Lin Zimik is indeed the fifth Chiranjivi.'

The priest leaned forward. 'Does it really?'

'Undoubtedly. This statue was crafted by the legendary Italian sculptor Benvenuto Cellini. Tell me, Atharva. What has been Lin's greatest victory so far?'

'The Summer Olympic win.'

'Yes. And what did she win? The bronze medal. Do you know what makes Cellini's *Perseus with the Head of Medusa* so unique? That he carved it out of bronze. A metal that had not been used as a medium for almost fifty years when Cellini conceived this statue. The one resplendent feature that makes that sculpture stand out.'

'Perfect.'

'And something even more direct. Besides statues, what is the other thing that Cellini is remembered for? Medallions. Iconic metal medallions. Again pointing squarely at Lin.'

The priest was getting ecstatic now but Suri still had a shadow over his face. He pointed at the frame again.

'If Cellini's sculpture held all the clues for Parashurama, why superimpose it on a fucking film strip? She could have just sent us a picture of that bronze statue. Why this cinema reel, Om?'

'Another clue pointing at Lin. Quite a literal one actually.' He fingered through his mobile and placed it before the officer. 'Aren't you forgetting this?'

An IMDB page displaying the name of the film in bold font.

LIN ZIMIK—THE BIOPIC

'The movie!' Suri cried out. 'The movie they have made on her life.'

'Releases tomorrow. And produced by Ashwin Tomar.'

The name suddenly reminding them how close the danger was. How Somnath and Mahira had bled before their eyes.

'It's as if Medusa walks the earth again,' the officer was saying. 'Ashwin has revived her as Yeva, and she is turning the Chiranjivis into stone.'

Patnaik had entered Google to fish for images of Lin.

Nilotpal…

His finger swiping dexterously. Juggling photos one by one.

'Is that the Buddhist Lotus wheel?' the officer poked at the image on their screen now. A shot of Lin's back displaying a vibrant blue tattoo right behind her neck.

'That doesn't count,' Atharva said. 'Artificial application of blue does not make you a Chiranjivi. The Nilotpal must be a part of you. Something you are born with. Wired into the very circuit of your being.'

'I understand that. All I am saying is this Buddhist Lotus is incorrect.'

'Incorrect?'

'I know the symbol. It's all over the Bodhi Temple. They always have eight petals signifying Buddha's Eight-Fold Path. This one has nine.'

Patnaik was peering at the tattoo now. 'Suri is right. Why nine petals? That's also a strange place to get a tattoo done.'

'People get tattoos done everywhere, Om,' the priest said. 'You would be surprised.'

'I know that, but this looks quite misplaced. A tattoo in this area is usually at the centre of the nape or the side of the neck. This one's neither here nor there. Somewhere in the middle and almost spilling over to her back.'

'I give you that. Strange place to choose.'

'Yes. Strange indeed. What if she did not choose it?'

'What?'

'Maybe Lin had no choice. She had to get the tattoo there.'

'Had to?'

'To cover something. See how the petals are a vibrant blue but not that central area. It's a different shade of blue. Both the blues trying hard to blend but not really. This lotus has been inked around something to make it appear aesthetic. Something already present. Already blue.'

He looked at them. Unspeaking as if relaying the information through his eyes. And watching them receiving it. One letter at a time. The buffering finally over. They had grasped the word.

Birthmark.

'Yes. A birthmark. A blue birthmark disguised as a blue Buddhist lotus.'

They gaped at the nine petals as if one of them would unfold and betray Lin's secret.

'How do we find out?'

'I think I can, Suri,' the writer opened his contact list. 'I recognise this style. I was in Imphal recently, researching Buddhist iconography. I know the artist.'

'Will he talk?'

'He will if I tell him Lin's life depends on it.'

The call was brief. It confirmed what the lotus was hiding. Also revealed that an extra petal had to be added to conceal the lopsided shape of the birthmark.

'But a blue birthmark, Om?'

'It's known as a Mongolian Spot. They are almost always pigmented blue.'

The officer picked up the film frame. '23 June. They are attacking her tomorrow.'

'And we know where exactly.' Patnaik indicated the reel. 'Premiere of *Lin Zimik*.'

'We can speak to Lin. She may listen to us.'

'No use, Suri,' the priest said. 'Remember what Mahira told us. The Chiranjivis are going with the flow. Embracing what's being thrown at them. She will not listen. We can only try and keep her safe tomorrow.'

'Yes. Tomorrow. Ashwin will also be there.' The writer's foot traced a wavy line over the grass. 'But I want to see Yeva.'

Chapter 39

THE BLACK BENTLEY WAS GLIDING INTO THE MALL PREMISES as if sailing on high waters. Forging effortlessly through a throng of delirious fans. Ashwin's hand protruding and waving. A messiah showering benediction on his flock. As his shoe touched the carpet, it seemed to press a button of hysteria through the multitudes standing behind the barricades on either side. The car moved making way for the convertible following it.

Lin Zimik.

The decibels she elicited were hardly as deafening as Ashwin's but still worthy of a national hero. Patnaik and Atharva were already there. And Suri with his posse of men lining the entire walkway from its entrance to the auditorium. Watching the queues on both sides chanting names. Waving posters. Watching a hundred mobiles flash like glittering confetti for stars parading on the carpet. Selfie sticks protruding like metallic limbs to grab a handful of pictures. Watching Ashwin and Lin interacting with the press. Greeting the team. Posing before the film standee.

The priest nudged Patnaik. 'Look at that, Om. Two Chiranjivis in one frame. If only these cameras knew what they were capturing.'

'I see good and evil holding hands. Happens very rarely.

I wonder why Lin agreed to associate with Ashwin. If what Mahira told you is true, his evil might only taint her more.'

'Why doesn't it happen the other way around? Good cleansing evil? Look at his body. That façade like silver paper glued over rotting cardboard.'

The actor was displaying his signature dance moves. Elated cameras flashing to craft a halo around him. Lenses moving in tandem now as if waltzing with a lover. As applause erupted, Ashwin headed towards the reserved lounge followed by Lin. The officer darted to intercept her.

'Excuse me. Parag Suri. Officer-in-charge.'

'I am aware. My team had intimated me. And Mahira.'

'Mahira?'

'Yes. She had messaged me about you that day before she went for the live. Informed me and the sixth Chiranjivi. We know that you and your friends know.'

The officer directed her to a secluded spot.

'I apologise. I failed that day.'

'No, Suri. You can only do what you can. Anything else now would be mere speculation. Don't fall into that trap.'

'Mahira did not defend herself. She willingly draped the Icchadhari around herself like a noose. Said perhaps all Chiranjivis had become impure and must offer their blood to atone. Are you planning the same?'

The boxer came closer. 'Frisk me. I am hiding no snakes.'

'Thank you.'

'And I will fight. Fight Yeva.'

Suri exhaled. 'I am glad to hear that.'

'But I think I shall fail.'

'Fail?'

She looked at him calmly. A calm that graced a face only

after it had braved a thousand storms.

'We the Immortals. We were truly blessed, officer. All six of us. Consecrated by the greatest powers above. Placed on earth to carry out the good work we had been doing. And we did. So much good has emerged from our multiple births through the ages. So much more we want to do. Make every incarnation count. But while we rejoice, we also ask ourselves too many questions these days. Are we as immaculate as we were? Still that sacrosanct? I don't know. I am not sure. Doubts have been surfacing over several lifetimes now. Have we become arrogant? Complacent within our cocoons? Has this world magnified the faults we already had or made us abuse our own gunas?'

'Is that possible?'

'Yes. One's guna can also become one's hamartia. The tragic flaw. Are we perhaps turning human? Failing to overcome our own selves? We Chiranjivis have battled many demons and vanquished them. But perhaps there are personal demons we have not exorcised. We celebrate our immortality but perhaps the cosmos no longer celebrates us. The attack on Akram jolted us all. A cursed creature had violated a Chiranjivi. It seemed like the gods were abandoning us. Elements refusing to nurture us. We waited for answers. When they did not come, we stopped asking questions. We surrendered.'

'Is that why you stand next to Ashwin today?'

'Yes. It pains us but we have yielded. Letting our fates take us where it wants. The universe weeds out the unworthy. Survival of the fittest has been its primal mantra. We are no one to argue with the cosmic arrangement. It can preserve us or dissolve us. But if it brings us back into action, we shall know we are still worthy. We shall then drag Ashwathama into the arena. Next time the six of us won't take it lying down.'

'I am sure you shall be back. No one can condemn gods like you.'

'Our own voices have been condemning us through many lifetimes now. If the divine plan wants me to bleed like the others, I shall. Perhaps we overstay our welcome.' Lin gazed at the afternoon sun sliding down the horizon now.

'The world needs Chiranjivis. What else is truly everlasting?'

'An idea. A concept that inspires nobility. Teaches compassion. Anyone can be a Chiranjivi if he can leave behind such thoughts that live forever. You can all be Chiranjivis. Your race is still evolving. Evolving faster in the last ten thousand years. Many say the planet is declining but what if it's the exact opposite? Maybe, you all are progressing towards the post-human. Maybe you will even challenge Kalki.'

'Kalki?'

'Why not? Perhaps this was what the Mayans really predicted. Mankind's rebirth to a higher consciousness. Perhaps you yourself are the Saviour you have been waiting for. Realising that power within all of you shall be the true Second Coming. Then maybe Vyasa will write a new epic.'

Suri folded his hands. 'Will you pardon me if I fail again?'

'Not me. You must accept that it was not meant to be. You could do only what the universe allowed.'

'That's comforting but I shall still carry the guilt of failure. You can help me. You say you shall fight.'

'I am Parashurama. That's what I have done all my life. My several lives. Never inert when a force arrives to ravage me. A losing battle today perhaps but fight till the end.'

The lounge door opened as the cast and crew poured out headed by Ashwin. It was time for the show to begin. The actor linked arms with Lin leading the way towards the auditorium. As they crossed the mall's skywalk, Ashwin pointed at his fans below.

'Look, Lin. All my power encloses you today.'

She saw them. The crowds on all floors. Spiralling through the mall like a giant reptile climbing up the structure.

'I see Ashwin. You look down but I look up.'

'Why aren't you carrying your axe, Lin?'

'Why aren't you carrying your wounds, Ashwin?'

Inside the auditorium, sniffer dogs were crouching low. Suri had planned a separate arrangement for the boxer. A solitary couch placed in the centre and four armed men deployed around it. His men were also positioned at the six exit points. Patnaik and Atharva were seated where they had a clear view of Lin. As the lights dimmed, a group of guards switched on flashlights and moved around like wraiths. Ashwin was smiling.

Smiling as the opening credits rolled, announcing the saga of Lin Zimik. Smiling through the narration of her intense devotion towards the sport. Her twenty-one tournaments where she had outdone her greatest opponents. Smiling at the martial secrets gifted to her by masters supreme. And her emergence as a mentor to others. But smiling a tad more when the screen announced intermission.

With the lights fading in, an eager bunch made a beeline towards Lin, clamouring for autographs. Suri stood like a colossus with Patnaik and Atharva by his side. The writer's eyes skimming through the auditorium.

Where is Yeva?

He paused as someone joined the autograph queue. A curious female figure covered from head to toe. Her face was partially concealed behind a netted veil hanging from her hat. Trying her best to merge in but only appearing more and more conspicuous. As her gloved palms hovered over Lin holding a notepad, the writer gripped her wrist. She yanked herself away losing her glove and revealing her hand.

Scales…Thick scales…

Patnaik lurched and ripped off her hat. Diamond shaped plates of thick fleshy skin, separated by deep cracks, covered her face and body. Blue eyes glaring from under a hairless shiny head. Her lips pulled back wide and ears and nose missing entirely.

'My god! The snake woman.'

The ladies standing behind her were shrieking. As an array of rifles flicked into action, she sprinted down the aisle. Dogs tearing behind her, baying for her flesh. Skirting every bullet, she ran headlong into the alarmed crowds and disappeared through the exit. Suri's men drained out of the auditorium with the officer's voice hounding them.

'Hold fire. It won't help.'

The audience had exited behind the officers to witness this real-life drama now. The mall transforming into a colossal *mise-en-scene* with more and more spectators joining in from every floor. Watching the cops hunting that phantasm. Dogs barking incessantly. Store owners pulling down shutters to prevent her from entering. Mothers clutching kids as her scales brushed against their bodies. Some recording footage for social media. Ashwin stood watching, too. The public hardly looking at him. They were looking at this new star flashing through the mall. The cops had cornered her against a balcony now. She cowered as Suri along with Patnaik and Atharva broke through the police circle.

'It's over, Yeva.'

She was eyeing them. Her eyes burning like those of a trapped beast.

'Raise your hands and walk slowly towards me. One step at a time.'

She did not budge.

'Do it. Raise your…'

She sprang at them hissing like a boa constrictor, wanting to powder their bones. Clawing at them in a desperate bid to escape, when her hands suddenly seized her stomach. A rifle had roared and her body was recoiling through the air. Tottering back from the impact, she grabbed the balcony railing behind but the blood on her palms slackened her grip. Unable to hold on, she slipped and tumbled headlong four floors down. Seconds later a crowd had converged encircling her. The three men were watching her body. Moving. Writhing. Still bleeding. A dog smelling her blood. Licking it. Still bleeding. Examined by a medical team but still bleeding. Carted out to an ambulance outside and still bleeding. Not healing. Not healing as her eye had healed when Suri had put a bullet into it.

Not healing…

Her blood dripping like acid into their brains now. Consuming everything inside except the revelation.

Not Yeva…

Suri spun. 'What is that thing, Om? That fucking snake like crea…' He froze. 'Look.'

Pointing at the sky outside. A red rainbow had appeared over it like a raised scar. The writer turned towards the auditorium.

'Lin!'

They darted towards the theatre. Suri kicking the empty seats in fury now at what they were seeing. Lin slumped on the floor. A horseshoe on her head and a gushing wound. Her body slick with perspiration. The four guards foaming dead and a name in yellow stretching across the screen.

PARASHURAMA

Ashwin walked in. He was looking at Lin's palms curved into fists. Running his finger over the boxer's forehead, he flicked her sweat.

'Looks like Lin fought.'

Chapter 40

'ICTHYOSIS? WHAT THE FUCK IS ICHTHYOSIS, OM?'

They were standing inside the hospital ward. Lin had joined the other Immortals as the latest exhibit in this gallery of the living dead. Five gods vegetating. Eternal life in suspended animation. In a room below them, that body that had lain shattered on the mall floor had just breathed her last. They were saying she was barely eighteen years old.

'A skin disorder, Suri. An extremely rare condition which causes the dermis to thicken five to ten times more than normal. The skin also grows at an accelerated rate which leads to frequent shedding and flaking. Dermal layers become cracked and covered with diamond-shaped hexagonal scales with no hair.'

Patnaik stood unsteadily as he spoke as if his legs were turning into jelly. The priest held him firmly.

'This wasn't your fault.'

'It was. I was too hasty. She did not fall. My own hands practically shoved her down that railing. And made sure Lin was attacked.'

'You are not alone, Om,' Suri said. 'We all share the blame. That teenager's blood is on all our hands. But this was too fucking unexpected. I mean a skin disease that makes you resemble a snake? Too bloody twisted. That bastard knew what he was doing. We were looking for a snake, and he placed one right before our eyes.'

The writer quaked. 'Ashwin? He planted her there?'

'Yes. The teen could barely speak much before she died. But quite enough. Told us that a woman found out about her. She came to her village in Solapur and brought her to the premiere to get Lin's autograph. A woman with blue eyes just like her.'

'Yeva.'

'It was the perfect distraction. Who would doubt a bait like that? We all filed out of the auditorium and the Ichhadhari bled the boxer.'

'Maybe I should have stayed back with Lin,' Atharva said.

'We would have found you foaming on the floor too. You were so right, Om. I was a fool. Bloody fool to think that Yeva's anger against humans was probably justified. They lured an innocent teenager and left her on a fucking minefield. They will do far worse if we do not stop them.'

'She could help us out,' the priest suggested. 'You said she came from a village in Solapur. Did she say which one?'

'Yes. Something sounding like sepal or petal.'

'Sepal,' Atharva latched on to the word. 'Shetphal? Did she say Shetphal?'

'That's it. Shetphal.'

'Of course. Shetphal. It had to be.'

'Do you know the place?'

'I do,' the priest spoke as if the name had transported him somewhere far. 'Shetphal is astonishing. It slithers and hisses. Coils all around you to touch you and love you. Why did I not think of Shetphal before? Maybe it called out to me, but I paid no heed. This teen shows me that way now.

Holds my hand and leads me there. Shetphal's calling me again. So late now but not too late. I must go.'

'Go?'

'Yes. It's time now to make that pilgrimage. Bow before that altar. Shetphal knows everything. It will speak to me. Give me the answers. That secret we seek.'

'Secret? You mean…'

'Yes, Suri. The nemesis for Yeva. Shetphal alone can reveal it. Whisper in my ears how to destroy the Ichhadhari. I must go. I must go now.'

Following Atharva out of the ward, they saw attendants wheeling the teenager's corpse to the morgue. Shrouded in a white sheet frayed at the edges from where peeked a scaly foot. The priest walked out still murmuring to himself.

'Shetphal cannot refuse.'

As they watched him leave, the doctor joined them. 'Sorry to keep you both waiting. Manu's a lot worse today.'

Patnaik turned. 'Manu?'

'Yes. The woman from the forensic team. I thought you knew about her.'

'Knew what?'

'She is wasting away. Not very long now.'

The two men looked at each other.

Manu?

Still processing what the doctor was saying as he led them towards her room.

Wasting away…

Not long…

Terminal case…

Standing before her now. Seeing what she had turned into. The young woman entombed in a glass case. That glass getting cloudy each time her breath collided with it. The writer saw Suri's face twitch. He knew it was not for Manu.

He's thinking about her...

When he had seen her lying on the stretcher...

Her skull bashed in...

Alia...

'Why have you encased her?' Suri placed his hand on the glass.

'She is contagious. Acute risk of infection. Biohazard Level Four.'

'Level Four? What has got inside her?'

'Parasitic infestation.'

'Parasitic?'

'Yes. Her body...'

He broke off. Manu's forehead was becoming agitated. Frenzied as if something was bubbling underneath. The skin suddenly cracked and a small jet of blood spurted out. Blue blood.

'Cyanosis,' the doctor explained. 'Since her infection, oxygen levels in her blood have depleted, turning it blue.'

'Is that normal? Skin rupturing on its own like that?'

'No. This has never happened before. That only occurs if...'

Something was wriggling. Wriggling out through that fissure in the centre of her forehead. Patnaik inched closer to the glass. 'What the...'

A worm.

A strand of white emerging out of that cavity.

Suri yanked his hand away from the case as if the worm would attach itself to his skin.

Another one now. And another one.

'What's going on here?' the officer screamed.

More and more worms pushing their way out now. Spawning from that hole as if hatching from a million eggs below. Infinite filaments breaking out unspooled by an invisible force. White threads as if a hundred bobbins were whirring inside her body. Crawling all over her face. Entering her ears and nostrils. Slipping into her mouth and getting swallowed. Rubbing against her swollen eyeballs like a throbbing sticky web blinding her.

Manu could hardly see now. She could only hear the writer's fists pounding that coffin.

Chapter 41

INDIRA WAS LYING ON THE FLOOR NEXT TO A SNAKE.

The colossal white serpent depicted on the school wall was perhaps as familiar to her as her own chalk drawings. This was not the only wall in Shetphal that clasped a painted serpent to its bosom. Walking through the lanes of this village a few hours ago, they had seen almost every wall exhibiting that same art as if it was a snake tank made of brick and lime. Announcing the presence of the actual serpent that lived inside that house. Every house in Shetphal.

'Cobras mostly though we have kraits and vipers too,' the headmaster was telling Atharva as they now lay on charpoys under the squeaking school fan. 'These are dry plains and snakes are everywhere. The roads. Sugarcane fields. This school. The homes. It is Nagoba. The village deity.'

'And all the houses here have an area for serpents to dwell?'

'Sure. That's what makes Shetphal so unique. Every house has a separate space in the hollow wooden rafters of the ceilings. We call it the Devasthan. In fact, each dwelling is modelled keeping snakes in mind. This particular architecture facilitates their movement in and out. In Shetphal we do not have sanctums in the heart of the house. It's high up under the roof holding a live deity. It comes and goes as it pleases.'

'And no snakebites?'

'Never. Neither I nor my father or forefathers have ever heard of a single case. This is that kind of place. You can find miracles if you look.'

'I am looking for answers.'

'Yes. I have heard what you told me. I probably would have rejected your story if I was someplace else. But Shetphal teaches otherwise. Denial stems from pride and I have seen quite a lot here that tells me to hold on to my faith.'

'So, whom do we approach?'

'The Nagatma.'

'Nagatma?'

'He who presides over the Nagnath Temple. The spirit of Shetphal. Its oldest inhabitant. Perhaps as old as the snakes themselves that crawl this village. If your question has an answer, only he shall have it.'

In the middle of the night, Atharva's eyes opened at the hollow sound of metal hitting against earth. He saw a copper pitcher spinning on the floor. Spinning like those prayer wheels outside Buddhist monasteries. He knew a snake's body had coiled around the pitcher while making its way up towards the rafters. He smiled and closed his eyes. When he opened them again, it was time to visit the Nagatma. Stepping out of the house, he saw the headmaster staggering towards him.

'What is it? You look ghastly.'

'A boy. A boy has been bitten.'

'Bitten? Here?'

'Yes.'

'How's that possible? Snakes in Shetphal never harm anyone.'

'No one knows why. We are all horrified. Many think maybe we have enraged Nagoba in some way. Displeased him enough to strike at us. Wondering if it's an omen for worse things to follow. Famines or epidemics. I have seen kids playing with snakes here. So many trained to become snake charmers. Ours has been a symbiosis baffling and endearing. Nothing for years and now suddenly this. Right after you arrive.'

The priest's face clouded. 'We arrive? Is the village blaming us?'

'Not openly, but I have heard voices. Many questioning why the wrath of Nagoba falls the day you step into the village. Wondering if Shetphal has reacted to your presence. Maybe it doesn't welcome whatever you seek.'

'What I seek? I am looking for a solution. A formula to kill a monster. This snakebite is surely confusing but then nature has always been fickle. Being random is one of its biggest strengths. It can take all the laws of physics that we worship and turn them around like an hourglass.'

'Are you not a part of that nature?'

Atharva was quiet. He glanced at the village. 'Is it really me? Have I damaged Shetphal?'

As they made their way to the temple, the silence told them that Shetphal stood traumatised today. Too shocked to mourn out loud. When God's fury was about to plague every first-born child in Egypt, Moses had instructed his people to mark their doors with the blood of a spring lamb. The spirit of the lord had passed over all those houses, leaving them unharmed. Perhaps Shetphal had a similar covenant with the serpents. Each house branded with the image of a snake to keep their children safe.

Had that pact been broken?

Were the villagers looking at him like a toxin that had entered Shetphal? A toxin making its way now to the very heart of Shetphal?

Nagnath Temple

The three-hundred-year-old sanctum rose from the ground like a mammoth block of white ice. Hewed in the front where the entrance glowed with a riot of green and orange. The doorway was flanked on either side by stone images of two black snakes coiled around each other forming a spiral. An artwork of Vishnu reclining over Sheshnag covered a wall. They saw Indira touching her head to the god's feet. Inside the *garbhagriha* towered a gigantic copper image of a cobra. A seven-hooded serpent sheltering Shiva.

The Nagoba.

Before the idol lay a boy wrapped in a sheet.

'Is that him?'

The headmaster nodded. 'Not dead yet.'

Indira knelt beside the body, placing her scarred cheek over his. The priest held up the boy's arm noting his pulse.

'But why here? I hear you have a dispensary.'

'The Nagtama asked him to be brought here.'

'Nagatma? Why?'

'We don't know. A snakebite in Shetphal is the darkest portent possible. The worst breach of trust. It has poisoned the very coexistence between man and reptile that defines Shetphal. Made us afraid to enter our own homes now. Perhaps the Nagatma knows something we don't. We can only seek Nagoba's mercy.'

Atharva bowed. 'I pray too. Pray to be forgiven if I have harmed this boy.'

'Shetphal does not believe in forgiveness. Only natural balance.'

The voice had come from behind them. They turned to see an old man by the sanctum door. He had more lines on his face than hair on his head. Dressed in white and eyes as black as coal. He was ringing a small copper bell in his hands.

The Nagatma.

He came closer to the priest. 'Balance. When the scales do not tip anymore. Aligned next to each other in perfect symmetry. When you replace what was taken. No more and no less. Only an equilibrium spreading throughout. That balance has tilted now.'

'Is it my fault? Am I responsible?'

'Not your fault, but you are responsible. Because of that which you seek.'

Atharva folded his hands. 'The secret. You know. You know what I have come to you for.'

'Yes. And I know what action that knowledge will lead to.'

'Am I wrong? Should I not seek to kill the Ichhadhari?'

'You must. She is a negative force and must be plucked out. Your pursuit is a noble one.'

'Then why did a snake strike this boy?'

'Because you are about to strike a snake.' The Nagatma placed a lotus flower on a tray as the bell in his hand rang louder. 'When you take a life, it upsets the natural order. Even if it is the life of someone as evil as the Ichhadhari. Order can only be recreated then by a similar event. A reaction exactly opposite to the action. When you resolved to kill the serpent, you created a crack in the balance. And balance will have to be restored again. So Shetphal allowed what it had never allowed so far. It allowed a snake to bite a human.'

'Shetphal sacrificed itself?'

'A barter. One life for another. That is how Shetphal can seal the crack.'

Atharva crumbled before the Nagoba. 'The villagers were right. I have destroyed Shetphal.'

'You are only doing what must be done. But since you are trying to kill a snake, a snake now tries to kill a man. That is how the universe achieves proportion. Violence has happened in the village today because you intend to perform a necessary violent act in the future. Someone had to pay the price to recover equilibrium. Shetphal has done that. You are here looking for help, and Shetphal never refuses.'

The priest looked at the shrouded figure. 'I have killed him.'

'He isn't dead yet, because you still haven't found out how to kill the Ichhadhari.'

'How can I find that out now when I know it will lead to this child's death? I have seen the pain on Om's face because his actions pushed an innocent teenager to a tragic end. That guilt he carries. I cannot have that. End such a young life for what I seek.'

'You end nothing. No man has the power to do that. It's Nagoba. Only Nagoba who can give life and take it away. You can only do what you must do. Come. See if you can gain the knowledge that you have come to Shetphal for. That's why I have placed the boy next to you. To see what Nagoba desires. If the boy has to live, you will not be able to interpret the Sadhan to kill the Ichhadhari. But if the boy has to die, you will decipher the Sadhan and find out the secret.'

'What Sadhan?'

The Nagatma picked something up from the feet of the Nagoba and placed it in the priest's hands.

'That's the secret you seek.'

The headmaster and Indira gazed at the object as the old man closed the sanctum doors.

'What is this, Atharva?'

'I don't have the faintest idea.'

Chapter 42

THE WRITER WAS STARING AT THE HOOVES OF THE HORSE now. In the air poised right above his stomach. They plunged in digging holes and scooping his innards out. Guts spilling everywhere soaked in his fluids. The horse bent over. Probing deep inside. Its mouth lifting his intestines with its teeth. Wrenching that coil out and sucking it whole. Patnaik woke up. Still sitting on the hospital bench. Watching Suri dragging himself towards him.

'Is she dead'

'Yes. Nine minutes ago. They say the worms ate up her brain.'

He got up and walked towards Manu's room. Still in her glass coffin.

'Lethal parasite infestation, Mr Patnaik.'

'What parasite is this?'

'That's the problem. We cannot identify it. Appears to be some kind of a hybrid and highly eccentric. It does not exhibit characteristics of any nematodes we have tested so far. Instead it shows compound properties. Characteristics of multiple parasites.'

'Multiple parasites?'

'Yes. Once inside the body, the larvae of this parasite latch on to bodily fluids for nourishment like pinworms.

As soon as the larvae mature, they migrate towards the brain like tapeworms. And like hookworms, their mouths are structured into hooks to burrow into the brain. From here onwards they do what no parasite has ever done so far. They start sucking the brain out.'

The doctor pointed at Manu's MRI scans.

'It began with mild headaches. As the infestation compounded, she started to suffer epileptic seizures. Our tests revealed the parasite colonies that had invaded her brain. Imagine hundreds of these worms writhing inside your head. We immediately isolated her, but none of our medications worked. She would tell me that she wanted to crack open her skull and pull these worms out one by one. As the parasites consumed more and more of her brain, her physical functions started to cease. One by one until her body finally shut down. But the worst came in the end. The end we saw yesterday when the parasites mimicked another worm. The guinea worm.'

'Guinea worm?'

'Also called Dracunculus, the nematode is native to Africa. It matures in the human abdominal cavity and feeds off the host for an entire year. At the end of its cycle, the female emerges out of the host's body by burrowing through the skin.'

'Like this parasite did yesterday?'

'Yes. The female guinea worm forms a blister on the host's skin. Once the blister ruptures, the worm surfaces through that lesion. It must then be mechanically pulled out of the patient's flesh. This extraction takes several days since any breakage only makes the condition worse. But the guinea worm always comes out through the patient's legs.

These parasites are not doing that. They are…'

'Bursting through the forehead.'

He was looking at Manu.'

Hole in her head

Forehead

'The pace of this parasite's life cycle is also baffling. The guinea worm takes a whole year to emerge out of the body but not these. Our cultures confirm that the infection occurred a little over three months back. Just hundred days to turn a human brain into sawdust.'

'But how did Manu get infected? How did these parasites enter her body?' Suri asked.

'We haven't been able to determine that.'

Patnaik was still looking. Looking into that cavity on her forehead as if it was a pin-hole camera showing him an image. A picture that suddenly swelled into an aspect so alarming that he seized the doctor's arm. 'You need to do something.'

'What?'

'Check those five patients in coma. Akram, Trehan, Somnath, Mahira and Lin. Test them for this parasite.'

'I don't understand.'

'I think I do. I have reason to believe that they might be infected with this same worm.'

The doctor shook his head. 'Impossible. Look at Manu. See how the parasite vandalises the human body. These five patients exhibit no such symptoms. Even if they are comatose, if this parasite invades them, their bodies will start flashing signals. But apart from the coma, they are all in perfect health. We are constantly monitoring their fluids.'

'But you have never tested them for this parasite?'

'Of course not. We had no reason to.'

'I have reasons. Do it.'

He gazed at Suri who gazed at the doctor.

'Do what he says.'

Forty minutes later the doctor confirmed it. All five of them were carrying the parasite. But the worm was not attacking them. Any of them. It lay dormant. An outsider simply seeking refuge in their bodies. The two men were standing in the hospital lab now. The blood of the Chiranjivis standing before them in five long test-tubes. And microscope slides of the parasite.

'How did you know the Chiranjivis were carrying the worm?'

'Because that's the only way Manu could have picked up this infection.'

'I don't follow you.'

'Trehan. She got it from Trehan.'

'Trehan?'

'Yes. Recall that day in the classroom. She was collecting Trehan's blood from his body and broke a test-tube. It was during the procedure that the parasite must have gained entry. Trehan was assaulted in March. Three months ago.'

'But that would mean Trehan was already infected. Where did he pick up the parasite?'

'Nowhere.'

'Nowhere?'

'He did not pick it up. It was introduced in his blood.'

'Introduced in his bl…' The officer felt the pit of his stomach churn. 'Yeva?'

'Yes. Yeva.'

Patnaik lifted the test-tube labelled *Lin Zimik*. 'Blood, Suri. We are back to blood.'

'Careful. That can infect you.'

'Not this blood. Lin was infected day before yesterday and the doctors have confirmed that the parasite takes three weeks to mature. If you remove the blood from the body before that period, the larvae die posing no threat. This tube has dead parasite but not the other four. Yeva is not only attacking the Immortals to acquire their blood. She's also contaminating it.'

'But she could also get infected in the process.'

'She's an Ichhadhari. Paranormal just like the Chiranjivis who are not affected by the parasite. It lives and breathes inside all of them but lies completely inactive.'

'But why, Om? Why infect the Chiranjivis?'

'Because Ashwin ordered her.'

'Ashwin?'

The writer indicated his head. 'Didn't you see Manu? A parasite that has been programmed to devour the human brain and then bore through the forehead. Centre of the forehead, Suri.'

The officer gulped a load of saliva. 'Ashwathama.'

'Yes. This has Ashwathama written all over it.'

'But where would Ashwin get such a parasite from?'

'He didn't need to get it. He created it himself.'

'Created it?'

Patnaik pointed at the sealed glass window. The Mumbai cityscape filling that frame. And one building standing closer than the rest.

'Kalpataru.'

'Ashwin's research facility.'

'Yes, Suri. His centre named after that wish-granting tree. It has granted Ashwin's wish.'

Suri took the test-tube from his hands and placed it back on the stand. 'This is getting more and more fucked up, Om. Is this what Yeva was hinting at? What Ashwathama is planning?'

Patnaik was offering him no answers. The officer lowered his eye into the shaft of the electron microscope to look at the slides of the parasite.

'Worms like snakes. Fucking snakes all over the brain.'

'What did you say?'

'Snakes around the brain.'

The writer was standing still as if an invisible idea had electrocuted him. Suri touched him gingerly.

'Om?'

Patnaik opened his website community page on the mobile and raised the screen before Suri's eyes.

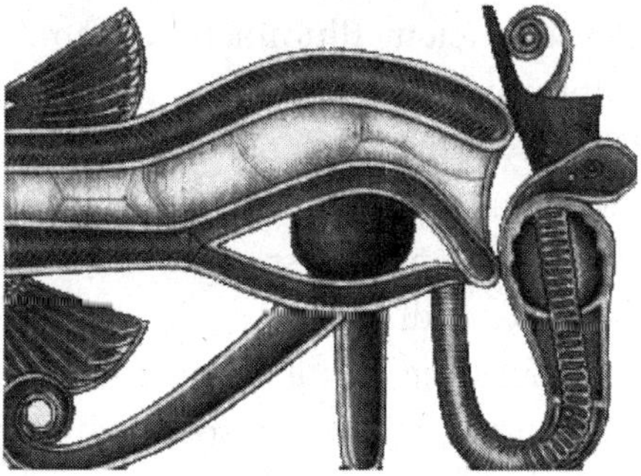

'Snakes around the brain. The last image posted by Zahak.'

Chapter 43

THE SADHAN LAY IN HIS HANDS LIKE A NEWBORN THAT had not yet learnt to speak. Tell Atharva anything about itself. He brought it closer.

What are you?

He was looking at a large circular piece of stone. The surface bare except a triangle engraved right in the middle. In the centre of the triangle was a black dot.

'A dot inside a triangle inside a circle,' the headmaster observed.

'Yes. And it makes no sense because this symbol you see here resembles an ancient Illuminati diagram.'

'What's Illuminati?'

'A secret society founded in the eighteenth century. The circle and the triangle denote the Illuminati New World Order. The dot represents the spiritual axis of the universe. The energy pivotal to all of us.'

'Looks similar to the triangle on an American dollar.'

'The Masonic Eye. That also originates from the Illuminati symbol of the Eye of Providence. The All-Seeing Eye. The Kabbalah borrows this diagram where the triangle symbolises the spirit. A hallowed pyramid of light. And for Rosicrucianism, this icon signifies creation. Triangle within a circle has also been adopted as a symbol for gay rights.'

'The inverted pink triangle inside a green circle.'

'Yes. Interestingly that triangle originated in Nazi concentration camps. Gays and lesbians were segregated by making them wear a pink badge shaped as an inverted triangle. That mark of shame was later reclaimed as an international symbol of gay pride.'

Atharva was rotating the Sadhan to invert the triangle. He paused.

'What is it?'

The priest's nails were grinding the stone. He placed the Sadhan gently on the floor as if it were a piece of glass. Picking up the lotus from the silver tray, he plucked the petals one by one and arranged them around the inverted triangle in an octagon.

'Look. What do you see?'

That dot. The inverted triangle. That ring of eight petals around it. The headmaster nodded.

'Kali Yantra. The most powerful Shakti Yantra.'

'Exactly,' the priest touched the geometric figure. 'This central dot represents Kali. The seat of Atman. The centre from which the cosmos emerges. The circle symbolises life and death while the eight lotus petals represent Prakriti or the manifesting universe. And the inverted triangle is the female genitalia. Is that where we need to attack Yeva to kill her?'

Strike her genitalia?

A screeching sound diverted him. He saw Indira squatting. The chalk in her hand moving round and round, depositing white circles on the floor.

Largest. Larger. Large. Small. Smaller. Smallest.

Smallest. Smaller. Small. Large. Larger. Largest.

The circles converging and diverging. Imploding and exploding.

Concentric circles

'Water. I need water,' Atharva exclaimed.

The Nagatma pointed at a copper bowl before the idol. The priest emptied it over the stone.

'Look.'

As soon as the liquid touched the Sadhan, the surface turned dark. Rings of striation marks suddenly visible to the naked eye now. Circles in a concentric pattern radiating from the triangle in the centre to the outer margin of the stone. It was as if water had turned sculptor and carved out these spheres throughout the Sadhan.

'All these concentric circles,' the headmaster peered. 'What does that mean?'

'It means it's not just a Shakti Yantra. It's also a Mehen.'

'A what?'

'Mehen. An ancient board game from Egypt where the board is shaped like a snake coiled into a circle. The body of the snake is divided into rectangular spaces to move the pegs. The Mehen itself is a serpent deity believed to encircle the sun. Similar to the Ouroboros.'

'The serpent devouring its own tail?'

'Right.'

'But I don't get this. Why are a Mehen and Kali Yantra fused together on this Sadhan?'

'Because both are pointing towards the same thing.'

'The same thing?'

'Yes. Shakti and coiled serpent. It can't be clearer than this.'

The headmaster's eyes were scouring the stone. He

lifted it as if he had heard the Sadhan whisper the word.

'Kundalini?'

'Precisely. That primary vital energy within all of us that remains coiled at the base of the spine. Denoting Shakti or the sacred feminine lying dormant. Only when that spiral fire is ignited can we attain true enlightenment. Various yogic practices induce the upward movement of this libidinal force which the Mayans called *coyopa*. Lightning in the blood. Like an electric current, it rises from the base of our backbone and reaches the brain through the spinal cord. Moving inside us sinuously like a snake to create altered consciousness.'

Atharva was hearing his own words.

Serpent ascending the psycho-spiritual conduit...

Nehushtan...

'And just as the reptile sheds its skin but remains unchanged, this wisdom manifests new forms but its core essence remains the same. Kali is the goddess of Kundalini. The female dynamic opposed to the male static. The ultimate aim here is the reintegration of the masculine and feminine inside our heart.'

'The harmony principle. Choreography of Shakti and Shiva,' the headmaster said.

'Right. The Mother Goddess. Matriarchal power reviled by patriarchy throughout the ages when they both actually complement each other. Even the Mehen is believed to envelope the solar god Ra into sexual communion every night which revitalises the sun to provide light the next day. An Immaculate Conception that leads to Christ-like consciousness.'

'Christ like?'

'Sure. Why do you think Adam and Eve were forbidden

to eat fruits of the Tree of Knowledge? The tree was the spinal channel and the coiled serpent was the creative force around. If they would have eaten, they would have become like gods.'

'Quite a dangerous energy to handle.'

'Yes. Kundalini can be dangerous but extremely crucial. So, Vishnu lies on a coiled Sheshnag at the base of the universe, sending out vibrations that animate its matrix. Similarly, the Kundalini vibrates through the seven chakras of the human body and awakens the super-sensory third eye. Our latent energy points wake up, leading us towards reawakening.'

'A transcendence of sorts?'

'Exactly,' the priest tapped the triangle in the centre of the Sadhan. 'That's the secret. The spine. We have to shatter Yeva's spine to destroy her.'

He was seeing that vision in his mind again. Yeva's wooden staff. She was not only invoking a new life for Ashwin. Also constantly reminding herself of the key to her own death.

Nehushtan…

Kundalini…

They were looking at the Nagatma like disciples who had answered a question. Waiting for the guru to applaud them. The old man's lips moved.

'So, the boy shall die.'

Atharva's heart sank again. 'Must Shetphal do this?'

'It has no choice. If a serpent must die, so must a human.'

'I hold the key now that I came for. But it's covered with this boy's blood.'

'A sacrifice for greater good. Nagoba has chosen you over him. It wants you to kill the Ichhadhari. Go fulfil your destiny as we all must fulfil ours.'

'But the child...'

The Nagatma opened the sanctum portal. 'He's not your concern any longer. Go. Let Nagoba accomplish through you what he wants.'

As the three of them left, the Nagatma slammed the door and turned towards the seven-hooded cobra.

'Not him lord. Not the boy.'

He fell on the floor prostrate before Nagoba.

'Let my death compensate. Reinstate the symmetry. Take me. Me but not the child. My bones. Not his flesh.'

He bent over the Mehen.

'My work here is done. They have the secret.'

Slitting his skin, he let his blood drip on the stone. Watched as the fluid charted through the Mehen, coating every circle red.

'I am willing now, Shetphal.'

The reptile around Shiva's throat was waking up. Slithering down the lord like a thread unclasping itself. Reaching the boy and sucking all the poison from his heart. The old man was placing the lotus petals on his chest. Ringing the small bell. The serpent looped around his wrinkled feet now. Climbing up towards his face.

The Nagatma smiled.

Chapter 44

PATNAIK HAD NEVER SEEN A MAN HANGING BY THE ROPE from a ceiling fan. He was aware of the unsavoury details that the rope ran over the throat leaving deep tyre marks. That eyes apparently popped out of their sockets and the tongue stretched out from the constricted gullet. He had often wondered how much was clinical fact and how much urban legend. Now he stood looking at the body suspended from above. The noose biting the man's Adam's apple. Cutting it into small pieces.

Suri's team had been way more resourceful than the writer had imagined. Based on Zahak's account details on the online forum and the photographs he had pasted all over the Internet, they had unearthed the man's identity and coordinates in a single day. They were bringing his body down now. Patnaik clasped the man's wrist sensing the ice within. Zahak's tonsured head carried a tattoo of the symbol. The same symbol drawn all over this room.

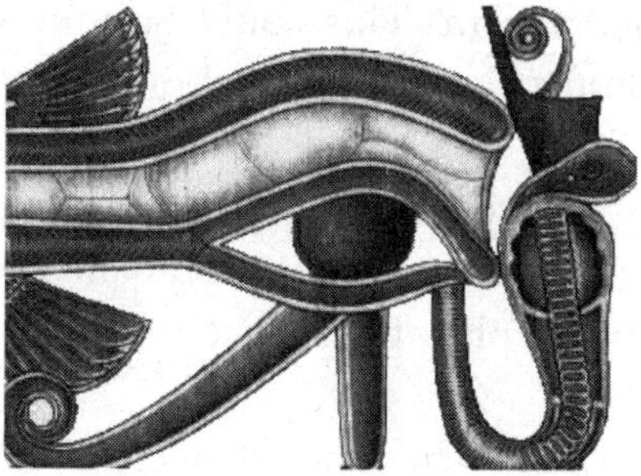

The medical team was pronouncing him dead for well over a month. Others were rummaging through the flat. Dipping into whatever Zahak had touched but found nothing. Suri asked everyone to step out. Just him and Patnaik with Zahak now.

'Nothing here, Om. Just that he was a junior researcher. At Kalpataru.'

'Exactly. What more do you want?'

'Lot more. This doesn't prove that Zahak knew about the parasite.'

'The username he chose for himself proves it quite adequately.'

'Username?'

'Zahak. It's the name of a Persian prince in a story by Firdausi. He had two snakes sprouting from his body instead of arms. The snakes had sworn never to kill him as long as he fed them brains. Human brains.'

'Quite the parallel but hardly conclusive that he knew anything or that Ashwin is involved.'

'Why did he post that symbol then? And why is he dead? He knew. He knew what was being manufactured inside that lab.'

'Still a theory, Om. This could be murder or suicide. Difficult to confirm anything based on a random image he posted online.'

'Random? Do you know what this is? It's the Eye of Horus. Horus was the ancient Egyptian deity of the sky and this symbol depicts his right eye denoting power and health.'

'Interesting but what's the connection?'

'Over the years, the Eye of Horus has been increasingly linked with a cardinal organ of the human body. Linked because this symbol looks exactly like that organ. A resemblance extremely uncanny.'

'Liver?'

'No. The brain. The organ that Ashwin's parasite is targeting.'

As comprehension spread over the officer's face, Patnaik went on. 'More specifically the hypothalamus. The Eye of Horus is almost a replica of the anatomical structure of the hypothalamus. And not just the shape. Even functionally, the Eye of Horus constitutes the five sensory perceptions of sight, smell, hearing, taste and touch. And that's exactly what the hypothalamus does. It interprets the incoming signals from our sense organs. That's the connection, Suri. A connection that was noticed even by Michelangelo way back in the sixteenth century.'

'Michelangelo?'

'Yes. Master of dissimulation, he blended many such images of human anatomy along with figures and symbols all over the ceiling at Sistine Chapel. Look at the Creation of Adam and you can make out the human brain in cross section. Another fresco called Separation of Light from

Darkness presents a ventral view of the brainstem and spinal cord. Whether these are subliminal messages or the entire ceiling is a giant Rorschach Test is a matter of debate. Perhaps he was suggesting that God not only gave us life but also intellect. For Michelangelo, God was perhaps nothing but the highest aspect of our own true self.'

'And the snake in this symbol?'

'That snake appears with the Eye of Horus in many Egyptian icons. Also called Wadjet or the Eye of Ra, it's a common image in funerary amulets for pharaohs to protect them in their after-life.'

'Snake around the brain.'

'Exactly. Does it all add up now? Zahak posted this symbol, and he worked at Kalpataru. He was silently screaming about this worm created to feed on human brains.'

'I see that, Om, but it's still circumstantial. Something a little more solid would help. We have turned this flat upside down but found fucking nothing.'

'There must be, Suri. Zahak was warning us all. He was surely aware that his life was in danger. He must have left something about the parasite.'

'Maybe we are reading too much into that symbol. Perhaps it was all in Zahak's mind.'

The writer looked at the Eye of Horus.

In his mind…

The tattoo on that bald head. A brain painted on top of an actual brain.

Like Sistine Chapel?

'Yes. All in his mind. You are right. You'll find nothing in his flat because it's all in his mind.'

'So, this was a waste of time.'

'I didn't say that, Suri. I said it was all in his mind.' He tapped on the tattoo.

The officer walked closer to the corpse. 'In there?'

'Dissimulation. I just told you about Michelangelo. Hiding information in plain view. I am sure Zahak has done exactly that. See how recent this tattoo looks. You can still see a hint of redness of the skin around it. I think our friend has stashed something right here.'

Patnaik's fingers were sliding over the image now. Groping all the colours. They paused.

'Here.'

Suri touched the spot. A horizontal scab hardly visible to the naked eye. Hiding in black ink. Ruptured skin sewn together. He picked up a knife from the kitchen. The blade was slicing through the threads now that sealed that fissure firmly. Digging into the lesion as the joint gave away. His fingers probing that hollow. Extracting a piece of plastic from congealed blood.

'Memory card wrapped in polythene.'

'Double entendre,' the writer whispered. 'See what he did? The symbol he was posting everywhere had a double meaning. It was not only warning us about the parasite. It was also revealing where exactly he had hidden the evidence for it. Literally inside his head.'

Suri was watching the video inside the card now. The dead man's monologue telling them how Ashwin got the parasite synthesised at Kalpataru. How three scientists were hypnotised by the Ichhadhari to carry out that task and how their memories were later wiped clean using her Mani. How he had found out about the biological terror the actor was going to unleash and tried to warn everyone by posting the image. How he had seen Ashwin emptying all that toxin into tiny crystal vials. His words blaring ominously through the headphones.

Six vials of venom...

'I think it's time we spoke to Ashwin,' the officer got up.

'No, Suri. We shall do nothing.'

'What?'

'Nothing. We do not tell Ashwin that we know about the parasite. Do not interrogate anyone at Kalpataru.'

'This is evidence, Om. Bloody evidence. We can drag him in for some serious questioning. Maybe even charge him.'

'I know. But you will not do that.'

'But why? What's wrong with you?'

'Because he's Ashwathama,' the writer erupted. 'Ashwathama. The horse who always kicks viciously when he's cornered. What did Ashwathama do when he was trapped in the end by Arjuna? He released the Brahmastra to wreck the entire universe. He destroyed the unborn foetus in Uttara's womb. He had even massacred the sons of Draupadi while they were sleeping the night before. He cares for no one but himself. What if he does the same now? Lets this parasite loose as soon as you confront him? Infects the whole world? Can we risk that?'

'But he might release the parasite today or tomorrow. We have to stop him.'

'No, Suri. He had the parasite since the very first day when Akram was attacked. Why hasn't he dispersed it yet? Don't you get it? Six vials. Six vials for six Chiranjivis. He won't do it himself. He's doing it through the Immortals. Making them the receptacle for this poison to smear them forever. He will not release the toxin. He is waiting for them to wake up. Waiting for the Chiranjivis to become unknowing weapons of his biological war.'

'What then?'

'We only have a single option left. We must thwart his final attack. Keep that last Chiranjivi safe and find out how to disinfect the other five. That alone will foil Ashwin.' He covered Zahak's face. 'Enough blood has been spilled. We cannot risk any more.'

The officer left the room as the body was carried out. He was ordering a full-blown investigation. Patnaik stood a little longer looking at the floor. That blue plastic board lying there.

Snakes & Ladders...

Chapter 45

YEVA'S JOURNAL—PG 108

The snake on my mobile screen seemed unquenchable. Every time I clicked the button, it wolfed a tiny morsel. Darting all over the screen in perfect perpendicular motion. Creating absolute right angles. Conforming to the contours of the screen. Respecting the prison of this game that confined it.

I made a face. I would never move like that in absolute straight lines. There was an elegance in being twisted. Curvilinear was delicious. The helix so divine. I closed my eyes and smiled. Thinking about how men loved to sport with snakes even inside virtual realms. On plastic boards. Thinking about how I had sported with a man who liked to call himself Zahak.

I had entered his house. At night through the window. Waiting for him.

As he entered and switched on the lights, I raised myself up. He saw the noose I had strung for him around his ceiling fan. I plucked a blue plastic board from his shelf and spread it out before him.

'A game.'

He lowered his eyes to see the lines on the board. Some straight ones. Some spiral.

'If your ladders save you, you live. If my snakes kill you, you die.'

I was looking at his bald head. The serpent tattoo. The dice rolled. Again and again. Somersaulting on the plastic like a veteran acrobat. We caged it in our palms but once we flung it on the board, it was free to go wherever it wanted. Display the number that it alone fancied. Like every creature in this cosmos, the dice took a life of its own once it was liberated. It knew we both were watching it. Pleading before it to bestow the numbers we desired. We assumed we were the players. The dice knew that it alone was playing.

The pegs were sliding fast. Hauled up by ladders and yanked down by snakes. Both our pegs stationed now at 98.

99 and the largest serpent of all would consume us.

He rolled a one. He watched as my long index finger pushed the peg on top of the snake's mouth. Twisting and turning all the way down like a morsel of food moving through its body. The prey being absorbed and digested and its remains deposited on number 9.

99 to 9.

'You lose, Zahak.'

Not Yeva now. A blue krait staring at him. He was hearing hissing sounds. Warm and clear like steam escaping from a kettle. Not me. He lowered his sight. The snakes on the board were writhing and wriggling. Trying to twist around the ladders and numbers. Drooling poison on the plastic board. Red, green, yellow and blue snakes. Black and white ones flicking the black and white dice. Their beady eyes glittering as they turned to face him. Raising their hoods now. Looking at him. Getting louder.

On the inside he was running. Running as fast as his pumping heart. Getting further and further away from these beasts. But on the outside he sat still. Transfixed by the snakes from that plastic board, climbing his arms. Swarming over his chest. Their scales rubbing against his skin. Leaving lashes of blue, green, yellow and red all over. Folding around his throat and breathing into his nose. He stood up trying to wrench the reptiles off his body, but they seemed *to have clung like leeches. Inserting their fangs into his nipples and hanging from his torso. Biting his tongue and licking his eyeballs. Sliding down his bald head like cascades of black water. His face dotted with sting marks now as they injected their venom. He flailed, brutally ripping them off his skin. Armpits and groin. Recoiling again and again as they struck. Frothing like a rabid dog as they covered him. The poison hacking his flesh into pieces. He was groping at the chair below the rope. Clambering over. His fingers pouncing on the noose and tightening it around his throat. All those snakes had entered his body now, swimming inside him. Tickling his brain and crawling over his spine. Sucking all the blood from his heart. His legs kicked away the chair. The last sound he heard was of the rope squeezing his life out of him.*

I was humming. Grinning at how this man had gone hysterical about so many snakes. I peered at the game-board.

I was the only snake in the room.

Chapter 46

'SPECTACULAR.'

The priest was holding up an X-ray image of the human backbone. 'Check out how organic our universe is. The serpent not only symbolises Kundalini but is also itself shaped like the spine. Tapering and undulating. And like the spinal cord controls our reflexes, the snake denotes the unconscious within us, manifesting itself without warning.'

'And now the serpent must consume itself?' Patnaik asked.

'Yes. Just as the snake's venom cures its bite, we destroy Yeva by destroying her spine. Shetphal has spoken.'

'You are absolutely sure?' Suri pressed.

'Shetphal never lies. It broke its own rule. We cannot let Shetphal down.'

The writer clinched Indira in his arms. 'Thank you. Both of you. I hope she realises one day what she has done for all of us. She is truly blessed.'

'You are no less, Om,' Atharva said. 'Only you could have worked out the calamity Ashwin is planning. Suri just showed me Zahak's video. One of Ashwathama's most powerful weapons during the Mahabharata war was an arrow that could shower snakes at the enemy. He hasn't changed.'

'He hasn't. Still playing with snakes. And infecting the Chiranjivis is a masterstroke. Beyond genius. It gives him two advantages. The biological demon he has raised in his lab finds the perfect body to lodge in. A body that shall never show any symptoms of the parasite that inhabits it. No one will even know this parasite exists. Not even the Chiranjivis infected secretly by Yeva. Like snakes carrying venom, the six Immortals shall poison everyone when they wake up, never aware of what they are doing. By the time patients start piling up, it will be too late.'

'And the second advantage?'

'His parasite has found carriers blessed with eternal life. It shall be an everlasting pestilence. Like an inexhaustible source of energy, the Chiranjivis will go on spreading the contagion forever. Poisoning generation after generation. Infecting others who in turn shall infect more until the world becomes one giant morgue.'

'The bodily fluids?'

'Yes,' the writer displayed four fingers. 'The parasite diffuses through four primary fluids. Saliva. Blood. Semen. And breast milk. The Chiranjivis would stand ignorant as everyone around them wastes away. Dead with gaping holes in their foreheads.'

'Like Ashwathama,' the priest shuddered.

A world full of Ashwathamas…

'Precisely. That's what he has planned. Not just to erase us but turn everyone into Ashwathama. Billions of cursed Ashwathamas everywhere. Festering bodies with cracked foreheads. It's a double-edged sword. On one hand, he destroys the earth that imprisons him. Strikes at the very heart of the universe by striking at man. Its most beloved creation. Satan planned maximum damage by going after what was dearest to god. Man. Ashwin's doing the same.'

'The highest terror attack possible,' Suri's voice turned flaccid. 'Targeting what one is most proud of.'

'And on the other hand, Ashwin's also lashing out at the Chiranjivis. That hallowed group that he was never a part of. Mahira told you that they had no idea what evil Ashwin was planning. He's turning these gods into his agents. They will wake up tomorrow unaware that their bodies have become instruments of his doom. Ashwathama had always hated how the Chiranjivis celebrated their immortality. But now their eternal lives will be as cursed as his own. Like him, they will also crave for their existence to end. They will undo all the good they have ever done as they go on infecting the world till the end of time.'

'Omega!' Atharva covered his mouth. 'The end of everything. And Yeva had looked up. Looked up when she had told us that we had no idea what Ashwin was planning.'

'Yes. Looked up at the horseshoe dangling from her ceiling,' Suri said.

'Not just the horseshoe. She was looking up at what was actually above all of us. Above that basement.'

The officer stiffened. 'Kalpataru laboratory. The fucking parasite.'

'Yeva had said she'll invert the pyramid. This parasite will pull man down to the very bottom of the food chain. Fodder for maggots. She had said Ashwathama will do nothing. Said we shall destroy each other. I see it now. Like that clan by the sea. Yeva had said like that clan by the sea.'

'What clan, Atharva?'

'Krishna's clan. The Yadavas of Dwarka. No outsider killed them. They themselves butchered each other in a single day. Ashwthama is not defiling us. He wants to defile Krishna. His final revenge against the god who had cursed his body. He now plans the same for him. What is this world but the body of Krishna. We are all the body of Krishna. Ashwathama infects us to infect Krishna. Can you imagine that chaos?'

'We saw some of that in Manu,' Patnaik said. 'It was unspeakable. If it hadn't been for her and Zahak, we would have never known. Five Chiranjivis lying now as ticking timebombs.'

'I heard what you told Suri about not questioning Ashwin,' the priest said. 'You are right. There's no telling what that beast may do.'

'Yes. We cannot interrogate him. But we can surely have a conversation.'

'Conversation?'

'I believe he's called for a presser tomorrow.'

'He has. Regarding his film and the attack on Lin,' Suri nodded. 'I'll be there.'

'Perfect.'

'What's on your mind, Om? Not the parasite?'

'Of course not. The parasite is off limits. But I can always remind Ashwathama that he himself is no better than a worm. We have discovered Yeva's soft spot. Now to bruise Ashwin's balls.'

'I don't understand.'

'The story of the blue jackal. The jackal dyes itself blue to become king of the forest. All animals hail it and carry it on their shoulders. But then the rains come, exposing its façade. I want to scratch some of Ashwin's blue paint tomorrow.'

He wrote three words on Indira's slate.

HOMICIDE
FOETICIDE
GENOCIDE
'I want to remind Ashwathama of his three cardinal sins.'

Chapter 47

THE CABLES WERE SLITHERING ALL OVER THE PLACE. Sprouting from television cameras like mammoth snakes towards OB vans parked outside to relay live feed. White, red and black snakes. Trampled underfoot by Ashwin as he entered leading his cortège. The actor was looking up from his mobile sporadically to joke with the journos. And the assembly was tittering back in chorus. Fearing perhaps that if they did not, the star would stop shining at them.

The PR person cleared her throat as they settled. The presser now in session.

'Before we open the floor to questions, Ashwin would like to issue a statement.'

The actor was posting a selfie on Instagram. He pulled the mike stem.

'Members of the media. Thank you, all, for joining us today. I also see my friend sitting right there at the back.'

All eyes turned.

'Chief Inspector Parag Suri.'

The officer nodded as Ashwin continued. 'I am sure everyone is aware of the issue at hand. What happened at the premiere of *Lin Zimik* was most unfortunate. I have known Lin for a really long time. She has always been strong, and I am sure she'll only emerge stronger. Given the extraordinary set of events, you will all appreciate the fact that we could not interact with the press immediately. There was just so much that had to be taken care of. Lin's coma. The shock to her family and fans. Our film's release. Mercifully things have settled down now, and we open this Friday.'

'This Friday?' a reporter frowned. 'Is that good timing given Lin's condition?'

'The film is a tribute to her. The fighter. A national champion. We are only doing what she would have wanted us to do. Not yield to tragedy but punch it right back in the face.'

'What exactly is Lin's state right now?'

'The latest update from the medical team says she's still comatose. They are constantly monitoring her.'

'Are they telling us when she might regain consciousness?'

'A coma puts you in a state of probabilities. Making estimates will be a futile exercise. We can only hope that it's sooner rather than later.'

A female scribe grabbed the mike. 'This is not a solitary case. In recent months, Guru Somnath, Lalit Trehan, Mahira Khan and Akram Qureshi have all been hospitalised in the same state of coma. All high-profile cases. What crazy epidemic is this? The police continues to withhold information, and many questions still remain unanswered. You say Lin was your friend, Ashwin. Will you be moving the machinery to shed some light? Why were these people targeted? Is there some sort of connection?'

The star's face deflected towards Suri. 'That's for the police to answer. She's asking vital questions, Suri. Is there a connection?'

'I wouldn't want to usurp your press conference, Ashwin,'

the officer smiled. 'This is about the premiere of *Lin Zimik*, and let's keep it that way. Regarding the other queries, I am glad the media realises that we are dealing with high-profile cases. This is hardly the platform to discuss or speculate about them. Information will be shared with the press as and when we deem fit. All I can say is that we are close. Very close. Not long now before we pull a few masks off.'

The actor clapped, but the scribe looked unimpressed. 'This attack on Lin. How could someone get away despite such large police presence at the premiere?'

'That's not fair,' Ashwin clicked his tongue. 'I am sure the cops did all they could have done. But I guess sometimes your adversary is just too fiendishly shrewd.'

'What about that teenager who died in the mall?' Another journalist chimed. 'There are reports that she was suffering from a skin disease.'

The PR nodded. 'Yes. The doctors are calling it ichthyosis. Apparently, it's an extremely rare skin condition that gives the body a scaly, snake-like appearance.'

'So, she was just a fan of Lin who got killed in all the confusion? Did the police drive an innocent person to death?'

No one spoke. The star's voice perforated the silence.

'You should've been careful, Suri. A life lost for nothing. I hope someone pays for it.'

'Someone surely will. Make no mistake.'

The voice had come from behind but it was not the officer. It was the man sitting right next to him. Om Patnaik.

'An act like that hardly goes unpunished. Do you know Ashwathama's story, Ashwin?'

The actor did not reply. He was putting his shades over his eyes. Patnaik continued.

'Ashwathama was the son of Drona. Born with a gem-encrusted forehead that kept him away from death and disease. But he sinned. And that evil coursing through his blood licked every bit of his divinity. They say he wanders by himself now covered with boils. Seeking nectar to heal himself. No one escapes justice, Ashwin. The universe is a moneylender most vile. It knows no mercy. Only its pound of flesh.'

The star's fingers were playing over his picture on his mobile screen. To and fro. Up and down. Expanding and contracting. The writer stood up.

'My name is Om Patnaik. Author and friend of Suri.'

'Yes. I have heard about you.'

'I was at the premiere that day. I am aiding him in his investigations.'

'So, you are his Watson?'

'We all have companions, Ashwin. Some out in the open. Some stashed way below the earth.'

The actor's fingers paused. He placed his cell gently on the table. Then leaning back, he crossed his arms.

'Yes, Watson. And you are right about justice. We all seek it. Seek justice for every wrong done. I hope you and Suri nab the offender. Or at least come up with concrete proof. One must be able to prove, Watson. Prove what they think they know. Even Christ had to perform miracles. No one believes you otherwise.'

Ashwin was grinning. Patnaik smiled back. 'Just three questions. Do you permit?'

The PR rep immediately intervened. 'We were only taking media questions here.'

'He calls me Watson. What I have is quite elementary. Three deaths.'

'Three deaths?'

'Yes. I am sure Ashwin will be intrigued. I read a recent interview of his where he said some fascinating things about death. Especially when asked why he indulges in such dangerous action stunts for his films, he said he had no fear of dying. Is that true, Ashwin?'

'Completely. One must not be terrified of death. It's life that can be much more frightening. Much more demanding. I would gladly embrace my death if it came for me.'

'But death seems to be coming for others surrounding you. That girl in the mall is just one of them. Three deaths have happened around you in the past few days.'

The PR rep opened her mouth again, but the actor halted her. He was seeing the press rumble. 'Go on. I want to hear this.'

Patnaik looked at his notepad.

Abhimanyu.

'A teenager fell to her death during the premiere of your film. A young life has ended, Ashwin, but you are going ahead with the film release. Some would say you are almost as indifferent to the death of others as you are to your own.'

'It's not indifference. Inevitability. The film is a labour of love about someone I truly admire. The teen's death is highly tragic, of course. And the fact that it happened during our premiere makes it even more distressing. I am pained beyond words, and I wish she could have been spared such a horrible fate. But sometimes you have to do what you have to do.'

'You call it fate but obviously some forces conspired. Dark forces plotting against her. Lin was attacked at the precise moment when the cops were chasing that teenager. In other words, the boxer was left unguarded because of this girl. That makes it quite obvious that the teen was deliberately placed at the venue to distract Suri and his men. A decoy.'

'Decoy?' A journo echoed.

'And it worked like a charm. Lin was assaulted, and the girl was mere collateral damage.'

Ashwin pursed his lips. 'This is ghastly.'

'It is. Who would do that to a teenager? Entice her into a trap. Make sure she was surrounded from all sides. No escape possible. End such a young life for personal gain.'

The actor sat still. Patnaik's words were conjuring an image before his eyes. A warrior pierced with swords. Countless swords like a porcupine. The writer's voice unstoppable.

'It's barbaric, Ashwin.'

The actor extended his hand and took a sip of water.

'Who would do that? Only someone utterly inhuman.'

The glass trembled. 'Inhuman may not be strictly correct, Watson.'

'Sorry.'

'That word means one who is not human. But unfortunately, it is humans who have been slaughtering children throughout the ages. No other creature on earth does that. Look at every war mankind has fought. Children continue to be the biggest casualties. And one can do nothing but mourn. Mourn for this teenager who got trapped and killed. Mourn for Anne Frank and Alan Kurdi. Mourn for millions of youngsters dead from war.'

The reporters were nodding. The writer stood muted for a moment. Then he spoke. 'You are right, Ashwin. We have butchered more of our young than anyone else.'

'Truly appalling.'

'Perhaps some of us relish killing a child.'

'No. No one would enjoy a thing like that. But war is a tricky business. Maybe it has its own morals and ethics. Its own conscience. Perhaps victory becomes the only dharma on a battlefield. We condemn a civilian who takes a life but we decorate a soldier who massacres hundreds. War celebrates death. Both sides fight to win. Win at every cost. They cheat. They lie. Everything blurs. Anything to triumph.'

'Even putting a young life to death?'

'As I said, we can do nothing but mourn. You will even hear voices trying to rationalise that. They will call it the victim's destiny. Say perhaps children are massacred for the faults of their families. Past generations who made grave mistakes. Provoked others into war, leading to such extreme violence. They will say death is never simple and cannot be viewed in isolation.'

'Voices like these are pathetic attempts at psychoanalysing wholesale murder. And I was talking about the teenager at the mall. Why are you speaking of war?'

The star loosened the tie around his throat. 'So was I. Her death is truly unfortunate. We can only hope that Suri and his men are able to catch those involved. And try to take solace from the fact that perhaps it was meant to be. Something that god willed. She had a cameo, and she exited. Cruel but unavoidable. All scripted up there.'

'No, Ashwin. This was scripted by someone not man enough to kill another man. A wimp who thought he also had courage because he murdered a teen. And then a foetus.'

The actor winced. 'Foetus?'

Patnaik was looking at the second item on his page.

Uttara

'Yes. I have news for you. For all of you. Everybody knows that Lin has slipped into coma. But no one knows that she was pregnant.'

The media exploded collectively. Turmoil swallowed the room and everyone present like chunks of morsel. The writer was staring fixedly at Ashwin. He had seen something that perhaps no one else had. That glorious face had convulsed brutally for a second.

He did not know...Ashwin did not know...

Did not know that he had done it again...

As they settled down, Patnaik spoke. 'Her family has permitted me to make the news public. They were planning to announce her pregnancy at the end of the premiere that day. You were not aware, Ashwin, were you? Aware that she was expecting?'

The actor was looking at his mobile screen again. A woman ripping her foetus from her womb and offering it to him.

'Ashwin?'

The actor's voice placid. Modulated without emotion. 'No. I was not aware.'

'Three months pregnant. It aborted this morning.'

'That's two deaths now,' the press sounded overwhelmed. 'Two deaths at the premiere.'

'Are you sure?' Ashwin's syllables still frigid. 'Sure, that it's dead? A foetus appearing to have died may sometimes come back to life.'

'That happened in the Mahabharata, Ashwin,' the writer said. 'Mythology.'

'But you mentioned Ashwathama. You almost sounded like those voices today that are constantly telling everyone that our epics are not fantasy. That these men truly lived and died. At least some of them.'

'No, Ashwin. Lin's foetus is gone. And all the gods and god's men cannot put it together again.'

'Horrible. I wish she had announced that she was with child.'

'Announced? You think the attacker would have spared Lin if he had known?'

Silence prevailed. The writer shook his head. 'I don't think so. A murderer who arranged for a teenager to be butchered would never think twice before wrecking a foetus.'

'Absolutely, Watson. I pray for Lin. And I pray for every mother out there who's being made to undergo the same agony.'

'Every mother?'

'Of course. It's dreadful to see foeticide becoming a rampant practice now. Hundreds of foetuses are being deliberately destroyed every day. Female foeticide clocking an all-time high. These figures are shaming humanity. How can man choke so many lives inside wombs? We must take this opportunity to condemn each and every human committing this crime. The worst crime as you put it.'

The gathering applauded aloud. Ashwin still speaking. 'This world has become a mess. Some are predicting it shall end soon. Lie rotting in space. Brains shrinking and bodies disintegrating. You say you are a writer. Can this world be saved, Watson? Can it be saved?'

'You are not the first to ask that question, Ashwin. And you won't be the last. And every time the answer shall be yes. This earth violated the most powerful cosmic laws to come into existence. Life here is the highest degree of probability. Why do you think the human DNA is coiled like a spring? We are all elastic. The harder you crush us, the higher we spring back. We are sinners. We are survivors. And we intend to keep surviving.'

A stringer whistled. The actor was clapping. 'Are we done?'

'Last one.'

Night Massacre

'Another death at the premiere?'

'No, Ashwin. This one is far removed but again connected to you.'

'Careful, Watson. Statements like that can land me in trouble. Who are you talking about?'

'The junior researcher at Kalpataru. He was found hanging in his flat.'

'The suicide. Another wasted life. We shall be calling a presser for that soon.'

'Not suicide. Murder.'

The PR rep was shaking her fingers. 'This press conference is about the premiere. We are not discussing other cases here.'

But the press had latched on to that word.

Murder...

Their decibels rising. Patnaik's third revelation had just tripled the thrill quotient of the presser. The actor looked at Suri.

'Why does he say it was murder?'

'Our investigations corroborate that. Someone entered his flat at night and overpowered him.'

The journos were clamouring for more now, but the PR rep postponed all queries to a separate presser for later. The writer took a step forward.

'Think about it, Ashwin. A secret attack at night. How

cowardly it is to ambush someone like that. Strike when someone's least prepared. Can offer least resistance. Unarmed and unsuspecting. Again, a contemptible weakling who dares not challenge in broad daylight. A worm, Ashwin. A worm crawling out after dark. A *pishacha*. Creature of the lowest order. Who would be so spineless to do that?'

'Hard to say. Sounds like a follower of Chanakya.'

'Chanakya?'

'Yes. The modus operandi you describe sounds like guerrilla warfare. And Chanakya who advocates war tactics in *Arthashastra* also endorses this technique. Apparently great leaders like Mao Zedong and Che Guevara also adopted it. Looks like our attacker was following their principles of combat.'

'Principles?' Patnaik laughed. 'I hardly think this attacker has any principles, Ashwin. Maybe his father had none too.'

Was the actor's forehead bubbling?

'So, this ignorant father taught his son nothing.'

Palpitating now. Was a deluge attempting to charge through Ashwin's skin? The actor's hands swallowed the mike. 'Let's keep the father out of this, Watson. This is no platform to abuse a parent.'

'Sure. Let's abuse the son who shames his father then. Scatters bodies of three innocent victims.'

'Victims? There you go again. The dead need not always be victims. I told you death can be a release. It can liberate you. Make you fly with air or flow with water. But life pins you down like gravity. Do not grieve for the dead. Those three have found a doorway. Grieve for those who go on living. Who must grab a handful of meaning from their own chaos every day. And believe me when I tell you this.

Nothing would make me happier than to bring those three back to life. Make all of you immortal if I could. Would that make you all happy? I know I would be happy.'

He watched the gathering looking at him. Whispering and scribbling in their pads. The PR rep speaking into his ears. He stood up to leave. Patnaik was standing before the dais now.

'No, Ashwin. I don't want to be immortal. You are right. Men have done wrong and will continue to do so. Kill children. Mutilate wombs. Ambush the innocent. But the world shall not end. It will simply ensure that every sinner is punished. Each one of them. I told you the universe spares no one. It never will.'

The star was descending now. A few mobbed him for autographs. As Ashwin obliged, he scribbled something on a piece of paper and handed it to the writer.

You may not be immortal...But you did bleed one.

Chapter 48

HE WAS SITTING IN THE SHADE OF THE NEHUSHTAN. BACK propped against the staff, and legs sprawled into Yeva's lap. Water was trickling from a pipe overhead, and he had moved under the wooden serpent to keep himself dry. Watching news reports of his presser on television.

'Om Patnaik. The one who bled Hanuman for you.'

'Yes, Ashwin,' Yeva was clipping his toenails. 'Writes esoteric.'

'He knows quite a lot.'

'They all do. Suri had told me about him and the priest.'

'The parasite? Do they know about the parasite?'

'I doubt that.'

He kicked her in the stomach. 'I had warned you not to send them those objects. But you wouldn't listen. You wanted to ridicule him. Supremely confident that he wouldn't be able to understand anything. They have sucked the marrow out and are hurling the bones at me in public.'

'It can't always be about you,' she hissed. 'This was about me. My pain. Healing some of my wounds as you seek to heal yours. How can you not see that?'

He pulled her into his arms as a film of water coated her eyes. Blue eyes melting like glaciers.

'So, what if they know, Ashwin? Have they been able to

save a single Chiranjivi so far? Can they stop the parasite even if they find out? They are mere humans. And knowledge might even precipitate action. They may themselves hasten their defeat and our triumph. Patnaik's just an author who questions anomalies. His interest in us would be purely academic.'

Ashwin smirked. 'Was that why he landed there to question me? I who am neither human nor divine.'

'From what you have told me, he seemed interested in reminding you of your sins. What the world calls your three cardinal sins.'

'And I reminded him what he had done. What his race had been doing. Committing exactly the same sins many times over. And sin is a relative term, Yeva. Who decides what's a sin and who's a sinner? If killing a young Abhimanyu was a sin, then so was killing the geriatric Bhishma. If we slaughtered that teenage warrior deceptively, they beheaded their guru dishonestly. If they are right, then even I am not wrong.'

'And the nocturnal massacre?'

'Ah! The genocide. What about how Bhima slaughtered one-hundred Kauravas? How his demon seed Ghatothkacha deliberately collapsed over our army when he died, crushing thousands? Not to mention the zillion holocausts carried out by humans. What exactly is the issue here? That I killed so many or that I struck at midnight? Besides, it wasn't really me. I believe it was Mahadev who possessed my body. My sword. I believe he directed me that night just as the Dark One directed Arjuna throughout the war.'

'Did Mahadev also command you to scorch Uttara's foetus?'

'What's wrong, Yeva? Do I smell maternal instincts? Sudden emotion for mankind?'

'Never,' she spat. 'I am simply awed at your mind that tried ending a human life even before it began.'

'Hardly as wicked as staking your own wife at dice. That was the only time the five Pandavas took a decision on their own and look what they did. Besides, technically the foeticide never even happened. The Dark One placed his hand over the debris inside Uttara's womb and made it whole again.'

'The media reports of your presser are rather interesting. Everyone has a different take.'

Ashwin chucked his mobile at the TV in rage. 'That bastard writer!'

'Calm down. You fielded Patnaik's questions perfectly.'

'Who gives anyone the right to question me? Remind me what all I had done? They are all his minions. The Dark One's minions. Out there to rankle me. They lament his death but know nothing of my deathlessness. The pain he suffered from that hunter's arrow was but a fraction of what I endure each moment. His evil eye follows me everywhere.'

'Not just him. That other woman's also trailing you these days.'

'Which woman?'

'Your leading lady. I found you both rehearsing inside your vanity van.'

Ashwin smiled. His toes climbed up to Yeva, tickling her nipples. 'Is someone feeling leftout? A tad jealous perhaps?'

She drove the nail file into his leg. Ran it along the thigh, lacerating his skin. Making wavy lines like the ones snakes leave on sand.

'No one knows you like I do, Ashwin. No one can own you like I do.'

'No one, Yeva. No one.'

She was licking him now. Licking the blood lining the scratch. Ashwin laid his hand on her head.

'You demolish me and build me again.'

'The Chiranjivis lie demolished too.'

'Not long now. They shall all awaken as apostles of Ashwathama. Do my bidding as Patnaik did yours. Did you have fun with the Immortals?'

'Most with Lin. She battled hard. But the rest welcomed me as if they were grateful. I can't seem to forget Mahira's face when she allowed me inside her. Spread her belt wide open as I entered. Joined to her at the hip, striking again and again. They all said the gods had sent me and they were prepared. Their devotion confuses me. Is such reverence possible?'

'Sounds like you have enjoyed.'

'I enjoy it when I remind Suri again and again how insignificant he is. When he saw Patnaik with Somnath's blood all over him. When he saw Mahira smack herself with that horseshoe on air. When he saw that girl's blood in the mall. Just one more left now. The last one. The final Charanjivi. And Suri has no idea what's going to hit him. None of them have.'

The star yanked her hair. 'Come. Serpents incubate gods during their death sleep in between incarnations. Envelope me so that when I awaken, I shall be Ashwathama again.'

A moment later, he opened his eyes. 'Will it be done, Yeva?'

'My father who art in hell. Thy will be done.'

He laughed as she picked up *Twilight*. 'Ashwin.'

'What?'

'Are vampires real?'

'Of course. Have you forgotten what Bhima did when he killed Dushasan?'

Chapter 49

If the ocean appears blue reflecting that sky overhead
The firmament above this field should have turned red
Hair, skin and rotting flesh were clogging all his toes
Stinking under a sweating sun as the dying bodies froze
Vultures pecking intestines and wolves fracturing bones
Animal noises drowning under shrieking feminine tones
Mouths filled with maggots like bodies coating the field
Asking the rancid martyrs what profit did the war yield
Both his soles crimson now and yet further did he tread
The Rishiputra back again for all his friends were dead
Stars watching corpse clusters creating their own zodiac
The night igniting funeral pyres that set ablaze the dark
Longing to avenge his friends and to set their souls free
He was suddenly distracted by chaos high up on a tree
An owl had pounced upon crows sleeping in their nest
Cawing in fear on being so violently aroused from rest
The bird of prey taking advantage of its nocturnal sight
Blinded in the dark the crows hardly putting up a fight
Shedding black feathers while the owl nibbled each eye
The thought scorched Rishiputra like a bolt from the sky
At midnight his naked sword ambushed the enemy camp
The sky closed its eyes and blew out its spherical lamp
He believed Mahadev was possessing his murderous blade

Was that massacre of the sleeping truly divine crusade?
The five brothers absent, but in the dark he hardly knew
Metal stabbing again and again as their five sons it slew
Many a dream interrupted as that sword sliced through
The grass next morning staring at that red tinted dew
The field now indifferent at the fresh blood on its breast
Forced by men to drink so much in this eighteen-day fest
Silver Prince and his brothers lost though they had won
They set out now to assassinate their dead teacher's son
As they advanced the Rishiputra hurled a weapon divine
Fierce missile that threatened to crack the cosmic spine
Vyasa appeared instructing both to recall their projectile
But Rishiputra had never learnt to turn that monster vile
Little knowledge they verily say is a most dangerous thing
For inside it nestles more poison than the scorpion's sting
He knew the Silver Prince's daughter-in-law was with child
Wife of the warrior lad they had butchered like coyotes wild
His malignant mind steered his weapon towards that womb
To demolish their race by making it their final seed's tomb
Krishna intervened and resurrected that dismembered child
Tore that jewel from Rishiputra and had him forever exiled
The grime within his very soul would drain from every pore
His face hiding itself in shame under layers of pus and gore
And so that night roams the earth searching for its moon
That curse seeking blue nectar tore model it into a boon

Chapter 50

'THE LAST ONE.'

'Bali. Who could be Bali?'

'This will tell us. Exhibit A.'

Nothing ostentatious about the final object but the envelope encasing it demanded attention. Motley paper displaying five colours. All the five colours that had arrived so far.

'The five serpents,' Patnaik said.

'No, Om,' the officer smiled wanly. 'The five times we lost. The five times Yeva won. The five Chiranjivis bleeding and lying in coma. She spits in our face one last time.'

'And gives us one last chance. The final one. Ashwin had asked me if this world can be saved. I want to tell him we did our best. Fought like Lin till the very end.'

The envelope had produced a piece of black chart paper. Coating all of it was a composition in water colours. Psychedelic shades dramatically contrasting against the background but the style strangely juvenile.

'Obviously hand-painted,' the writer observed.

'Not just hand-painted, Om,' Atharva said. 'Painted deliberately in a childish hand.'

'Yes. Bumbling figures and colours all over the lines.'

'It's her. Yeva. She's drawn this.'

'You think so?'

'Childish doodle on black paper. She's mocking Indira's slate drawings.'

Suri lifted the painting. 'Indira? How would Yeva know about the child's drawings?'

'She knows everything.'

They were looking at the image of an enormous serpent right in the centre of the sheet. It was coiled up vertically. Coils resting above one another like a towering pillar. Above the reptile's head hovered a circular disc with serrated edges. A large gold-coloured expanse rippled beneath the snake. The upper surface of this area had fires burning. Deep below that inferno were blobs of red, blue and green sprinkled all through that golden stretch.

'The last Chiranjivi, Bali.' The officer tapped on the envelope, 'Tell me about Bali.'

'This is not the Bali who was Sugriva's elder brother in the Ramayana,' Patnaik said. 'This Bali or Mahabali was a benevolent emperor of the Asuras. He was the grandson of the ardent Vishnu devotee Prahalad. Such was Bali's prowess that he vanquished Indra and many other gods to bring all the three worlds of the universe under his banner. A just king whose long rule was marked by peace and fortune.'

'Until Vishnu tricked him,' the priest chipped in.

'Yes. When Bali conquered heaven, the gods pleaded with Vishnu to reclaim it for them. Vishnu took the Vamana or dwarf avatar and reached Bali's Ashwamedha Yagna seeking alms. Requesting him for a piece of land as large as three strides of his feet. As soon as Bali consented, the Vamana grew gigantic. His first stride covered earth and the underworld while his second stride covered the heavens leaving nowhere to place his third stride. Bali realised that this dwarf was Vishnu himself and offered his head as the third stepping stone.'

'His head? Bali offered his head?'

'Yes. The only thing he could do to honour his word. Vishnu obliged and his foot pushed Bali into the underworld. The king desired to meet his people on earth once every year which was granted by the lord and is celebrated as Onam.'

'Bali's attribute?'

'Power. The power he held over heaven, earth and hell. The power of a ruler who was kind and compassionate. Power that he knew came with much responsibility.'

'So, a man of power. Obviously politics.'

'Power is no longer exclusive to politics, Suri,' Patnaik countered. 'Like knowledge, power has evolved into a broad terminology. We are in a millennium now where power poles have massively shifted. New frontiers have opened up exercising influence like never before and Bali could be any one of them.'

'What's this fucking painting telling us then?'

'The serpent here is obviously the central clue. This stretch of gold underneath could be land. Or perhaps water. But water on fire?'

'It is water,' Atharva declared.

'Are you sure?'

'Yes. Look at the ripples. That's a water body. And I think it's the Yamuna.'

'Yamuna?'

'Yes. And that would make this snake Kalia.' The priest bent over the chart paper. 'You must be familiar with the tale that serpent Kalia had poisoned the waters of the Yamuna in

Vrindavan. Krishna tamed the monster and commanded it to leave. Look at the painting. The water is on fire. That is how Yamuna boiled due to Kalia's venom. The flying disc on top is nothing but the Sudarshan Chakra symbolising Krishna who danced on the serpent's head.'

'And these coloured chunks inside the water?' the officer asked.

'Can't figure that out. This is the best I have unless you have something better.'

'I do,' Suri said. 'This golden expanse below the snake is surely water but not the Yamuna. It's no river. I think it's the fucking ocean.'

'Ocean?' the writer echoed him. 'Are you talking about…'

'Yes. Churning of the Ocean. The story in the Puranas where the gods and demons churned the ocean using a snake.'

Patnaik lifted an eyebrow. 'Someone's evolving. Suddenly our cop here is an expert on mythology.'

'Hardly, Om. Came across this story in the paper yesterday. The headline had something about snakes and that caught my eye. Didn't they use the serpent Vasuki to churn the ocean?'

'They did.'

'I feel that's what this painting depicts. That's Vasuki. These coloured blobs are gemstones. The Ratnas that emerged from the waters. And the ocean fumed and smoked when venom rose to the surface with all that churning. Hence these fires.'

The writer shook his head. 'You are both wrong.'

'Both of us?' Suri sputtered. 'We can't both be wrong. You mean there's a third possibility?'

'Indeed. And most probably the right one. This cannot

be the Kalia legend because it does not explain these jewels. And as for the churning episode, Vasuki was tied to Mount Mandara horizontally. The snake here is coiled up vertically like a giant column. Also, the venom that floated up was blue in colour. It turned Mahadev into Neelkanth, but Yeva here has coloured the water golden.'

'Fuck Yeva. What's your take then?'

'This serpent is neither Kalia nor Vasuki. It's Vasuki's elder brother.'

'Elder brother?'

Atharva pulled the sheet. 'Sheshnag?'

'Exactly,' Patnaik slapped his thigh. 'The one that lies coiled at the base of the universe. Remember we are talking about Bali here. He also resides in the netherworld like Sheshnag. And this chakra atop denotes Vishnu who reclines on this great serpent as it floats above the ocean. The disc also symbolises earth or the entire galaxy that Sheshnag balances upon its head.'

'And the fires? These jewels?'

'What you see here is one of the lesser-known stories of Sheshnag. Have you heard of a place called Manikaran, Atharva?'

'Of course. That famous pilgrimage in Himachal.'

'Yes. This painting depicts the legend of how that place was created.'

'What legend?'

'They say Shiva and Parvati were once travelling through that valley when the goddess dropped one of her gems into a stream. The lord summoned Sheshnag to retrieve the stone. As soon as the mighty serpent hissed, the fire of its breath boiled the waters of the region. Much of that stream evaporated revealing gold and silver and hundreds of sparkling jewels, pleasing Parvati.'

'And so, the gold and these stones in the painting?' the priest indicated the paper.

'Yes. And this fire depicts the scorching waters of Manikaran. Very interesting because the place is famous now for its hot-water springs.'

'True. Those springs are believed to have curative powers. I have known many families flocking those banks with sick members, hoping for a miracle.'

Suri struck the table. 'We need one here too. Three different versions and we are not even fucking close. Let's say your story works, Om. This is Sheshnag creating Manikaran. What now? How do we locate Bali?'

'We have identified what Yeva has sent us,' the writer said. 'Bali's guna is power. That should to be the key here. What power motifs can you make out in this picture?'

Atharva circled the disc on top. 'The Sudarshan Chakra is an icon for the entire universe. Rotating on Vishnu's finger, it symbolises supreme individual power. One man controlling everything.'

'I remember a 2013 report that the Indian Army was developing BrahMos II along the principles of the Chakra,' the officer added. 'An intelligent hypersonic missile that shall destroy the target and fly back to the base to be reloaded. Is this painting talking about military power?'

'Possible,' Patnaik shrugged. 'The other element here is the serpent coiled up vertically like a tower. A skyscraper. This might suggest the Indian construction sector which has several power players. As for these jewels down here, they seem pretty obvious.'

'Wealth?'

'Yes. Massive wealth.'

'So, Bali's fucking loaded?'

'Seems like it, Suri. And if you are that loaded, you will surely find your name on a certain global list.'

They watched his fingers drumming over the computer keyboard. Watching what had materialised on screen.

Forbes List—The World's Billionaires

'This should narrow things down,' the writer moved the cursor to *Countries* and selected *India*. The page instantly returned a roll-call of the richest in the nation.

'Eighty-four names,' the priest exclaimed. 'This will take forever.'

Suri yanked the keyboard. 'You are looking at the wrong list, Om.'

'Wrong list?'

'Bali's attribute is Power. One may have all the wealth in the world and one may still not wield much power. The list we should be looking at is this one.'

He was jabbing at what he had pulled out of the Internet.

Forbes List—World's Most Powerful People

'Let's see how many of those eighty-four moneybags feature on this list.'

The officer clicked on *India*. They were waiting. Another second later the page changed.

'Two names,' Atharva exulted. 'Just two.'

'Actually just one,' the writer touched the screen. 'Only one man from that billionaire list has also made it to this power list. The other Indian here hardly has that kind of money. He only exercises maximum political power.'

The billionaire was business magnate Kiran Kripalani

positioned at thirty-six.

The other man was Samar Bedi. Prime minister of India ranking nine.

'This is good,' the priest rubbed his palms. 'The two most powerful men in India right now. If Bali is really all about power, we should strike gold here. It must be one or the other.'

'Obviously not the PM?' Suri balked.

'Why not?' Patnaik queried. 'You were talking about politics. Bedi with all his de facto power would be the most obvious answer.'

'Too impossible. Ashwin would not dare this far.'

'Ashwin has no choice anymore. He will do whatever needs to be done now to acquire that final drop.'

'But you are talking about the PM. A near assassination attempt. This is fucking suicidal. Where will they even begin?'

The officer's voice had risen high as if to drown out the sound of his beating heart. Atharva placed the painting before him.

'Pertinent questions, Suri, but I am also convinced that they are targeting Bedi. The Chakra on the top here surely denotes military power. Constitutionally, the president of India is the Supreme Commander of the armed forces but the actual executive power for defence lies with the PM. It has to be Bedi. Even Om agrees.'

'I don't,' the writer shook his head.

'Sorry?'

'I said the prime minister was the perfect choice. And that's precisely why I disagree. It's too obvious. Too much of a cliché. My money is on the billionaire.'

'But the Chakra?'

'That disc can have various interpretations. Besides, how do you account for the jewels? They can only mean enormous riches and that has to be Kripalani.'

Suri picked up the chart paper. 'Looks like we have a deadlock. Only way out for both of you now is to own as many of the remaining elements on this painting as you can. The more you own, the stronger your claim shall be. Let's start with the serpent.'

Patnaik was already eyeing the reptile. Sheshnag all coiled up. Coils above one another. He took the sheet from the officer's hands. He was counting something.

'What is it?' the priest asked.

'I think I can stake a claim on the snake.'

'Tell us.'

'Its body is wound up into coils standing upon each other. Standing vertically like a tall structure. A tower or a high-rise.'

'Yes. We have discussed that.'

'But we never counted the number of coils. There are twenty-five of them. And that would denote a building with twenty-five storeys. You both have surely seen Kripalani's house.'

The men spoke not, but the writer knew the vision flaring inside their minds right now. The billionaire's home was a soaring skyscraper comprising twenty-five floors. Named Ionia, the mansion dominated the city's horizon and was regularly featured among the most expensive private residences in the world.

'Not to mention, the house is located in South Mumbai,' Patnaik traced the serpent standing perpendicular to the water body below it. 'A building by the sea.'

Atharva instantly retorted. 'If you are talking numbers then I can do that too. You say the twenty-five coils specify Kripalani's house. Two plus five equals seven. And that gives you the PM's house. The official residence of the Indian prime minister.'

The officer nodded, '7 Race Course Road.'

'Exactly.'

'Thin ice,' the writer clinched his fingers. 'Wafer-thin ice. And I have much more than numbers. What is Kripalani's company called? Balance India. Sheshnag balances the universe on its head. And just as Sheshnag is the eldest serpent, Kiran is the eldest of the Kripalani brothers.'

The priest's face was collapsing now. He pointed at the painting. 'And the fires? If Bali is Kripalani, how do you account for that water on fire?'

Patnaik gazed at the sheet.

Water on fire…

Water never catches fire…And water is never golden…

But these ripples…

Something like water then…And something that burns…

Golden fluid that ignites…

Inflammable…

Kripalani's golden liquid…

Gold that pleased Parvati…Uncovered by a snake…

His eyes flickered. Burnished as if they were reflecting a lightbulb that had suddenly lit up over his head.

'I can account for it. Except that it's not water.'

'What do you mean?'

'It's oil.'

'Oil?'

'Yes. Oil. One of the largest components of Kripalani's

company is oil and natural gas. Especially that large oil rig installed by him in that river basin in south India.'

The writer was keying into the computer again. He swung the monitor towards them. As they looked at the online photograph, Patnaik propped Yeva's painting right next to the screen. The two images side by side. Almost identical. Kripalani's oil platform towering above the river just like the vertical serpent rising above that golden stretch.

'Both go underwater fishing for treasures. One draws up oil while the other unearthed jewels. This painting has so many layers.'

The priest yielded. 'You win. It's all piling up in your favour. You were right. Kripalani is Bali. We must connect the Chakra with him now. The last element here. That'll settle it beyond doubt.'

Suri had opened up the man's biography on the Net. 'What else does the billionaire do that can help us? Textiles. Petrochemicals. Telecom. Cricket India League. Life Sciences. Retail…'

He paused. Light had filled Patnaik's eyes. A light the officer knew only too well.

'You have it, Om, don't you?'

The writer logged into the Cricket India League website. Kripalani's team represented Maharashtra and had been christened Bombay Boys. He placed the cursor right above their logo.

Sudarshan Chakra.

Atharva cried out in delight, but the officer hushed him.

'Not yet. We still need the blue.'

The blue. They had forgotten the Nilotpal. Minutes passed, but they found absolutely nothing.

'Can we talk to the man directly?' Patnaik asked Suri.

'Speak about what? How will you even frame that question?'

'We are running out of options here. Besides, Kripalani knows you.'

'Hardly,' the officer protested. 'Just met him once last December at his birthday gala. One of my senior officers had been invited, and he dragged me along to...'

'Birthday?'

'Yes.'

'December?'

'Right.'

'Kripalani was born in December?'

'Yes, Om.'

'Why didn't you tell me that?'

'Tell you what?'

'December.'

The writer was hammering away at the computer once more.

'Here you go.'

Birthstones. Twelve precious stones assigned to the twelve months of the year. Patnaik's finger underlined the jewel for December.

'Turquoise. Kripalani's birthstone is blue.'

The officer seized the envelope.

Exhibit...

Name...

Address...

His blood congealed. His fingers strangulating it.

'What is it?'

'No date, Om.'

'What?'

'Date,' the officer turned. His breath fell from his mouth and crashed on the floor. 'Date of the attack. Not mentioned on this one.'

'Impossible.'

'Not here.'

'We have to speak to Kripalani. We have no choice. But will that Chiranjivi listen to us?'

'Not in India. He's in Moscow.'

Suri spoke again.

'Kiran Kripalani is going to be attacked. And we don't know when.'

He saw the white scroll fluttering. The one that carried the lines by D.H. Lawrence. The poem that had arrived on the very first day when it had all begun.

For he seemed to me again like a king,
Like a king in exile, uncrowned in the underworld,
Now due to be crowned again…

Chapter 51

THEY WERE BACK IN THE HOSPITAL WARD.

The priest's arrangement may have looked like a five-pointed star from space, but the truth was purely clinical. Five bodies had been stretched out in five directions like a human pentacle. The Chiranjivis still unmoving. Five MRI monitors had been installed next to each of them. Their screens imaging cross sections of their brains as if the organ had been pulled out and plastered over them. Indira was standing in the centre of this pentagram. The axle of this alignment. Watching the five immortals and the three mortals.

Patnaik. Suri. Atharva. Standing before a monitor each.

A triangle enclosing the pentacle.

'Will this work, Atharva?' the officer switched his mobile off.

'I don't know. I have only carried out what she wanted.'

They were gazing at her slate drawing again. The pentacle with a dot in the centre.

Patnaik's eyes were riveted to the child. 'I am worried. She's exceptional, of course, but can she handle this?'

'Have faith in the Indigo, Om,' the priest reassured. 'Clairaudience is not a myth.'

'Clair…what?'

'Clairaudience, Suri,' the writer pronounced the word slowly. 'The psychic ability to receive information from another realm or dimension without sensory channels. Purely through the medium of the mind. One of the most celebrated traits of an Indigo. Indira will invoke it to contact the Immortals and obtain any possible data about the final attack.'

'You mean telepathy?'

'Telepathy happens between two minds existing in the same realm,' Atharva explained. 'But the Chiranjivis do not inhabit the same dimension as us. Their mortal body is simply a vessel holding forces of nature that dwell on a much higher territory. Indira will try to reach them there. Perhaps communicate the way Joan of Arc had interacted with divine voices.'

'Joan of Arc?'

'Sure. Maybe she was an Indigo too.'

The officer's eyes circled the five prone bodies. 'What about them? You are certain they will respond? Tell us if they know anything about when Kripalani will be assaulted?'

'We shall find out. Coma is not death, Suri. More like a computer that has hung. The body may be inert, but the brain remains wakeful. Active. Open to every stimulus and signal. Since communication here shall be purely through the psyche, it should work.'

'Does she need to be restrained? Tied up or something?'

Atharva smiled. 'No. Even if we did, she'll pull the rope to pieces.'

Indira was walking around inside the pentagram. Touching the Immortals one by one. Vibhishan's feet. Kripacharya's mouth. Hanuman's bosom. Vyasa's head. Parashurama's arm. Completing her revolution, she stood still at the centre. Eyes closed. Still like water in a backyard pool. Her scar staring at them. They were waiting. The men and the monitors. Waiting and watching. Not a sound or word.

And then her eyelids burst open, as if a bomb had gone off within her body. Her eyeballs stared. Grey eyeballs glinting like metal ball bearings. Threatening to fly at them like shrapnel. But then the eyeballs travelled upwards. Slowly and steadily up north as the eyes rotated. Vanishing completely into her sockets. Leaving behind nada. Two white vacuums.

'Her eyes...'

'She has found her way,' the priest yelled. 'Making contact now.'

A face without eyes like a Roman bust with blank sockets. Seeing nothing and everything. Standing there but existing somewhere else. No longer Indira. She was a portal now. A pathway between this dimension and another. The men were trying to look away and yet kept coming back to that face as if sucked in by those white holes.

A beep gored the silence.

Patnaik turned towards the MRI monitor in front of him mapping Somnath's brain. A section of that digital image was glowing bright red.

'He's responding ba...'

Beep...Beep...Beep...Beep

Four more. One by one.

All of them red now. Five brains activated in a single sequence.

'They have forged a link,' Atharva tapped on the part of the brain image that was throbbing red. 'That's the medial prefrontal cortex. The Me Centre, or, what we call in Tantra, the self-referencing centre. The region where memories are stored. The Chiranjivis surely know something about the intended attack on Kripalani. They are digging into this area of their brains to share the information with Indira. Like a computer scanning through its folders. As the Immortals respond, their memories are getting stimulated, triggering this neural response that we are seeing on screen.'

The red pulsating harder now. The chalk in the child's hand was whirling like a dervish on the slate. Information flowing freely through this highway. Ascending and descending. Invisible arteries above them channelling knowledge. She had become a human fax machine generating a page.

'Does she have it all?' Suri was getting impatient.

They were waiting. Her eyes still empty. The five brains glimmering like glowworms.

'She must.'

The red flares were dimming. Darker and darker. Indira lifted the chalk and made a cross on her forehead.

'What's that?'

The lights faded and died one after the other. Indira's eyes were thawing. As her body drooped, Atharva's arms clinched her, handing the slate to Patnaik. The images the Indigo had produced.

A snake devouring the sun...

A snake devouring the moon...

She was drinking carrot juice from Atharva's hands. The officer tugged at the slate. 'What is this, Om?'

'Can't you make out?'

'Tell me.'

'Rahu and Ketu. Serpent demons in Hindu mythology

who swallow the sun and the moon causing…'

'Eclipses,' Suri finished the sentence.

'Yes. Both these demons were beheaded by Vishnu for consuming the nectar that had surfaced from the Churning of the Ocean. Their bodies perished, but their heads remained immortal due to the Amrit. Rahu devours the sun while Ketu gobbles up the moon.'

'The eclipse. The solar eclipse tomorrow,' Atharva murmured. 'A total solar eclipse. They are saying it shall be one of the longest in history.' He pulled the slate. 'Tomorrow, Suri. It's going to happen tomorrow. The attack on Kripalani. Tomorrow when the sky goes dark.'

'Is that what the Chiranjivis are telling us? The final attack during an eclipse?'

'Maybe all the attacks were.' Patnaik said.

'All?'

The writer's eyes were gyrating over his mobile. Running through cyberspace. They appeared loaded when he looked up.

'Yes. They were. All five of them. An eclipse had occurred during every assault.'

'Are you sure?'

'Look for yourself. All those five days. Each assault happened when an eclipse was on.'

'Five eclipses in one year?' the officer frowned.

'Sure. You can have as many as seven in a single calendar year.'

'But surely we would have noticed these eclipses?'

'Not these ones. These five were all partial.'

'Partial?'

'Yes. Such an eclipse covers just a fraction of the solar or lunar diameter. Hardly visible.'

'But surely the media?'

'Why would the media bother when you have something way more dramatic happening in the sky on the same day?'

'Red rainbows!'

'Precisely. Dotting the sky on all those five days. They make a much more exciting visual than a partial eclipse. But the one tomorrow is the magnum opus. A total solar eclipse.'

'But why attack during a fucking eclipse?'

'For a very good reason,' the priest said. 'An eclipse increases an Ichhadhari's power many times over. As the sun or moon is swallowed by one mythical snake, it instantly vitalises another. Serpents in the sky invigorating the one on earth. Recall how she completely hypnotised you or overcame Lin. She is already powerful, and an eclipse further compounds that. But there's also a handicap.'

'What handicap?'

'An Ichhadhari cannot shape-shift during an eclipse.'

'Interesting.'

'It is. Radiations from the photosphere prevent that conversion of energy. She will remain literally locked in the form that she was in when the eclipse began until the eclipse ends.'

'That explains it!' Patnaik observed. 'Yeva was in human form throughout during Somnath's attack. And a reptile when she bled Mahira and escaped.'

'Precisely,' Atharva nodded. 'It also explains something that's been bothering me. Ashwin found Yeva many years back. Why wait all this while and start attacking only now? They knew about the eclipses. Waiting for this year when the six eclipses would take place. Striking at the exact hour.'

'Ashwathama's signature all over again. He attacked the

Pandava camp in the middle of the night. He attacks now during eclipses when it gets dark. The eclipse tomorrow is scheduled for 11.52 a.m. Zero hour, Suri.'

'11.52 a.m.?'

'Yes.'

'Guess where Kripalani is going to be then.' The officer pulled out a full-page ad from the newspaper.

'*Maquillage*!'

'Yes. *Maquillage* 2019. Ashwin has cordially invited him as the chief guest. The tycoon's returning from Moscow tomorrow morning and will be at the show by 11 o'clock.'

'The stage,' Atharva spoke as if he could see the curtain shrouding Kiran Kripalani's body. The arclights burning it and the chorus singing a requiem. 'The actor is setting the stage. The grand finale. Ashwin is placing Bali in his own arena. The Chiranjivi will embrace his fate as Yeva strikes him in the dark.'

Patnaik flicked the ward light on and off tensely. 'Twenty-four hours to the eclipse, Suri. We must...'

His finger jammed. No longer switching the light on. He heard Suri's voice fumbling in the dark.

'What happened, Om?'

'Did you see that?'

'See what?'

'The cricketer.'

'Cricketer?'

'I think he raised his hands.'

The writer slammed the switch on. Was this an apparition that the light and dark in the room had procreated?

Akram's hands were covering his eyes...

Still comatose, but his palms shielding both his eyes. Lying still. Suddenly Lin now. And Trehan. And Somnath. One by one it was happening again. The remaining Chiranjivis doing the same. All of them in clockwork motion.

Hands rising and covering their eyes.

Chapter 52

THE ACTOR'S LATEST TROPHY LOOKED A LOT LIKE HIM. Yeva installed it on his shelf.

Face of the Year—Ashwin Tomar

She was looking at all the Ashwins around her. So many of him surrounding her in his living room. His enormous framed photographs. A life-size replica of his wax statue at Tussauds. His songs airing on the television screen. His interview playing on the laptop. His face on magazine covers on the table. She had read that Krishna always performed Raasleela with one hundred and eight gopis. And every time the god would split into one hundred and eight Krishnas so that each gopi could have her own personal consort. He had again divided himself into sixteen thousand Krishnas when he had married his sixteen thousand wives. Yeva grinned as she gazed around the actor's apartment.

Ashwin Tomar had been doing exactly that.

The star splitting into a million stars for his lovers everywhere. They each could possess a piece of him as images or videos. Fragments like so many relics. Their own personal Ashwin in numerous avatars. But all shadows. Mere mirror images. Only she was the sky that cradled the true nova.

Om namahshivay

Om namahshivay

Om namahshivay

The mantra was spiralling around in circles in the adjoining room. Yeva stepped inside. Three words filling that chamber with the hum of the universe. Stuffing it with more and more of the divine. The actor sat anointing a massive granite lingam before the idol of Shiva. He had already daubed it with curd and was now anointing it with rosewater, ghee, honey and sandalwood. Garlanding the lingam with a glistening chain of bel leaves and applying three horizontal lines of vibhuti and kumkum. Placing a lilac arka flower. The man stood up now holding a large pot of water from the Ganga. She watched him pour it into the copper vessel suspended directly above the lingam. Water seeping through the perforated metal and dripping over the granite.

Drop by drop.

Sounds from the television outside were sneaking in. A Hindi news channel doing a special feature on Ashwathama. The reporter's voice echoing through a remote village.

'…widely believed that this is where Ashwathama comes every night to…'

Ashwin was laughing. She moved closer to the idol. 'Both blue. Shiva and Krishna. Could they be one, Ashwin? Born of the same mother?'

'You blaspheme, Yeva.'

'Sorry.'

'I don't believe the Dark One ever had a mother.'

'What do you mean?'

He closed his eyes. His throat bulged as if certain words had tied themselves into a thick knot.

'What is it, Ashwin?'

'Nothing. You think I despise him for what he did to

me? My father? Kauravas? Bhishma and Karna? I do. I will always do. But most of all for what he did to a mother.'

'Mother?'

'To Gandhari.'

'I know. He got her one hundred sons killed.'

'Not only that. He did something far more brutal to her the night the war ended. Something so demonic that even Vyasa avoided mentioning it in his epic.'

'What can be more inhuman than getting all her sons massacred?'

'Nobody knows about it, but I do. I saw it with my own eyes.'

'Tell me, Ashwin.'

'Gandhari sat mourning by Duryodhan's body. Thrashing about a wooden rod in the dark to keep the wolves from tearing her son's limbs. That woman had given birth to a piece of flesh from which her hundred sons had sprung. And now they had all been reduced to lumps of flesh again. Rancid corpses turning into dust. Such was the volume of her tears that they flooded the cloth over her eyes enabling her to see through them. She covered her eyes with her hands in terror lest her lifelong vow to her husband broke. And therein entered the Dark One.'

'What did he do?'

'He embraced her and asked her why she clung to her son's cadaver. And she replied that he would never understand a mother's pain. He argued. Said every pain was temporary. One pain remains only until a bigger pain comes along. But she replied that this pain of losing her sons was everlasting. Nothing would ever replace it. He left.'

'Left?'

'Yes. I thought that was the end, but something happened. I saw Gandhari clutching her stomach. I imagined it was another spasm of motherly ache, but I was wrong. It was hunger.'

'Hunger?'

'Yes. She was hungry. Craving for food.'

'That's strange.'

'It was. An abrupt hunger had assailed her out of nowhere. Possessed her body like a ghost. She was writhing. Salivating like the wolves who were watching Duryodhan's corpse from a distance. He entered again. The Dark One. He was carrying a luscious mango. He held it right before her blindfolded face. The fruit's scent was overpowering. Gandhari groped. Pounced viciously and finally grabbed it. Tore that ripe skin and gnawed at it. Devoured all the pulp and juice. Sucked the stone dry. At last satiated, she sat by her dead son licking her lips and fingers. Suddenly she froze. He was laughing. Looking at her and laughing aloud. He left, but his laughter remained. And his words biting her soul again and again:

One pain remains only until a bigger pain comes along.

Yeva trembled.

'It was that sadist. He had induced that terrible hunger in her to drive his point home. Teach her a lesson. Defeat that mother one more time.'

Sliding forward, she gathered Ashwin in her embrace.

'Gandhari howled. Howled like an animal.'

She clutched his shivering frame tighter.

'I hear it all the time, Yeva.'

Cradling him.

'All the time.'

Cradling him for long.

'She cursed him. And he cursed me. Do you see, Yeva? Do you see? I have been cursed by a cursed creature.'

They sat buried in each other's arms. Then she took out the Mani she had brought along. Almost saturated now with an iridescent shade of blue.

'Look, Ashwin. Just one more drop of human dew.'

He wiped his tears. Kissed the stone repeatedly. Slurped it as if wanting to drink all the nectar from that lozenge.

'Gandhari's curse only destroyed his Dwarka. We shall demolish his world.'

The final drop tomorrow…

Chapter 53

MUMBAI'S MORNING SUN WAS SAILING OVER THE ARABIAN Sea. Watching Suri's SUV speeding through Marine Drive. Although affectionately called Queen's Necklace, this elliptical stretch of road appeared hardly set in stone. Vehicles drove to and fro like mobile jewels of the necklace. A spiral kaleidoscope shape-shifting every moment. The officer was looking at *Maquillage* hoardings on every billboard. Pushing the pedal harder. He was not motoring towards the twenty-five-storeyed Ionia. He knew Kripalani was not at home. The tycoon had landed from Moscow and headed straight to his private yacht anchored along the city's coastline. He glanced at his watch once more.

198 minutes to darkness...

The sequence of the past few hours was looped around his brain like a reel of film. Playing the same montage over and over again. A barrage of noisy telephone calls since sunrise. Agitating his superiors. Swooping down on Kripalani's team and urging a firewall of secure confinement. Attempting to the point of hysteria to jolt them into some kind of action. Even considering for a moment to divulge everything. But he knew they would only cast him out.

Like he had cast her out in that case...

Alia...

And so Suri had reminded them of the five high-profile attacks and informed them that the tycoon was most probably next in line. That he had intelligence data that *Maquillage* could be the venue to target him. He knew the Chiranjivi himself would be immune to every precaution he suggested. So, the officer had frantically appealed to the people surrounding Kripalani. Hoped that the threat would terrify them adequately to mount a wall around the man. Prevent him from going for the show. But Bali had predictably shot everything down. Official word had arrived that Kripalani was attending the theatrical as planned. He had refused to be sealed inside his residence or marooned at sea. Suri had pleaded with the tycoon to allow for security cover at the auditorium, but that had been overruled as well. The officer strangulated the steering wheel.

Bali was all set to be the final martyr…

Suri had ultimately requested Kripalani for a meeting before he left for *Maquillage*, and he had surprisingly agreed. The officer could see his white vessel now bobbing at sea. Hoping that he, along with Patnaik and Atharva accompanying him, could reason with the Chiranjivi. Or at least stall him on the yacht until the eclipse passed.

Until the snake devoured the sun…

Minutes later, Suri was seated in the central cabin looking at this strange mosaic of characters under one roof. The writer and the priest on either side. The Immortal in the centre with the Indigo perched on his lap. She was playing her toudri. He looked at his watch.

162 minutes to darkness…

Kripalani gazed at him. 'You are silent, officer.'

'Just wondering how your PA, Kaul, would react if I

told him who you were. He hardly looked happy when you sent him and your guards out of the cabin.'

'Who am I?'

'Chiranjivi. Bali. We know. And you know that we know. Lin had told me that Mahira had messaged both of you about us.'

'Sure. That's why you are here. I wanted to meet all of you in private.'

'I met you last year on your birthday. Not that you would remember but..'

'I do, Suri. I forget nothing.'

'And you will still not let me do anything to safeguard you.'

'You tried to keep Mahira and Lin safe,' the tycoon made quote marks in the air as he spoke the last word. 'Did it work?'

The officer flushed as a grin dimpled Kripalani's face. 'Man considers himself almighty, but there's so little he can do. Give it up now. These forces are beyond all of you. Don't you hear the gods calling out? It's my turn now. I shall walk into that theatre and cling to my fate.'

'Bali,' Patnaik scoured the billionaire's face. 'Power. And here you are. One of the most powerful men in the country.'

'Power is an oxymoron. It's like the elements. Warms and chars. Slakes and drowns. Becomes your breath but also blows you apart. I see men extracting much power from the universe but they are still too fragile to hold it.'

'All the more reason why you cannot visit *Maquillage*. You are too vital for us. We have already lost those five and you cannot join them. The Immortals themselves want you secured.'

'What are you talking about?'

'The other day they raised their hands and covered their eyes,' the writer displayed the gesture. 'It was frightening but so compelling. None of us knows what that means, but it seems like they were asking us to shield you. Or a signal for you to close your eyes. Not watch Ashwin's show.'

'All of them did that?'

'Yes.'

The man's face twitched jubilantly. 'Are they awake? Out of coma?'

'No. That movement happened for less than a minute. Doctors explained it as some kind of involuntary muscle motion. They are reporting that the five bodies have healed remarkably but the coma still continues.'

'Maybe you are reading too much into a spasm.'

'Possible,' Suri flung his hands impatiently. 'But there's a more critical reason why you cannot allow Yeva to assault you. It's not about drawing your blood alone. She will infect you with a parasite.'

'Parasite?'

The officer rushed through the details as Kripalani listened. Indira had fallen asleep. The tycoon gripped the bamboo flute. Pulled it slowly from her fingers and placed it aside.

'Uncanny how you figured it all out.'

'So, you shall stay?'

'I hear what you are saying, but I must still attend the show.'

'Despite the massive risk involved?'

'Yes, Suri. I had thought this was only about us. The Chiranjivis. Cosmic forces devouring us one by one for reasons best known to them. But this is about humanity too. All of you. Perhaps your collective sins piling down the ages. Your apathy for everything the universe has done for you. Your hearts rot and now your minds must too. We cannot stonewall anything now. Let the events unfold. Men have been deciding their own destiny. Let Nature decide for once.'

The officer opened his mouth again, but Kripalani silenced him. A woman had entered bearing a tray.

'One must do what has to be done. Have tea, gentlemen. Then I must leave.'

She was pouring out coffee and chamomile tea. The tycoon pushed her hand away.

'Just milk for me today.'

Another woman was placing the day's newspapers on the centre table. Photographs of the recent Moscow Summit covering the front pages. As the attendants left, Indira snuggled closer to Kripalani. He caressed the scar on her face.

'Extraordinary child.'

Patnaik pointed at the sea outside. 'This must remind you of Kerala, Mahabali. The country you ruled. The people you loved. The land that was claimed from these very waters by the other Chiranjivi.'

'Which other Chiranjivi?' Suri asked.

'Parashurama. The Puranas tell us that the entire Konkan and Malabar landmass was submerged below the Arabian Sea. Parashurama clashed with Varuna, the god of water. As the battle raged, Parashurama flung his mighty axe. The steel tore through these waves, forcing the waters to recede as far as the axe went. The area that surfaced was saline and barren. Parashurama invoked the serpent Vasuki who sprayed its venom to neutralise the salt and transform it into a green paradise.'

The tycoon slammed his cup on the saucer. 'More like an ecological hell.'

'I am sorry?'

'The legend describes what's known as land reclamation today. This process of claiming submerged areas for human use is a violent process. It wrecks the natural balance.'

'Are you condemning Parashurama? A fellow Chiranjivi?'

'He shall be forever venerated for everything he did. But I can never excuse crippling a habitat. I always debate with Parashurama over this.'

'Habitat. The home. Obviously matters to you.'

'It does because we forget how brittle our ecosystem is. Reclaimed land is constantly prone to flooding and sinking. If you raze my home, yours is not safe either.'

'And you have two homes, Mahabali. Vishnu placed you in the netherworld, and yet you are also on earth as a Chiranjivi. How do you stride both these dimensions?'

'I have always balanced opposites. Subconscious in the intestines of the earth and yet supremely conscious of everything on its surface. Perhaps it is inhabiting this interim zone that makes my transitions possible.'

They watched him smile as he continued. 'That's power given to few. Very few.'

Patnaik nodded. 'And as you pointed out, not everyone can handle power.'

'It's getting late. I must leave for *Maquillage* now.'

'Last question.'

'Yes, Om?'

'Where is Kripalani, Yeva?'

Chapter 54

YEVA?

Suri and Atharva sprang as if knocked unawares by a tidal wave. But not the one who sat cradling Indira. Sitting unfazed like a boulder against which that wave had crashed and shattered into a million drops. Patnaik asked again.

'Time you got out of your costume, Yeva. What have you done with Kripalani?'

'Yeva?' the officer sputtered.

'Indeed,' the writer's finger slowly sliced the air before the tycoon from head to toe. 'It's the shape-shifter.'

Suri gawked at the lantern clock on the wall.

135 minutes to darkness...

Kripalani looked up. 'You do realise whom you are pointing at?'

'I absolutely do, Yeva. I have been noticing ever since I entered that you haven't blinked even once. You may wear the human form but you remain a stranger to the eyelid.'

Atharva peered at the man's face. 'Snakes don't blink. They have no eyelids.'

'And then there's the milk,' the writer indicated the cup in Kripalani's hand. 'You also remain a stranger to our food. Still no taste for the common beverage. But it's the newspapers that betrayed you.'

The officer picked one up. 'Papers?'

'The Moscow Summit photographs. Look at the tycoon shaking hands. He is left-handed. But Yeva here picked up the cup with her right hand. Added sugar to it with her right hand and sits holding the cup in her right hand.'

They watched her fingers. Fingers curling around the cup like claws of a reptile.

'All the signs before my eyes, but I had to be sure,' Patnaik lowered his face. 'And so, I went for the kill. Ecology. Land reclamation. And your mask crumbled, Yeva. Your pupils dilated and you just could not resist. You allowed your heart to ruin your head. It was not Bali speaking. It was the serpent waving her green placard. Condemning both mortals and immortals. Your master has quite obviously infected you with his hatred.'

They watched him rise carrying Indira in his arms.

Still he. Still Kripalani.

Then he spoke, and they shrank. Still the tycoon but not his voice anymore. Yeva's voice cutting through the male body as if it was possessed. A woman speaking from inside that man. A snake hissing from inside that woman.

'Shiva symbolises us. The martyr who holds all the venom of the universe inside him like we do. He's austere. Organic and ascetic. No gold or silk covers him, like Vishnu. We are his ornaments. He makes us adorn him while the other one makes us serve him. The natural anoints Shiva while the synthetic sticks to Vishnu.'

'You are blind, Yeva. Open your eyes and see what's being shown to you. Vishnu is clad in finery because he symbolises civilization. His silk and gold denote weavers and craftsmen. The world of human occupations that he preserves.

His form celebrates the pinnacle of human advancement. Evolution of our society.'

'And once you have scaled the peak, you can only go down. Even your Chiranjivis are collapsing one by one. Collapsing like every social institution you have ever created. Not long now before your evolution flips into extinction. Once the Immortals awaken, your world shall become a necropolis. City of the dead.'

'That's why you got so excited when you heard that the Chiranjivis had made a sign. You thought they had awakened and would now start transmitting Ashwin's parasite. I hardly believe that's going to happen.'

She laughed. 'But I had heard you are a believer, Om. Why such little faith in me? I am divine too. A goddess who has transcended. My avatar walks this earth to cleanse it. But you are not fascinated. You never paid me a visit like the others did. You disappoint me.'

'Not as much as you do, Yeva. My faith remains intact. I have seen the universe constantly validating my beliefs and it has done so again. But it shows me now that even the divine can lack morality. Like Ashwathama, you too were an evolved being. You could have evolved further. Turned this into an opportunity to do good, but you remain an animal that only seeks revenge. Slave to evil now. Unconscious of the true magic within you and that you could have been even more miraculous. Perhaps even become my Muse, but you stand corrupted.'

'Maybe it's the star I was created under. I cannot grow the conscience you look for.'

'I know. You disenchant me and so I stay away.'

'You are here now.'

'I am here for Bali. Where is he? Have you already attacked him?'

'Not yet,' Suri spoke. 'Not until the eclipse. She must have stashed him somewhere on this yacht. You knew Kripalani was coming here from the airport, Yeva?'

'I know everything. I have been tracking everyone. That man had no idea I was waiting for him here. I took his place as soon as he arrived. And then calls from your precinct started pouring in.'

'Yes. My calls offering security measures for Kripalani. And you rejected them all. You obviously wanted to be alone with the tycoon here. But why, Yeva? The man was going to be at your show today. Why are you here then? Were you going to drain his blood on this yacht? Was it never about *Maquillage*?'

The Ichhadhari hissed. 'It's always about *Maquillage*.'

The girl stirred in her sleep. She nuzzled Indira's face.

'Sleep, my Red Riding Hood. Sleep well.'

Atharva wrenched the child away from her. The Ichhadhari forked her tongue. 'Your priest is outraged. The man who comes here to escape his drab life. Looking for excitement. Seeking in Mumbai what Manipur cannot offer.'

The officer was gazing at a mirror on the wall. He heard her giggle.

'Mirror mirror on the wall! Who's the most pathetic of them all? You think the glass shall reflect the real me, Suri? Show you a shimmering blue krait?'

'I may not see you, Yeva. But I can certainly fucking crush you.'

He placed his index finger at the nape of her neck and ran it down. Slowly. Gently. Curving inward. All the way over her backbone. Right down to her sacrum. They watched her face twitch. Watching what she was realising.

They know…

She was looking into their eyes. Reading what they were spelling.

We know…

'Careful, Suri. I look human, but I am still cold blooded.'

He clutched her by the head.

'I will crumble your spine.'

'Can you?'

'Right here. Right now.'

'Can you?'

He brought her down on the table.

'Can you?'

Ripping the shirt off her back.

'Can you?'

Taking his revolver out and aiming at her vertebrae.

'Can you?'

The officer suddenly recoiled as if the snake had struck him between his eyes.

Her shape shifts…

He was gaping at the figure that lay before them now. Gaping at Patnaik and Atharva and seeing his own horror turning them catatonic.

Not Kripalani anymore…

She is…

Suri looked at the mirror again. The figure's lips moved.

'You like what the mirror shows you now?'

He stood mute.

'You cannot kill me. You love me. You have always loved me.'

He turned.
'Take my name, Suri.'
Took a step towards her.
'Take my name.'
His lips trembled.
'Alia.'

Chapter 55

ALIA...

Alia...

Suri was mouthing the name again and again but no one could hear a sound. He wanted to pounce on her and envelope her in his arms lest she burst like a bubble. He stood static, not daring to move a limb. His face too numb to betray the typhoon in his blood.

'No, Suri. Not Alia.'

Patnaik's voice clawing at the officer.

'You know it's Yeva.'

Trying to drag him back with a thread terribly fragile.

'Yeva.'

They saw her move. Gliding towards him, she stretched out her hand at his revolver. Her fist closing over the weapon.

'Touch me, Suri.'

He remained still.

'Hold me.'

She guided his other hand along her waist.

'Put your arms around me. Feel me. Feel my body next to yours.'

She was brushing her bosom against his. Stroking his mouth. The man pulsed. Her voice stabbing his heart like a hypodermic needle.

'Kiss me, Suri.'

Her breath colliding with his now. Smelling each other's skin.

'Kiss me.'

As he bent over her lips, she yanked the revolver from his slackened grip and smashed it against his head. Watching his temples bruise as the capillaries underneath broke. Still no word from Suri. Then his mouth moved.

'You are not Alia.'

She was laughing.

'Not Alia.'

'Alia! Your love. Your strength. I just turned her into your weakness, Suri. Disgusting how you hang on to that shadow.'

She had morphed again. Her own self now. The Ichhadhari with blue eyes.

'You are wrong, Yeva. Alia is reality. You are the bloody myth.'

'Myth? You know what else they call a myth? They say the image of a snake's enemy remains imprinted on its eyes.'

She pulled his face close to hers. 'Hardly a myth. Look into my eyes. See how they reflect your face. Reflect your vile bloodline.'

'I am not my grandmother, Yeva.'

'You are. You all carry the sins of your lineage. You smell of her evil.'

'Like you reek of Ashwathama,' the writer countered. 'Living out a fate crafted by a self-serving outlaw?'

'Self-serving? His punishment was a thousand times greater than his sin. But does he seek a cure only for himself? No. He seeks to heal the whole of earth. And for that to happen, mankind must perish. Even the elements agree or we wouldn't have come this far. You call it violent. Wicked. But there's simply no other solution.'

'Are you convincing us or convincing yourself, Yeva?

'I was convinced the very day Ashwin saved my life. Stop labelling me right or wrong, Om. Don't you see that I am neither of that anymore? I have surpassed. Beyond categories now. One of the Chiranjivis once called me Karna, but I have become Arjuna's arrow. Linear without any arc. I only see the bird's eye now that must be destroyed. Everything else is invisible.'

'But Arjuna also evolved, Yeva. When he stood before the Kauravas at Kurukshetra, he no longer saw them just as targets that had to be vanquished. He saw family. Kinsmen. His perspective had widened. You cannot be Arjuna because you lack that moral struggle. That sense of judgement. You are Yeva. Eve who always succumbs.'

'Some acts are so pure that they are above morality, Om. Arjuna performed his karma, and I am doing mine. I know the universe shall judge me when it's all done. And I am prepared.'

'Stop ranting, Yeva. Where the fuck is Kripalani?' Suri inched forward.

'Quiet.' She shoved the barrel into the officer's mouth. 'To bleed or not to bleed? Not to. You are a failure, Suri, but you just don't give up. It's your nature to hunt like your grandmother. You shall hunt again and fail again. Prove once more how overrated that human brain is. Mere meal for our parasite. It's over for all of you now. And it begins for us. No more of you. And more and more of us.'

'Where is the tycoon?'

She backed away keeping the revolver aimed at them. 'Today is all about blue. Dark blue. Once the sun and moon blend, the blue shall bleed for all to see.'

Reaching the side door that opened to the main deck, she aimed at the mirror. They flailed in horror as if that would block the bullet, but she fired and vanished. As the glass splintered, Kripalani's men stormed the cabin.

'KK?'

The writer and the officer had ducked while the priest was shielding his terrified child. Security guards pointed their rifles. Kaul was barking.

'Where's KK? We heard a gunshot.'

Patnaik and Atharva stood speechless, but Suri strode towards the open door.

'Possible assassin on board. The shot came from here and smashed the mirror. Kripalani rushed out to investigate.'

'All by himself?'

'He left before we could react.'

The PA lunged out of the cabin followed by everyone else. All eyes scanning the main deck.

KK?

Yeva?

'Where's he? Where did he go?'

'He just took off when the shot rang out.'

'KK would never do that. He knew we were outside. He would have waited for us.'

'I thought the same, but when we looked up, he was gone.'

Kaul's face darkened. 'You were right then. Someone's targeting him.'

'Exactly. Our information was watertight. He should

have listened and agreed for security cover.'

'But you informed us that the danger loomed at *Maquillage*. This yacht was never supposed to be...'

'Post-mortem can wait, Kaul. We need to secure Kripalani first. He must be here somewhere.'

'And the attacker as well.'

'How many hands on deck?'

'Five more. Two attendants and three security guards. The family's at Ionia. Just KK on board.'

'Round up everyone. We need to locate the tycoon. Locate him fast.'

As the PA bolted ahead, Atharva grasped the officer's hand, speaking in hushed tones.

'You have just lied through your teeth. Compromised Kripalani.'

'Action reaction. One of the survival kits this job teaches you. And I am not lying. I am handling this fucking crisis in the only way possible. We haven't compromised him. Nothing shall happen to the man until the eclipse takes place.'

'What now?' The writer asked.

'We know Kripalani arrived here from the airport. Yeva switched places with him to make sure no alarm was raised until the eclipse. She must have rendered the Chiranjivi unconscious and stashed him somewhere on this yacht. With Om exposing her, she's gone into hiding. Waiting it out until she can strike Kripalani. We must find either or both of them before the eclipse.'

'She has your revolver, Suri. You have revealed the Kundalini to her. She realises we can kill her now and will do anything to protect herself. '

'She was being fucking cocky, Om, and a cop doesn't

take that well. Did you see her face when I poked her spine? Terror. Mortal terror.' His knuckles clicked as he curled his fingers into a fist. 'Let's get her and grind her.'

Within minutes, the action on the yacht had become one of relentless manhunt. Security guards armed with walkie-talkies had spread all over the main deck, probing saloons and suites. Attendants scouring swimming platforms and the lower deck while Kaul was up on the sun deck. Patnaik was frisking crew quarters while Atharva was scuttling through staterooms with Indira in his arms. And a singular message crackling from every walkie-talkie.

All clear…All clear…All clear…

The officer growing restless on the upper deck bridge. His watch counting down.

108 minutes to darkness…

107…

Same words over and over.

All clear…All clear…

Over and over. Suri cursed.

Like fucking raindrops.

He stiffened. Not his words. He was hearing drops. Actual drops. But the sky above was as blue as the sea below. The firmament had rubbed every cloud away as if they would obscure the cosmic drama that was about to unfold. But he could still hear the water.

Drip…drip…drip…

The man bounded across the deck chasing that sound.

Drip…drip…drip…

It had not been there before. Where was it coming from?

Drip…drip…drip…

Closer now. Much closer. And louder.

Drip…Drip…Drip…

Kripalani sending an SOS? Yeva luring him into a trap?

Drip…Drip…Drip…

Turning left now.

Drip…Drip…Drip…

There.

Drip…Drip…Drip…

He saw it.

DRIP…DRIP…DRIP…

He was looking at the yacht pantry. The main galley was on the deck below and this was a smaller one being used more as a storage hold. Water was trickling from under its door and falling on a metal railing below. He had seen the priest checking the room and noticed no leakage then. Suri shoved the door open. The place was crammed everywhere with longitudinal units and stocked overhead cabinets. Baskets of fruit stood on the table next to a refrigerator. Sealed cartons heaped upon each other and a chest freezer running along the wall. The drops were seeping from a gap between the chest edge and the lid. A gap because the freezer had been improperly shut.

Suri stood watching the water percolate.

Because the freezer had been improperly shut…

Staggering through the galley, he hauled the lid off the chest.

'Kripalani!'

The man lay on the bed of ice. White crystals clinging to his hair and face. Frosting around his closed eyes and thawed water edging dangerously close to his nostrils. The sub-zero temperature had stained his skin and lips faint blue. As the officer yelled from the bridge outside, three words teetered on the tip of his tongue.

Just in time...Just in time...

And a question.

Where is Yeva?

Everyone had converged inside the galley now, carting the tycoon to the neighbouring suite. Rubbing his palms and soles. Kaul examining the whites of his eyes and hollering at the attendants to call in medical aid.

'He'll be fine,' Suri assured.

The PA did not reply.

'Wasn't in there too long.'

The man still feeling Kripalani's pulse.

'Just a bit of chill, Kaul.'

'A lot more than you think, officer.'

'Sorry?'

'He's gone.'

'Gone?'

'KK's dead.'

'What?'

'Dead.'

All noises ceased. The gathering hushed as if their brains had failed to recognise the input. Process that information hurtling towards them. Disbelief. Confusion. And terror. The quiet growing quieter and quieter when Suri suddenly laughed.

'Dead?'

'Yes.'

'He cannot be dead.'

'He is.'

'You don't understand, Kaul. Kripalani cannot fucking die.'

'He fucking has,' the PA erupted. 'KK's gone.'

The officer veered towards Patnaik and Atharva. His voice laced with amusement and alarm. 'What is he saying?'

Both men were gawking at the man's body. They knew he could not be dead. Supremely assured that Kaul was wrong. But hearing footsteps of another voice within them. An opposite voice. The writer dived and touched Kripalani's arm.

'Cold dead,' the PA said.

'This is just hypothermia,' Patanaik spoke. 'His temperature has lowered drastically since he was shoved into the freezer. His body may have gone into shock, but this can hardly kill him.'

'I know. The cold did not kill him. That did.'

Kaul was pointing at the tycoon's neck. Patnaik squinted. His body coagulated brutally as he saw the marks. Two puncture holes.

Snake bite

'What is it, Om?' he heard Suri asking.

'He has been bitten. Bitten by a snake.'

They were looking again at the blue that had spread all over his skin. Not from ice. It was venom running through his veins. The three men lashing themselves with another question now.

Why would she bite him?

The writer looked at Kaul again. 'A snake bite does not kill instantly. I am sure Kripalani's alive. We just need to restrict the flow of the poison inside his body until the medics arrive. They will revive him.'

'Can they also revive his heart?'

'Heart?'

The PA grabbed Patnaik's palm and curled it around the

tycoon's wrist. 'No pulse.' Then he brought it near his nose. 'No breath.' And finally placed it on his chest. 'No heart.'

The writer's fingers throbbing. Running over that damp bosom. Slipping and falling but getting up once again. Fumbling here and there to detect a single heartbeat. Nails digging into that cold flesh to register any seismic activity deep down. His own heart beating like a tom-tom now as if that would awaken the other.

Nothing

His hand swallowing Kripalani's wrist again to detect any motion animating it.

Nothing

His palm standing before Kripalani's nostrils again to feel that life-affirming breeze blowing.

Nothing

Patnaik looked at Suri and Atharva and shook his head. Saw them walking out of the suite. Joined them by the railing on the deck. Twenty minutes later the medical team arrived and confirmed it. Kiran Kripalani had succumbed to snake venom.

Chapter 56

THE WRITER WAS LOOKING AT THE BODIES IN THE ARABIAN Sea below. Somnath with a bleeding liver. The teen at the mall with a cracked skull. And now Kripalani with a blue face.

Pointing at him…

'But Yeva's painting,' the officer was gnashing his teeth. 'It has to be the billionaire.'

'Not anymore.'

'Was she screwing us? Handing out wrong info?'

'She has never done that before. Why now? We were wrong about the painting. Dead wrong.'

'But the links. The Nilotpal.'

'All wrong.'

'You could still be right. Maybe Yeva has killed the last Chiranjivi.'

'She cannot,' the priest lowered Indira. 'No one can. It's simply not possible.'

'But then it makes no fucking sense,' Suri shrieked. 'If Kripalani is not Bali, why is Yeva here? Why did she impersonate him? Where is she gone?'

The sea breeze was blowing those questions away. Their hearts still rebelling but their minds genuflecting now before the truth.

Kripalani was not Immortal

Not the final Chiranjivi

Patnaik's brain was scanning the painting again. Suri was right. It had quite neatly fitted with the tycoon. But now his lifeless body lay blue with Yeva's venom.

Dark blue…

The words floating over the sea water like bioluminescent plankton.

Dark blue…

He was hearing Yeva hiss.

'Today is all about blue…Dark blue.'

The words staining his tongue as he spoke them.

Dark blue…

The Arabian Sea now looking like a reservoir of dye.

Dark blue…

Blue dye.

Dark blue…

One of the rainbow.

Dark blue…

The writer gripped the railing.

Dark blue?

Dark blue?

Wringing the metal with both hands.

Of course…

His brain getting smudged as the colour trickled deep inside.

It has to be…has to be…

But immediately rejecting that epiphany.

Can't be…it can't be…

Staring once more at the bodies floating below.

No…no…

But making sense. Making so much sense.

Blind...have we all been that blind?

Answering Suri's questions also. Every question. All of them.

But the painting...Only some of it.

He paused. Not just blue. Another colour. Yeva had named another colour.

Red...

Red...

Patnaik let go of the railing. They were all emerging from him like threads of ectoplasm. Coalescing now. Weaving a face before his eyes. A face terrorising him more than any other face ever had.

What have I done!

He grasped the priest. 'Indira. Where's Indira?'

'Indira?'

'Yes. Where is she?'

'She was here. Right here.'

'Where is she, Atharva?'

'Right by my side.'

Words hanging all around them. Letters of the alphabet strangled to death. Lines not completing themselves.

'There...look there...her toudri...lying down there on the deck below...by the cabin...'

The writer had gathered Suri and bolted. Atharva followed them as they raced down towards the cabin. Nearing it, he saw both men standing at the entrance. Looking at something across the room. Hardly moving as if what they saw would tear them apart if they went near. The priest touched Patnaik's back.

'What is it, Om?'

The two men parted. The cabin was empty. The mirror

still shattered but the glass bearing a name now. The final name in dark blue.

BALI

Atharva had picked up the flute. He turned. 'Where's Indira?'

'Gone,' the writer barely audible.

'Gone?'

'Yeva's taken her.'

'Taken her?'

'Kripalani was not Bali. It was Indira.'

The priest walked towards the mirror.

'Indira?'

The fractured glass splitting his face into fragments.

'My Indira?'

'Yes.'

'My child? Bali?'

'Yes, Atharva.'

'Not just an Indigo? A Chiranjivi?'

'The last one.'

Suri banged the door shut. His eyes swerved towards the clock.

90 minutes to darkness...

'But how's that possible, Om? She was right there by the railing.'

'Does it matter now? The Ichhadhari's taken her.'

'But Indira? Bali? Bali symbolises power. Power. Indira is a kid.'

'A child with phenomenal power. A child who shall probably grow up to wield more power than anyone ever has.'

Patnaik sliced the air in a circular motion.

'The human cycle. That's the one thing we did not

take into account, Suri. That some Chiranjivis could still be infants. Not in the prime of their lives yet. Not yet functioning in society. Still walking towards the path that their guna had destined for them. Who knows what Indira would grow up to be?'

'How do you know you are not fucking wrong again?'

The writer pointed at the colour of the name on the mirror. 'Dark blue.'

Yeva's voice booming inside that closed cabin again.

Today is all about blue...Dark blue

'What's another word for dark blue, Suri? Indigo.'

The officer gulped. Seeing now what Patnaik had seen on that deck. 'Indigo child.'

'Yes. Her aura is her Nilotpal. The colour splashed on her soul. The colour that springs from the very pith of her being. Perhaps that's why Bali chose in his present life to be born as Indira. Perhaps as an Indigo, Bali will grow up to be truly Mahabali. More powerful than ever. It would be fascinating to wait and watch what she goes on to become. And not just blue. Yeva also spoke about another colour. Red.'

'Red?'

'Yes. What did she call Indira when she was sleeping in her arms? Red Riding Hood.'

'Yes.'

'The red denotes the colour of the girl's hood in the story. But over the years it has been interpreted to mean blood. The blood of a virgin.'

'Yeva said she will bleed. The blue shall bleed.'

'That's why Yeva was on the yacht. Not for Kripalani. For Indira.'

'How would she know we were after the tycoon?'

'She said she knew everything. Been tracking everyone. Yeva obviously knew that we thought Kripalani was Bali. She knew you would reach out to the tycoon and offer protection. She killed him as soon as he arrived here and took his place. Rejected your security offers but agreed to meet us all. She knew Atharva took Indira wherever he went. She was waiting. Waiting for us to deliver Bali to her. And we did.'

'Yeva had stroked her face and called her extraordinary,' Suri murmured.

'She is. Way more extraordinary than we imagined.'

'But the painting, Om. Does it specify Indira?'

'Its style was a deliberate imitation of her slate drawings. Also, Atharva had added up the coils of Sheshnag to seven. And the child is seven years old.

'That's not enough. Shouldn't there be an iron-clad bond?'

'There is.'

It was the priest speaking. He had sagged into the couch. Clutching the toudri as if he wanted to stab his own throat. Patnaik knelt.

'I am sorry, Atharva.'

'No, Om. You did nothing. This is perhaps my doing.'

'Yours?'

'Yes. You were asking about Yeva's painting, Suri. It has a profound link with Indira.'

'What is it?'

'We told you that the pilgrimage Manikaran, depicted in the painting, is known for its hot springs. That water is believed to be highly therapeutic.'

'I remember.'

'Last year Jupita began insisting that we take the child to Manikaran.'

'You have visited Manikaran?'

'Yes. Jupita was hoping that the springs would improve our daughter's condition. I tried deterring her, but she just wouldn't listen. We reached Manikaran the night before Indira's sixth birthday. The next morning...'

His voice trailed off as tears bubbled in his eyes. The writer clasped his hands, but Suri snarled.

'We are running out of time, Atharva. Speak up.'

'I was by the shore and Jupita entered the water with Indira. She was pressing her down gently to immerse her entire body into the spring. Immersing her and releasing her. The place was getting more and more crowded by the minute. She turned her back to me. I saw it then. Saw what Jupita was doing. She was holding the child's head underwater. Holding it forever. I kept waiting. Watching. Thinking I was panicking for no reason, but minutes passed and she wouldn't budge. Not a sound from either of them. I leapt into the spring and pulled Indira away. She was numb but breathing.'

'And Jupita?'

'She seemed in some kind of stupor as if the hot water had frozen her. Her eyes like glass hardly reacting. Like she barely knew what her hands were doing. I touched her and she throbbed. Suddenly conscious of everything around. I think she saw something in my face. Something that screamed at her what she had tried to do. She balked in horror. Grabbed Indira and clasped her tight in her arms. We just kept standing there. Jupita's tears flowing down that spring. Stinging the gash on the child's face.'

'That scar,' Patnaik said. 'That scar on her cheek.'

'Yes. That's where she got it.'

'You think Jupita tried to…'

'Kill Indira? It seems pretty obvious. But then I watch how she dotes on her and I wonder. Her feelings for Indira are too intricate for me. I know she loves her, but I also see Jupita's rage towards the child. Is she angry because her daughter's condition pains her? Or is it an irrational fear? Or helplessness? Too many emotions overlap here and I think one of them overpowered Jupita for a moment that day. I remember wondering for days how Indira survived the spring.'

'Now you know why.'

'Yes. How can you kill what cannot be killed? But I should have been more watchful at Manikaran. Prevented Jupita from harming the child. None of us ever begged forgiveness of our daughter. Never sought an absolution. Jupita still ties a rope around Indira like all those coils of Sheshnag in the painting. And now Yeva's got her. The gods are punishing me.'

'It's not your doing, Atharva,' the writer stood up. 'It was Bali. He positioned himself in the centre of this battle. Born as an Indigo, he already had greater consciousness. That's what spawned those slate drawings. Indira began reacting when the Chiranjivis came under attack. She knew what was going on and she revealed it to us.'

'Did she know from the beginning that Ashwathama was also infecting them?'

'No. Mahira clearly told us that none of the Immortals knew what Ashwin had planned. Indira knew nothing about the parasite. She discovered that bioterror much later along with us when we tested the Chiranjivis. But as an Indigo she had that higher perception which was always warning her that Ashwathama was plotting something heinous. And so, she engineered everything. Navigated you here so that you could show us the way. Communicated with the five Immortals about the eclipse and absolutely refused to reveal their identities to us. She was being true to who she was. Telling us like Mahira that this was our *purushartha*. You must rejoice even more in her now. Rejoice that she chose you to father her.'

The priest ran his fingers over the toudri. 'Like Vasudeva. Like Joseph. Touched by the divine. I knew her only as an Indigo. Never saw that she was notches above that. And now she'll bleed.'

'She will not,' Suri lurched and opened the door. 'We'll get her.'

'But how? Yeva could have taken her anywhere.'

'Not anywhere. *Maquillage*.'

'*Maquillage*?'

'Yes. Yeva told us it was always about *Maquillage*.'

'She was lying. How will they assault a child in public? In a packed theatre?' Patnaik reasoned.

'You forget what else she said, Om. The blue shall bleed for all to see. All to see.'

The writer stared at the skyline outside as if he could see the auditorium. '*Maquillage*. They are going to bleed her on stage. Right there before everyone's eyes.'

'It's the perfect security cover,' the officer said. 'Camouflage like they did with those envelopes. Hiding in plain sight. Ashwin will make the assault a part of his fucking spectacle and his audience shall stand and whistle. He's making a statement and he wants the world to watch. And once he become Ashwathama, he shall no longer be answerable to anyone.'

'How much time, Suri?'

'The show has begun. You both need to leave now.'

'We both?' Patnaik spun. 'You aren't coming?'

'Kripalani's dead, Om. I cannot leave the yacht right away. Things here have to be taken care of. But you both must reach the auditorium. I'll join you with my men.' He looked at the priest. 'It's time, Atharva. You say you failed Indira at Manikaran. Don't fail her at *Maquillage*. The final act now. Let's bring the curtain down.'

Minutes later the officer watched the two men cruising towards the coastline. He looked at his watch.

63 minutes to darkness...

Chapter 57

THE AUDITORIUM HAD OPENED ITS EYES TO LOOK AT THE firmament on top. The ceiling had disappeared and in its place today spanned a gigantic expanse of glass. A transparent dome arching marvellously upwards as if dissolving into the morning sky. Above it shone the sun. Peeping like an underage voyeur denied entrance. The hermetically sealed hall had transfigured into an amphitheatre today. No longer a veiled woman. It had become a Roman nude that had discarded all its trappings. Raising crystal arms to make love to the solar deity.

MAQUILLAGE 2019

A glass barrier had also been installed between the stage and the audience. Clear glass rising high and stretching across the entire perimeter of the podium. The barricade encasing performers within and keeping all others out. Injecting cinema into theatre through a strange hybrid of live action and inanimate screen. The show had arrived at its climax. Actors had come and gone. And now stood the greatest of them all.

Ashwin Tomar.

Swathed in daylight streaming through the glass ceiling and a single arclight on top. Clear yet obscure. Primal but plastic. The audience leaned forward. He was wearing what they had never seen him wear at *Maquillage* before. A steel face covering his own. Strapped all over as if nailed to his skull. Had his face been dipped in hot metal and left to solidify? Or had that façade grown out of his own flesh like a canker? Skin callousing and turning metallic?

'I was the man with the iron mask,' he spoke.

They shrank as he split that metal and tossed it away. This was not the face they had come to see. The crescendo they had been awaiting. The actor was offering them something else. Not the Ashwin who would stand there and dismantle himself. But the Ashwin who had already done that. Already defaced. His forehead squirting gore. Fibres hanging loose. Congealed blood clumped everywhere. Not a face but a shell of bones and flesh.

'The mask hides me no more.'

Had they experienced time lapse? Was *Maquillage* inverting its phantasmagoria? Had Ashwin Tomar already performed the ultimate sacrifice?

'Today we do not ruin. We repair.'

The star was smiling. He was dressed as a Mayan priest in breeches and a shawl of animal hide. Jade necklaces hanging from his throat and his head crowned with turquoise feathers of the quetzal. Raising his macauahuitl towards the sun, he thundered.

'Hail Kinich Ahau.'

As that sword with blades of obsidian stabbed the air, another spotlight beamed, illumining a marble platform. An enormous white monolith sitting on the stage like an arctic iceberg. The stone was carved on all four sides, depicting a continuous motif of snakes coiled around an egg. On the platform sat Indira. Dressed in a white huipil almost blending with the marble. Lilies wreathing her head and a stalk of maize flowers in her hand. The actor's voice boomed again.

'When we Mayans raise a temple, we make an offering. An offering of our young to invigorate the shrine we build. We do not erect now. We resurrect. Ages ago a temple had been demolished. Its jewels robbed. Its body racked and ruined. Today we anoint that carcass. Consecrate what was desecrated. Gather its bones and rinse them with this child's blood. The time has come to sanctify that sanctum again. Today we do not sacrifice the living. We only raise the dead.'

The auditorium darkened. Ashwin looked up. The sky was turning a shade deeper.

'Behold! The curtain rises. The stars are with us today. They are conjuring the ultimate phenomenon that shall empower our sacrament.'

Everyone craned their necks to see. They had been provided with eclipse glasses and soon the entire audience was watching the celestial drama unfolding above them.

'Not long now. When the sun lives and dies, we shall die and live.'

The firmament had gone from blue to dark blue. More and more stars were popping out as if rudely awakened from their sleep. They could hear wings flapping against the dome. That glass had become a screen, and the motion picture it played was assuming epic proportions now. The sun was becoming anaemic. Was a finger rotating a screw somewhere to turn that cosmic lantern dimmer and dimmer? Suddenly a chunk of the solar circle vanished as if someone had taken a bite. The actor gestured wildly.

'It arrives. The lunar serpent.'

The moon had reared its head. A concave shadow creeping across that brilliant rim. Sunlight was passing through lunar valleys, now casting iridescence over *Maquillage*. Ashwin pointed at Indira.

'When the moon plunges into the sun, I shall plunge this macauahuitl into her. The blade shall impale her liver and dig deep into the fountain of her purest blood. Elixir worthy of the temple, it shall rejuvenate. She shall be K'i'ik. Virgin nectar heralding the return of the monarch long banished into exile.'

Music reverberated from speakers now. Violins chanting an opera of death and rebirth. The sun was becoming an ever narrowing crescent with the moon consuming it bit by bit. That black circle clambering on top like an impatient lover. Wanting more and more of the solar body.

'I hear the moon snickering. It never realises how fleeting its triumph is. How insignificant within the mechanics of the universe. Darkness coats light but for a moment. The lunar disc will melt. Flee in terror to make way for that cosmic renaissance. That primordial orb of fire ascending once more to rule.'

As the audience kept gazing upwards, the door of the auditorium flung open. Two men standing there unsteadily. Eyes adjusting to the twilight. Perceiving the actor and the child. The next moment they were tearing down the aisles. Darting towards the stage. Almost making it to the podium when their bodies recoiled brutally, colliding with an unseen force. Dazed with this sudden impact, they tried once more, only to be repelled again. Their hands groped the invisible wall standing in their way.

'Glass, Om. A glass barrier.'

'Covering the entire length of the stage. No opening. We cannot go up there.'

Atharva was pounding on that glass now. Curled palms battering it mercilessly. The barricade shivered but hardly yielded. The clamour of his fists further dissolving in the orchestra of the violins. A few eyes in the front row strayed, observing his antics. Patnaik seized the man.

'Hold on. This won't work.'

'But Indira...'

'I know. I see her too. We need to get hold of the theatre manager. Get this barrier down or access through the backstage.'

'My child...'

'She's fine, Atharva. We are on time.'

'The Mani. I don't see the Mani. What's Ashwin up to?'

'Calm down. Just wait here and keep watch.'

As the writer turned, the moon blew out the galactic candle. The sun had vanished. In its place now gleamed a ring. The famed diamond ring reproduced by the perfect intercourse between the two heavenly bodies. The corona around it shimmering like a blue halo. Viscous blue tinting the whole auditorium. The sun had become an actor for *Maquillage*, covering itself with a black mask.

The eclipse was total.

Patnaik had paused like everyone else around. His senses still negotiating with this abrupt shift in light. The death of sound. Almost dark now and all noises had ceased. Hysteria had made way for hypnosis. Mass hypnosis exerted by the eclipse. The writer could make out men and women sitting enchanted with the spectacle. The diamond ring illuminating hands, eyes and faces. Rows and rows of human statues turning *Maquillage* into a theatre of the macabre. He had barely taken ten steps towards the exit when he winced.

What the hell…

A sudden inferno had exploded above him, forcing his eyes to seek refuge behind his hands. His pupils boiling with confusion now. Was the sun already out? Had it just charred his vision? That was impossible. He knew the eclipse was going to be long. What then had manifested in the air to shine a blinding torch into his face? Patnaik splayed his fingers to peer through the crack.

Yeva

Chapter 58

YEVA...

Is she flying?

The Ichhadhari seemed to have materialised out of the dark. Dressed in Maya blue, she was floating right above him. Aerial as if a cumulonimbus cloud had blown into the theatre through a crack in the glass ceiling. As she inched closer to him, Patnaik saw that she was standing on a flying stage. That theatrical device hoisted by ropes and pulleys, enabling her to glide over the auditorium. The serpent no longer subterranean. Not even terrestrial. *Maquillage* had made her airborne.

Ashwin held up his sword with both arms and bowed. 'Hail Akna. Guardian goddess. The deity of birth. Behold how Akna carries the seed in her hands. Hallowed kernel of the renaissance that you shall witness here. Rejoice. Repent. Prepare for the Second Coming.'

Nestling in her palms, the Mani was flaring magnificently. With the sun extinguished, this seed had now become the star of this galaxy. A brilliant blue with just a sliver of white like venom with a drop of milk. The writer had never seen a Mani before. He was watching it flaunt that incredible alchemy that the blood of the Chiranjivis had wrought upon it. Transforming it into a reservoir of nectar that could cure the cosmos. Watching Yeva spraying its blaze on everyone like a lighthouse. Watching her face utterly rapturous that a part of her could be so beatific. But also reminding himself how she had bled. Killed. Hypnotised. He gasped.

Again?

Was she doing it again?

Because his legs were walking backwards. Retracing every step he had taken a minute ago. Taking him in the reverse direction but not of his own volition. He was trying to propel himself forward. Make his legs halt but in vain. His brain no longer dominating his limbs. Relinquishing all control, he found himself stapled to her eyes again. Dissolving into her once more and unable to extract himself. Powerless to reach that exit door and seek help for Indira. Yoked to the single neural command of Yeva's mind, his flesh was obeying. As that flying stage advanced closer and closer above him, his body was marching further and further back. All the way down the aisle as if literally pushed by that approaching contraption. Everyone was staring at Yeva but her eyes were fixed on him alone. The writer was back at the glass barricade again. His body touched Atharva's skin behind him. Ice cold as his own.

Hypnotising us both...

The flying machine had stopped atop the barrier. Hovering right above them. Her eyes dousing the two men with a radiation that seemed to grow more and more toxic. Their senses splintering all ties now as they were made to turn. Turn around to face the stage. Look through the glass at Ashwin and Indira. The audience still gazing at that jewel in her raised palms. The Ichhadhari still rendering the two men below immobile. Making them stand and watch.

The actor genuflected.

'The seed.'

They watched a white dove fluttering over Yeva's fingers. She placed the Mani in its beak and released the bird. As the auditorium cheered at the dove flying towards Ashwin, he spoke.

'I shall first anoint the forehead of the sacrifice. Following that, when my macauahuitl enters the child, she shall bleed. Her blood will water this seed. Nourish it and germinate it. This stone shall become one with her core. Flesh of her flesh. Imbued with her ambrosia, this blue shall revive the dead. The sun that gestates above us shall witness the greatest reawakening ever.'

The Mani was with the star now. He placed it on the marble, irradiating that platform. Lighting up every detail of his ravaged face. Lifting Indira in his arms, he laid her gently on the slab. The audience watched the sword descending. Obsidian blade perforating her skin and leaving a red dot at the centre of her forehead.

'The symbol for One. The Supreme. The Absolute. The Primary.'

He was uncorking a miniature crystal vial. The liquid inside shimmering in the halo of the gem. And Patnaik and Atharva hearing Zahak's voice resonate from his grave.

Six vials of venom…

Their tongues lifeless but brains squawking.

The parasite…

The priest looked on as Ashwin emptied the vial over the child's forehead wound. Every drop entering her bloodstream.

'Consecrated. She is prepared to receive the seed.'

The actor was binding her now. Black rope snaking all

over that white marble, securing the child's torso to the platform. The knots were resting on her bosom and her belly. Indira turned her face. Turned left to look at her father. Atharva behind the glass. Locked inside his body by Yeva. Screaming silently at his daughter.

Do it, Indu…do it…

Invoking her. Beseeching her.

Untie yourself…

Her fingers clasping that stalk of golden maize flowers tighter.

Knots…

Open the knots, Indu…open how you always do…

Words burning holes in his frozen body. His heart punching as if sending her a Morse code.

I am here…

Watching…

Snap that rope…

She raised both her hands.

Yes…

Good girl…good…

Raised higher and higher in a parabolic motion.

Right there…

But not taking them near the knots. She brought her palms over her face and covered both her eyes.

Indira!

The child lay still. Fingers over her eyes.

What are y…

Words ended. No longer needed. The priest was not watching her lying there with her eyes covered anymore. He was seeing someone else. And another one. And another. Five of them prostrate. Five bodies who had also raised their hands.

The other Chiranjivis that day…

And covered their eyes like Indira.

One by one…

All of them…

Why had they done that? And why was she replicating it now?

What are these six Immortals telling us?

Atharva was looking at the empty crystal vial by her head. The parasite was inside her body now. Inside all the six bodies. Ashwathama waiting for the Chiranjivis to rise. Awaken and put men to sleep. The final holocaust. Waiting for them to open their eyes.

Open…

That visual flashing again.

Chiranjivis not opening their eyes…

Looking at Indira.

Covering her eyes…

The five Immortals that day.

Covering their eyes…

Hearing another voice now. The doctor monitoring those five in coma. Hearing his words again.

Healed remarkably but not awaking…

Ashwathama waiting.

Waiting for them to awaken…

The priest seeing it now.

Not awaking…

Not awaking…

So simple. So clear. So beautiful.

Not opening their eyes…

He knew now. Knew what the Immortals were doing. What Indira was telling everyone right now at *Maquillage*.

Not rising up…

Watching again how she had communicated with the five that day. Realising that it had been a barter of information. She had not only received but also transmitted. The Chiranjivis had informed her about the eclipse. And she had informed them what their blood test had revealed. What Ashwathama was planning. Enlightened them about the biological terror inhabiting their bodies. She had warned them what would happen if they woke up. And they had acknowledged.

Covered their eyes…

Like Indira was doing today after Ashwin infected her.

Covered her eyes…

The six Chiranjivis choosing to remain paralysed in a state of coma. Defending humanity. Defeating Ashwathama.

Healed but not awaking…

His child lying motionless. Waiting for the macauahuitl to penetrate so that she may turn comatose too. That Indigo no longer defiant. No longer tearing ropes. Willing to be the final sacrifice.

The K'i'ik…

Bali doing it once again. Doing the only thing that he had done before Lord Vishnu.

Offering himself…

Tears were drowning Atharva's eyes. That film of saline turning *Maquillage* blurry. Smudging for him what was happening on stage now. The child was still shielding her eyes. Ashwin caressed her head and whispered.

'Sleep, Bali. It's dark. Let me bleed you while you sleep.'

Looking up at the sun still chained by the moon, he raised his macauahuitl over Indira's torso. Uttering a chant that was hardly Mayan.

'Tat saviturvrinimahe...Vayamdevasyabhojanam.'

The sword shuddered as a sudden gunshot echoed through the auditorium. A bullet had come hurtling and crashed into the glass barrier. Yeva spun atop the flying stage. She saw Suri standing at the entrance.

The officer aimed and fired again.

Chapter 59

THE SHOT KNOCKED YEVA OFF HER PERCH. AS SHE LANDED on her limbs, she jerked her head towards Patnaik and Atharva. Both bodies were pulsating. Electricity jolting their congealed muscles as spasm after spasm knifed through. Her mental link had ruptured. The officer had intruded upon the trance. His bullets puncturing that magnetic field. The men deflating now as that which had possessed them was draining out. Suri advanced down the aisle, directing his revolver at the superstar.

'Walk away from the child, Ashwin. Put that weapon down and raise your hands.'

The actor did not react, but the audience was cowering in fear. Many sitting dazed in the dark, unsure of what to do with this new spectacle. That bullet lodged in the barrier. That glass chipping and cracking. Action no longer confined to that cloistered podium but spilling over to the aisles. Lights had come out now. Incoherent sounds floating around feeling every prop. Trying to separate truth from this tableau.

'Drop that sword,' the officer commanded again.

The theatre manager had entered, questioning Suri while the director appeared from backstage, standing next to Ashwin. The officer pointed at Indira.

'We are here to confiscate the child.'

'Confiscate her?' the manager queried.

'She's a minor and is being used in *Maquillage* without the legal consent of her parents. You can carry on with the show, but you must surrender the child first. Her father demands that she's immediately returned.'

'Father?'

The priest banged on the barricade. 'She's mine.'

'And that entitles a cop to shoot inside a packed auditorium?' The manager scowled at Suri. 'Are you insane?'

'I realise what I did, but your actor was dangling a sword over Indira,' the officer addressed the audience. 'I apologise. Please remain seated. This is a police matter. We are here for the child.'

'My daughter,' Atharva echoed again. 'That girl covering her eyes.'

He turned towards Patnaik who nodded. The writer had also figured out why Indira was doing it. He gazed through the bullet crack. 'Give her up, Ashwin.'

The star still silent. His macauahuitl poised above her torso. The blade descended slightly.

'Beware,' Suri marched up to the glass barrier. Standing next to Yeva and the two men now. 'Don't even think about harming the child.'

'Harm her?' The director's voice snapped.

They heard laughter. The actor on the proscenium laughing. His diseased face shivering. *Maquillage* looking down upon these mortals and cackling.

'You are standing in a theatre, Suri,' Ashwin spoke. 'The universe of artifice. A landscape of mirages. We are all apparitions. Mere phantasms flitting about in light and dark. Nothing here is real.'

Patnaik nodded. 'Indeed. The drama stage where glitter covers rotting wood. And who knows that better than you?'

The star smiled again. 'This child's safe. Nothing can harm her.'

'Prove it then,' Suri said. 'Hand her over.'

'Enough!' the director on the podium burst. 'Take the bloody girl. I am not having her ruin my show. I should have never let you change the finale, Ashwin. All this Mayan crap. I'll have her off the stage and you can get on with your act.'

He began undoing the knots.

'Come on.'

Heaving the child up but she was resisting.

'What's wrong with thi...'

The director's words exploded mid-air as a furious blow shattered his right eye. He reeled back clawing at his socket. Fingers trying to plug the bubbling blood. Scraping that hollow accidentally. His other eye gaping at the jade necklace Ashwin had used to lacerate him. Its locket caked with the pulp of his eyeball. As he whimpered violently, horror swirled through the auditorium. They were watching that man's face. Blood as fake blood could never be. Pain as drama could never manufacture. A growing realization now that this was no longer theatrical. That the actor was no longer acting. That the willing suspension of disbelief could no longer be trusted.

'Ashwin!' the manager hammered the barricade. The glass chipping and cracking. The star's forehead quivering. Skin in the centre swelling up like a ripe boil. They cringed collectively as it erupted, draining more sewage down his face.

'Not Ashwin,' the writer said. 'Ashwathama.'

'Ashwathama?'

'Yes. Just Ashwathama.' He grabbed Suri's hand. 'And more dangerous now than he ever was.'

'What do you mean, Om?'

'Don't you see? He's no longer the idol. No longer Ashwin now. He cares no more for that image of Ashwin or that his audience is watching. He demolished Ashwin Tomar when he struck that director. Only Ashwathama now. And Ashwathama will do anything, because he only cares for that final drop.'

The assembly was staring at their fallen hero. The star disintegrating before their eyes. Those behind the podium were pulling the director inside. The actor hovering the macauahuitl threateningly over Indira again. Commanding everyone at the rear to vacate backstage.

The officer turned and aimed the revolver at Yeva. 'Leave the child, Ashwin.'

The sword trembled. Many were getting up from their seats now, clamouring to leave. Suri looked at the manager.

'It might get ugly here. We must remove the audience. My men stationed outside shall help you evacuate.'

Suddenly a rapid succession of sounds scissored through the theatre. All the doors were closing. All seven of them bolted now. The Ichhadhari smirked.

'Your team can't help you, officer. No more entrances or exits. I have ensured that no one comes in and no one leaves.'

The gathering was in terror now. Some back in their seats while others grouping near aisles. Unable to call for help since *Maquillage* still prohibited mobile phones. The scenery before them had morphed into a different dimension. Demanding a vicious shift in perspective. As the cacophony increased, Suri's arm shackled Yeva. Seizing her by the throat, he rammed her face into the barrier. The glass chipping and cracking. Handcuffs bound her wrists and the revolver jabbed her backbone.

'Let Indira go or I shall fucking shred your Ichhadhari's spine. She can't escape, Ashwin. The eclipse is on, and she can't shape-shift to save herself.'

Yeva hissed. Not at them. At the one standing before her on the proscenium.

'I had warned you. Told you we should have taken Bali somewhere else. It would have been all over by now, but you wouldn't listen. You wanted the world to witness your revival.'

'This was the perfect setting, Yeva. The perfect play. But this is not how it's supposed to end. The ending has applause. Applause as I became Ashwathama. And before long everyone will turn into Ashwathama. A world full of festering Ashwthamas.'

The writer clapped. Ashwin raised the macauahuitl at him.

'There. He applauds. He relishes the idea of becoming Ashwathama.'

'No, Ashwin. I clap because you are so naïve. Don't you see that you don't need to turn men into Ashwathamas? We already are. All of us. Ashwathamas. You insulted your divinity. We humans have been doing the same forever. We hold power, and we abuse it every day. Not god fearing but fearing each other's gods. Pouring poison into the earth and running out of Neelkanths. Bringing generations into a plastic universe that only isolates. You want to shrink our brains, but our technology is already doing that. We don't value anything. Cherish anything. Running out of conversations.

Making it a crime to express. To dream. To even love.'

He spread out both his arms.

'Look at us, Ashwin. All Ashwathamas before you. Wholesome beings bleeding inside. Cracks and chaos blistering within. Foreheads oozing lines. Each cast out of his own paradise and craving for that final release. Seeking refuge in cyber avatars that hide our actual rot. In constant pain and yet desensitised. Perhaps you infected us long back when you began wandering the earth. Or perhaps we have done this to ourselves. But then I look at the Chiranjivis. If these divine beings find our world worthy to make it their home, there's surely much beauty left. Much truth.'

'Truth? If there was truth on earth, why was my father lied to and killed at Kurukshetra?'

'Maybe Drona did not deserve truth any longer. All his life he suppressed the true voice within him. Kept rejecting every truth and, in the end, the truth rejected him.'

'And so, he was beheaded? And I was cursed?'

'Even Krishna was cursed by Vrinda for stealing the Shaligram stone. Also cursed by Gandhari and Bhrigu. And the lord bowed and accepted every curse with folded hands. But you could never do that. Forever defending your sins. Even the six Immortals bowed before the will of the universe. That's why they are gods, and you are not.'

'Your gods are my slaves now,' the actor proclaimed. 'They are my third eye like Mahadev. When they awaken, they shall annihilate.'

Patnaik shook his head. 'They are not waking up. Not as long as your toxin flows in their veins. See what Bali's showing you. You cannot make Yevas out of them. They shall rather lie in eternal sleep than become your tools.'

Ashwin held the child's hands and laid them back gently on her body. 'Not Bali. He knows I love him the most among all Chiranjivis.'

'Love him?'

'Bali suffers like me. Both of us robbed by the same Dark One. He came pleading for three feet of land and snatched everything Bali had. That's exactly why Duryodhan kicked that devil out when he came begging for five villages for the Pandavas. Bali will never betray me. He knows my pain.'

'He knows your evil. You say you both were persecuted by Krishna but look what he's doing and what you are doing. Bali has now brought you to a point where you must choose. Do you see it, Ashwathama? Bali wants you to make a choice.'

'Choice?'

'Yes. If you bleed Indira, you will surely complete your Mani, but your parasite shall be rendered useless. Forever locked in six comatose bodies that shall never awaken. And if you want your toxin to be transmitted, you will have to spare Indira which means you can never fortify that Mani.' The writer paused and asked again. 'What will you choose, Ashwathama? Destroying us or deifying yourself?'

The face on the stage stood unblinking. The writer's words sinking into his festering flesh. Fingering that hole in his forehead. Was Ashwin waiting for a cue? Someone to prompt?

'A very intriguing juncture,' Patnaik continued. 'When the Ocean of Milk was churned using a serpent, it yielded Ratna and Halahal. You can't have them both, Ashwathama. What will you choose? The Mani or the venom?'

'Choose? Why must I choose? Why not everything I

desire? Have I not suffered enough?'

'And now you want to see everyone suffer. For you it's always about you. Your misery. Your life. Your narrative. Incapable of perceiving the other. Incompetent to comprehend multiple voices. Is that the reason you wish to devour us? Your singular mind horrified to confront plurality. The idea that others could also be right. As legitimate as you. You cannot tolerate the polyphony, and so you plan to silence us.'

'The man's rambling,' Yeva shrieked. 'Stalling you until the eclipse passes. Men will never change. They will keep bleeding the earth. Do what you must do. Stab the child.'

Suri drove her body into the barricade again. 'Don't you dare, Ashwin. Walk away from Indira, or I will fucking punch holes in Yeva's spine.'

The blade lingering in the air. Obsidian edges shimmering like a blue comet in the glow of the Mani. The Ichhadhari's finger shot upwards.

'The eclipse is about to end. Do it.'

'But he will kill you.'

'It's no longer about me. It's about what you have pledged me. What Mahadev has pledged you. Those covenants override everything. You owe it to me. You owe it to yourself.'

'He says the Chiranjivis are not waking up. Bali won't come out of coma.'

'Lies. They are lying like they lied to your father. They want you to drop your guard like he did. Terrified that you will reclaim your form. Become immaculate. Invincible. You can make the Chiranjivis wake up. Make them do whatever you desire. Just plunge that sword. Now. Right now.'

The auditorium throbbed as the officer fired into the floor. He was shaking his head menacingly at Ashwin. The barrel once more on her spine. Yeva's voice still scalding the glass.

'Have you been unsexed, Ashwin? Are you not the same warrior who slaughtered so many in the thick of night? Look up. The skies are dark again. What's hindering your blade? Are you not the same man in action as you are in desire? Why did you dispatch me to strike at five of them when you are too weak to bleed the sixth? The youngest one. Is this why I plucked my Mani out of my flesh and laid it at your feet?'

'That revolver, Yeva. It will murder you. Murder that flawless body you own. That body you took so long to attain.'

'This body is hardly mine. Just an unreal form wrapping me. An Ichhadhari changes forms like a piece of cloth. I am your guardian spirit and that can never perish. Stab her. My body is a lie, but your body is your supreme truth. Your karma. Your bhakti. You cannot lay down your arms now. Do what you have to do. Raise that macauahuitl and slash Bali.'

The sword still suspended in doubt. Staring at everyone standing before it. Yeva looked up. The eclipse was breathing its last. Merely a minute or two. She glanced at Ashwathama and closed her eyes. The next moment a violent motion of her wrists dislodged the officer's finger from the trigger behind her and inserted her own. Suri squealed but she fired.

Again. Again. Again.

Men and women crouched. Suri still swearing and Patnaik and Atharva processing what had just happened. But not a word from the podium. The actor had not heard the shots. Only the sound of her backbone cracking. That sacrum blown to bits. Her body had slumped on its knees. She opened her eyes one last time. Blue eyes beholding that brilliant blue jewel. Watching it fade. She fell, giving in to the earth that was pulling her close. Yeva no more. A krait lying dead.

Ashwin roared. A ghastly noise emanating from his insides like a beast mortally wounded. His face crumbling more. The glass above them convulsing as his decibels threatened to slice the dome. His fingers squeezed the macauahuitl's neck as it soared.

'Ashwathama,' the writer folded his hands. 'You could not stop your Bramhastra from impaling Uttara. You can do that today.'

But the blade had plunged into Indira. The audience leapt in horror. Patnaik and Suri gaped at the child and then Atharva. He stood silently watching that metal tearing his daughter's skin asunder. Dissecting her flesh but hitting her rib-cage. Ashwin pulled the sword out and drilled it once more. Sawing the bones and carving the liver. Indira's eyes were closed now, but the others were watching. The frenzy possessing the man on stage. The blood diffusing through the white marble. Soaking the carvings of the snakes around the egg. Simmering like every face looking at it.

The actor clenched the hilt again. As he drove the macauahuitl harder, a jet of blood from the liver splattered across his face. He laughed and cupped his palm before that faucet. Collecting a fistful, he picked up the blue stone with his other hand. The Mani still luminous but the actor's eyes more electric now. Holding that jewel above the blood. Holding it for that infinitesimal second and then dropping it as he yelled.

'Har Har Mahadev!'

The priest stirred. Patnaik and Suri heard his voice.

'He cannot have the Mani.' Atharva looked at them. 'If Ashwathama heals himself today, we lose. The Chiranjivis lose. My child loses. I cannot let her lose. He cannot have that Mani.'

Inching closer to the barricade, he began pounding it. Pounding it with his head. Pounding again and again. Pounding it as if nothing else mattered now.

The glass chipping and cracking.

Ashwin's palms had clamped shut. Incubating that stone as he anointed it. The raging audience no longer watching him. They were watching the child's father combating the barrier. The other two men joining him now.

The glass chipping and cracking.

They were all getting up. Walking down the aisles. Getting closer to that trio wrestling with the glass. Glaring at Ashwin's palms opening up like an oyster. The gem inside covered in blood like amniotic fluid. They wondered if it would blind them again, but it was no longer on fire. No longer that phosphorescent body. Just a block of blue.

But Ashwin gazing at it as if it was someone he knew...

Ashwathama gazing at it as if it was someone who knew him...

The audience had gathered around the three men now. Breathing all over the glass. The actor was walking towards them. Till the point where the stage ended. Indifferent to that trinity assaulting the wall. Standing at the very edge of the podium, he lifted the Mani and lodged it inside the cavity in his forehead. As that void held the jewel in its arms, the sun broke free. Incandescent light revealing a red rainbow arching above the dome.

The eclipse was over.

The solar god watched as the crowd exploded. A tidal

wave surging against that barricade. Men and women fiercely battering. The Mani installed in its niche was taking root now. Drinking up Ashwathama's pus and filling up his vacuum. Tissues and fibres enmeshing it to make that crater whole again.

The glass chipping and cracking.

Ashwathama's eyes sparkling and skin stretching over his face. Boils flushed out to divulge a countenance so pure that the sun was falling in love with him.

The glass chipping and cracking.

Lusty arms like those of a tiger now. Knuckles bursting. Septic flesh of his bosom cleansed and enlarged. The Mani fumigating his core. Pumping an ecstasy into his heart that he had never encountered.

The glass chipping and cracking.

The elixir of the jewel flowing through every nerve now. Disinfecting his blood as if purging him from all sins. Scouring his very essence. Absorbing and getting absorbed.

The glass chipping and cracking.

He was howling like a horse now. The nectar almost brimming over. Gratifying his loins and flowing down his limbs. Reaching out and just about to touch his feet.

The wall crashed. They wrenched the Mani out and then his face.

Chapter 60

Many a slip they count betwixt the chalice and the lip
The blue gemstone scratched out by a furious fingertip
His forehead's womb mutilated to bleed and rot again
Multiple hands disrobing him as he cursed god in vain
His face hung in ribbons as they stabbed his bare back
Eyes clamped never showing who vandalized in the dark
Their nails red as they mauled the lord of their pantheon
Night snuffing out the star that had dared to be the sun
Stinking miasma rising from the decay of his rancid core
Orgasmic for the mob as they peeled him more and more
Cops stormed Maquillage *and scanned that theatre round*
His bits and pieces everywhere but he himself never found
Every arclight above still in heat for that lover to make love
Even that curtain in a limbo neither falling nor staying above
They pronounced him fugitive as cinema disowned its hero
Some say despite such dark evil the price he paid was zero
They forget that for a Mani, the Rishiputra will again grope
What can be a greater hell than that undying flame of hope?

Epilogue

THE IMMORTALS WERE IN A CIRCLE. THEIR RIGHT HANDS radiating out and joined. Piled upon one another like spokes of a wheel in arrested motion. The hand on top was Indira's.

'Raise the gods. Place the Mani, Atharva.'

'Not me, Om. I am waiting for someone. I think that's her knocking.'

Suri opened the door. Jupita was standing outside. She crossed the threshold and entered. Standing before that coven of Chiranjivis now. Looking at her daughter. The priest handed her the blue stone.

'Do as I had told you.'

She deposited the gem on the little palm. Watched it spark as it touched that circuit of arms. Its aura gleaming. Swelling into a blue haze of osmosis. That aerosol reaching out to all the six beings. Befriending their flesh and sucking out the contagion like a sponge. The Mani was drinking their poison now as it had drunk their blood. Healing their bodies. Making love to their wounds. The nebula depleted and died.

Patnaik opened the door as their eyes opened.

He was watching the nine of them. Watching the child drawing again. The Chiranjivis talking about creation, destruction and creation once more. Suri handing over the

Mani to Somnath. That chunk of ether warming itself in its own halo as if hatched by a celestial bird.

An egg…

Walking out, the writer opened the web page on his mobile once more that he had been reading last night.

…subsequently the Takht-e-Taus was constructed and the jewel was placed upon it. And when Shah Jahan was confined to house arrest by his son…

He touched the words once more.

Takht-e-Taus

The Peacock Throne

Peacock egg…Atharva was right…Peacock egg

Patnaik smiled.

Koh-i-Noor

Minutes later he was looking at the horse Indira had drawn and the diamond flashing on its forehead.

About the Author

Satyarth Nayak is an author and screenwriter based in Mumbai. A former SAARC Award-winning correspondent with CNN-IBN, Delhi, he holds a master's degree in English Literature from St. Stephen's.

Satyarth's latest book, the national bestseller *Mahagatha* (2022), is an epic collection of the 100 greatest mythological tales from the Puranas of Hinduism. Containing stories of gods, demons, sages and kings in a unique chronological order, the book has been described by Anand Neelakantan as 'a must-have in your home library'. His bestselling biography, *Sridevi—The Eternal Screen Goddess* (2019), which charts the journey of the screen legend from child star to becoming India's first female superstar, met with high acclaim. *The Emperor's Riddles* (2014), his debut novel, was a bestselling thriller and earned comparisons with Dan Brown's works for its engaging 'history meets mystery' narrative. Satyarth also scripted Sony's epic historical TV show *Porus*, touted as India's most expensive series, which aired from 2017 to 2019. His short stories have won the British Council award and have been featured in Sudha Murty's anthology, *Something Happened on the Way to Heaven*.

Satyarth was named one of the Top 50 authors to follow on social media and is a regular speaker at national and international literature festivals. He is currently scripting a sci-fi film for one of Bollywood's biggest franchises and working on his next mythology book based on the Mahabharata.

ALSO BY SATYARTH NAYAK

Praise for *Mahagatha*

'He [Satyarth] is truly a phenomenal storyteller.'–Ashwin Sanghi, author

'An extremely readable book with beautiful illustrations.'–Namita Gokhale, author

'Very well written. More people should read these stories.'–Bibek Debroy, author and chairman, PM's Economic Council

An Om Patnaik Thriller

Praise for *The Emperor's Riddles*

'Fantastic blend of myth, imagination and mystery.'–Amish Tripathi

'Intelligent. Intriguing. Imaginative. Intense.'–Ashwin Sanghi

HarperCollins *Publishers* India

At HarperCollins India, we believe in telling the best stories and finding the widest readership for our books in every format possible. We started publishing in 1992; a great deal has changed since then, but what has remained constant is the passion with which our authors write their books, the love with which readers receive them, and the sheer joy and excitement that we as publishers feel in being a part of the publishing process.

Over the years, we've had the pleasure of publishing some of the finest writing from the subcontinent and around the world, including several award-winning titles and some of the biggest bestsellers in India's publishing history. But nothing has meant more to us than the fact that millions of people have read the books we published, and that somewhere, a book of ours might have made a difference.

As we look to the future, we go back to that one word—a word which has been a driving force for us all these years.

Read.